Message
of Lies

Hostage
of Lies

Maxine Thompson

URBAN BOOKS
www.urbanbooks.net

This is a work of fiction. Any references or similarities to actual events, real people, living or dead, or to real locales are intended to give the novel a sense of reality. Any similarity in other names, characters, places, and incidents is entirely coincidental.

URBAN SOUL is published by

Urban Books
1199 Straight Path
West Babylon, NY 11704

ISBN-13: 978-1-59983-095-7
ISBN-10: 1-59983-095-7

First Printing: December 2009
10 9 8 7 6 5 4 3 2 1

Printed in the United States of America

Dedicated to Michelle Burroughs

Acknowledgments

First, I want to thank my Heavenly Father for the muse.

I also want to thank my writer family, Michelle McGriff, Shelia Goss, Monica Carter, Suzetta Perkins, Leola Charles, Roslyn Wyche-Hamilton.

I want to thank my publisher, Carl and Martha Weber, the Urban Books Family, Brenda Owen and Natalie Weber and all the others.

I want to thank the ancestors for surviving and leaving behind their stories.

He that is without sin, cast a stone at her.
                                        —John 8:7

*I have borne thirteen children, and seen most all
sold off to slavery, and when I cried out with my
mother's grief, none but Jesus heard me! And ain't
I a woman?*
                                    —Sojourner Truth

Prologue

Shallow's Corner, Michigan, April 1993

When the old folks used to tell blossoming young girls, "You must be smelling yourself," their words surely had been coined with Titi in mind.

Echoing down through the rush of the years, Isaac can still hear Big Mama Lily's booming voice, dovetailed by Mannish, her rooster, when he would crow at dawn. Her voice would float over the fence, which separated their properties, as she chided Titi in the morning.

"Lil' Bit! Make sure you wash under your arms and in your pocketbook, too. And make sure you use that lavender water I made you."

But no amount of soap or lavender water could disguise that newly minted, girl-turned-to-woman smell. Because even now—more than twenty-six years later—he can still smell her lavender scent in the air. This year, it's as if spring has ushered in a welcome mat of lilac blossoms for Titi, who is back in town.

1

"Now, I done put up with your daddy till he died. I even put up with your crazy stepbrother. But enough is enough. I know you ain't been interested in setting foot in church after all these years. Who you think you fooling, man? You must think I'm somebody's brand-new fool. My mama didn't birth no fool. You must think I was born yesterday."

As he slammed his way out of his Palmer Heights tri-level, Isaac could feel the heat from his wife's termagant accusations darting at his back. Without looking back, he could see how her head wobbled on her neck and swayed from side to side like a palm tree. All she needed was a drum as she went on the warpath, her hip bone jutted out, her arms held akimbo. *All right, Sapphire.* Isaac was comparing her to the shrewish wife, Sapphire, from the old *Amos 'n' Andy* TV show, which was on reruns when he was growing up in the 1950s.

Although he did not answer her, if he'd wanted to, he could take his words and wrap her up in a winding sheet. Instead, clambering into his Mercedes, he mumbled to himself.

"It's a funny thing how you didn't talk all this lip when you were breaking up my marriage to the only woman I ever loved. Oh, you were as sweet as a candy apple then, making me think I was missing out on something. Keeping me out all night. Promising me the moon. But you ain't nothing but the Devil's daughter. Made me think that Titi didn't know how to please me. But you the one don't know how to please your man."

That morning, when he woke up, a prickling-on-the-neck uneasiness spooked Isaac. On the one hand, he wondered why his recurring dream started out differently than it usually did. On the other hand, not being one given to introspection, he didn't question it. Like a bird dog drawn along by a hidden scent, before he knew it, he wound up standing in Reverend Godbolt's church.

It had been five years since he'd been in his ex-father-in-law's church, yet Isaac could still smell the subtle aroma of her skin and hair right there in the pews. He just knew it was her fragrance. He'd know his ex-wife's scent anywhere. Even in his dreams.

Over seven years ago, Titi moved away from Shallow's Corner, and nothing had changed.

Isaac's nose held the history of every scent it had ever sniffed. Although Miss Magg, his ex-mother-in-law, had told him Titi would be at the church delivering flowers, he could tell by his nose that she was either in the church, or had been there earlier. Running his cupped hand across the pew to drink up her scent, he thought about how funny it was that every woman possessed her own unique wild perfume.

As he inhaled the lingering waft of Titi's perfume, he thought, *Mmmm. I smell you, girl.*

Was that her signature Nina Ricci L'Air du Temps still lingering in the air? Not that it mattered. Even the death odor of the yellow chrysanthemums garnishing the church's altar was no match for the life scent of Titi. If Isaac could bottle her essence, he'd call it Lilac. He thought back to the last dream he'd had last night.

No wonder he'd had such a crazy dream. He could smell Titi's presence in the air, the same way people said that animals were able to sense coming earthquakes. More than the smell of her, he needed to see Titi's eyes. Her eyes never lied. He hatched an excuse to get out of the house. When he left, Roshanne was just getting wound up and working her way to throwing Titi up in his face. That woman could be a bloodhound. Always accusing him of other women. Mighty funny she hadn't said that when she'd been sneaking around with him when he was married to Titi.

Well, he didn't care what she said. He just hoped it wasn't too late to try to win Titi back. Just like he could still be young in his dream, he could fly if he wanted to. He only had one problem clipping his wings: Roshanne.

Titi was nothing like Roshanne. That Roshanne was full of lip, if you asked him. Just this morning, when he'd informed her, "I have to run over to the church and help my mother set up the tables for Reverend's birthday party," she stood blocking the doorway, her mouth as grating as a hawk's beak.

He could still hear Roshanne's bleating voice. "Do you hear me, Isaac Thorne? My mama didn't drop me out of a banana tree. Like I said, my mama didn't birth no fool."

Naw, Roshanne. I know your mama didn't birth no fool. We don't even have to go there. But my mama didn't hatch one, either. Don't you know my mama was the talk of the town in 1958? So we don't even have to play the dozens.

"Hi, son."

Startled from his reverie, Isaac turned and nearly bumped into his mother, Calissa. Standing in the church aisle, so close to him he could smell the salty beads of sweat sliding down her forehead, Calissa looked surprised to see him. He stared straight into her eyes, which were scribbled with wine-stained streams of pain, yet fortressed by a bulwark brow, which bespoke her arrogance. As if each watermark of her aging was a badge of arrogance, a diagram of "I did it my way."

In a blink, the warring in Isaac's soul almost surfaced to his face in a scowl, but then he dissembled his cheek muscles into a lukewarm flag of peace. Momentarily their eyes locked. Stalemated. Then Calissa dropped her eyes from his— as though she genuflected in guilt whenever she saw him.

"Excuse me," he mumbled. "Hello, Calissa."

"Hi there, Isaac."

Calissa didn't miss a beat. The corners of her mouth crumpled like someone suffering with a toothache. She was hurt. They both knew that old pain—that fiery sleet pelting the skin—would always be between them.

"What are you doing here?" Isaac asked. His scorn butchered each word.

"I came to set up the altar," Calissa said, "and yourself?"

Isaac paused before answering. Try as he would, he knew he could never forgive his mother for what she'd done. He couldn't help himself. He'd only been nine years old going on ten at the time when his mother abandoned him.

"I just came to see if I could help. Maybe I could order a case of champagne." He would do anything to get next to Titi. He just wanted to talk to her. Even if it meant playing up to his mother, whom he despised.

"You know we don't drink in the church."

"Well, I heard the dinner was going to be at Haven House Restaurant after the service at church. Can't I have it sent over there?"

"Suit yourself."

Isaac studied his mother. Her pious demeanor seemed sincere. She'd become "sanctified" in her late years. Since the death of her second husband, "Pay Dirt," he'd heard that Calissa was very involved in the church now, often changing the altar linen, setting out the wine, and even being a member of the usher board. How come she had waited so late? Why hadn't she been like that when he was growing up?

He tried to figure out a way to ask his mother if Titi had been in the church, and if she was coming back before the dinner, but he couldn't find a nonchalant way to do so. Through his son,

Isaac Jr., he'd learned that Titi was coming to town. When he called his ex-mother-in-law, she told him that she sent Titi to church to drop off the flowers.

"Well, I guess I better get started," Calissa said, disappearing into the sacristy on the right-hand side of the altar. Isaac remembered that the Reverend usually kept his elaborate purple, magenta, and scarlet robes, yellow banners, and pristine white altar cloths in the cupboards there. Even when they were kids, Reverend had always dressed in the regalia of a Catholic priest.

When Pharaoh Curry pulled up in front of the Solid Rock Baptist Church in his bashed-in 1982 Cadillac, he saw his stepbrother's car in the adjacent parking lot. A new Mercedes 450SL in aubergine. Without looking, he knew the car came equipped with a mobile phone. He'd seen Isaac driving, as cool as you please, and talking on the phone at the same time. Show-off. Doggone his time, that Isaac had always been the lucky one, Pharaoh mused. Not that he'd appreciated it. Looking back, when they were younger, Pharaoh thought Isaac probably believed Pharaoh was the one who'd had it made.

Now, whereas Pharaoh was "just another blood"—one of Shallow's Corner's many anonymous black cabdrivers—Isaac's plain face was the one that graced the front cover of newspapers like the *New York Times* and magazines such as the *New Yorker.* Who would ever know Pharaoh's name? He was a nobody. Another black face in the trash pile of failures. Except for his disability check, he was an entity in the lost dregs of humanity. One whose mark had never been and, most likely, would never be made on the world. And to think he'd possessed so much promise as a young man.

The irony of it all was that as a kid, Isaac had been the misfit. The one last called to be on anyone's baseball team. The one everyone beat up on just for practice or to build their reputations. But Pharaoh admitted one thing to himself. Isaac had always been able to get the one thing Pharaoh himself was never able to garner in this town— respect. Because Isaac's mother had wronged his father, Deacon Thorne, Isaac got sympathy.

On the other hand, Pharaoh, the dubious offspring of that "scandalous, wife-stealing Pay Dirt," only gained suspicion. He'd been considered "Bad Blood" before he even knew Pay Dirt was his father. Now he understood why people used to look at him cross-eyed.

At thirteen, Pharaoh was considered "an outsider," "country," even "foreign" to the other blacks. By the time he was sixteen, he'd become a citizen, both bodacious and citified.

Pharaoh was surprised how the church had mushroomed since his last visit. Its steeple leaped against the sky, appearing threatening— bullet-shaped—almost phallic. This was the new church that was rebuilt after the fire during the '67 riots. Somehow, he'd liked the church better when it sat side by side with the Thorne Family Funeral Home. It seemed more real then. Now it even looked sterile. Like it was made of dead bones of steel and glass.

Echoing his thoughts, the church bell pealed a mournful requiem for the past. Inside the church's walls, afternoon sunlight streamed through the stained glass of the lancet windows, casting rainbow shadows on the floor. The Black Madonna, holding the dying Black Christ, smiled down from the Pietà scene. A new expensive organ replaced the old piano that Pharaoh remembered. Hand-hewn beams, crisscrossing the ceiling, glistened in the afternoon sun. They resembled twenty-two swords at attention. The coffered ceiling over the pulpit cast purple shadows onto the altar.

Pharaoh couldn't remember praying, let alone attending church—with the exception of his father's and Deacon Thorne's funeral—since he had gone to Vietnam. His stepmother, Calissa, told him earlier that Nefertiti was delivering the flowers to the church for her mother, whose hands were busy. He didn't know if he was an atheist or what. Candles, incense, and the death smells of the mums were powerless to block his sorrow. So much sadness overwhelmed him, he felt like crying when he looked up at the baby Black Christ on the wall. Seeing the baby made him think of his first and only child who was given up for adoption without any consideration for him being the biological father. Back in those days, the father had no rights.

How old would Nefertiti be now? About thirty-five? Or was it older? He wasn't even sure. Following his daughter's birth, he'd been shipped to Vietnam. After his return to the States, he was battling mental problems and had lost complete count of the years passing by. Whenever he thought about it, he felt like a bullet lodged itself near his heart, like the one that took out his road dog, Cornelius, over in 'Nam. It was like his mind was playing tricks on him. Was one little girl posing to be another? He didn't know what to think anymore.

Why couldn't he get Nefertiti out of his mind? From the time Moms told him that she was bringing flowers to the church, he'd been swirling in a space of craziness. Leave Nefertiti alone. Let it go. Can you ever forgive what she did to you? What's so good about her?

Even when she was young, she wasn't all that cute. Her eyes were set too far apart. She was a little bowlegged. Pigeon-toed. Kind of short and thick. Nefertiti possessed a haughty "I'm black and I'm proud" slant to her head, long before it was popular to be blue-black among black people. And dimples that you could stick your fingers into on each cheek. Dimples in which a man could melt and drown. Her full lips looked as if they were stained in indigo. She didn't even have good hair. Just a lot of bushy hair. But it was her eyes. Almond-shaped, and a kind of camel brown. The irises always reminded him of golden oases. That's what gave Nefertiti her exotic look. No matter what, he still wanted her.

2

"Why did you cut your hair, Titi?"

Nefertiti couldn't believe her mother. She had barely stepped off the plane, and here her mother was, starting right in on her head—both literally and metaphorically—as they walked through the airport's terminal. Instead of commenting on the cadmium yellow or the Hansa red of her African outfit, her mother went straight for her head.

When she didn't answer, her mother continued. "You know I like your hair long-long, gul."

Just hearing her mother slip into the patois from her mom's Creole-Louisiana upbringing was welcome enough for Nefertiti. She was home. Still, she balked at the little-girl role her mother automatically assigned to her.

"Mother, I'm over forty years old. I don't need hair hanging down my back." Nefertiti tightened her grip on her laptop case. As she and her mother walked through the baggage section, she was a little perturbed, so she was unaware of the heads that turned in her direction. To an untrained observer, one would not have thought that the older woman, as saffron-colored as a persimmon, and the younger, as purplish brown as an eggplant, were mother and daughter. But upon close examination, they both had the same high cheekbones and full-lipped mouths.

Yet it was Nefertiti who had a presence that commanded attention. Although she was only five feet four, she was queenly in her self-possession, and had a skin tone that, albeit dusky, showed hints of ochre and amber. She wore earrings in the shape of Africa, but if one were to look closely at them, they held the faces of Frederick Douglass, Harriet Tubman, and Sojourner Truth engraved on them. Nefertiti's was a face that attested to some irretrievable loss, yet one that still had survived the cataclysm.

Her carriage was so erect, and she held her head so high, one could easily imagine her lithely sauntering through some remote African village with a large pot balanced on her head. At the same time, there was a fierceness in her eyes, a drumbeat of battle, from which one could easily see the Dahomeyan female warrior.

While the two women stood in the crowd, waiting for the baggage orbiting around the turnstile of the claim center, her mother was crestfallen.

"Well, you sure don't need those little corkscrews, either. It reminds me of the horrible Afro you wore back in high school." Her mother picked up the thread of the conversation.

"I beg your pardon, but these are dreads. I am wearing my hair natural, the way it was meant to be in the first place. And with all due respect, I've had enough straightening combs and perms to last me for the rest of my life. The last time a hair-dresser messed my hair up, I said to myself, 'I'm not paying good money to go bald-headed anymore.'"

"Well, you know how men love hair." At sixty-five, her mother still wore her hair in the page-boy style that was popular when she was in high school in the 1940s.

"Well, they can *un*love it."

"Don't get cheeky now. I can still slap you in your mouth, gul. You can grow tall as a telephone pole and I can still chop you down to size."

"Oh, Mother." Nefertiti hugged her mother in an effort to parry off any more of her criticism.

"And when did you start calling me 'Mother'? I know this can't be my child. Lookin' like an African, but sounding like a white girl."

"All right, Miss Magg. Is that better? Give me a kiss. You know I'm just tired of people talking about my hair. If my ancestors hadn't come from Africa and been raped by white men, I would never have had so much hair in the first place. Now this is me."

As Nefertiti held her mother in her arms, she realized how frail her mother's rib cage felt. She could see by her mother's hand that the vitiligo had spread since she'd last seen her two years earlier—the time Nefertiti had mailed her mother a plane ticket to come visit Los Angeles. Even so, when she looked at her now, she didn't see an old, carping woman. All she saw was love.

In spite of her mixed feelings of resentment about her mother, she still loved her. She wished she could tell her mother she loved her—the way that her longtime girlfriend "Sweet" had often told her mother, before her mom passed away five years earlier. The way that Nigel Ford, her husband, often told his own mother, Mother Leah—casually, informally, spontaneously. But in her family, there had never been an open demonstration of affection. She could only hope her mother felt her love in her awkward hug.

"What does Ford think about all this back-to-Africa stuff?" Everyone called Nigel by his last name.

"Oh, he loves it. Now he runs his fingers through the wooly jungles of my hair all he wants."

A silence fell over the two women as they headed for Miss Magg's car.

Nefertiti was thinking of her argument with her husband, Ford, over her hair. How the cutting of her hair—even more so, the growing of dreadlocks—was beginning to drive a wedge, among the many other unspoken chasms, between them.

Ever since Nefertiti had opened her boutique selling African attire and African art, it was as if the couple had begun moving in two different circles. But the cutting, then the wearing of her hair naturally, had been like the final crime—the statement that declared war on their relationship—and had added more tension between them.

Oddly, the first thing Ford had told her when she met him twenty years earlier, during that one year she lived on campus at USC, was "I love your hair." At the time, she had been wearing a cloudburst of a natural. Nonetheless, he seemed to love her hair even more when they met years later, and her locks were straightened, hanging below her shoulders.

In any event, the leap from employee to self-employed had been a watershed that had changed Nefertiti's life in many ways. For one, things were much simpler. Less Eurocentric. Less mainstream. More Afrocentric. More holistic. The hair was only an outward expression of her new attitude. Through happenstance, she'd even become involved in different community grass roots groups, such as Recycling Black Dollars, and a reparations group. It seemed that the more she was moving away from her earlier bourgeois way of living, the further she and Ford were growing apart. And the more she was turning to her roots, the more truths about her own life, which she didn't want to face, were surfacing.

"Anyhow," Nefertiti continued, "I don't see what men find so attractive about hair."

"What's in that little case you're carrying? I've never seen a handbag that looked like that."

"Oh, that's my laptop. You know Savasia and Junior have already e-mailed me twice while I was up in the plane."

"Girl, I don't know nothing about these computers. You young folks are too much for me."

Having thought of her children—twelve-year-old Savasia and fifteen-year-old Ike, she called them as soon as she made it to her mother's house. The children were staying at her sister-in-law Yolan's house in Santa Monica, California. Yolan had two teenagers, Buffy and Tyler, and the two women usually switched carpooling the kids to their different activities. Nefertiti spoke to Savasia first.

Although it was ten-thirty in the morning in Michigan, it was only seven-thirty in California. Her children were due at school at nine in the morning.

"Hi, Mom." Savasia was as bubbly as usual. "We're going to Medieval Times tonight, and then we're going to Disneyland this weekend. We're having a ball."

"Good. Where's Ike?"

"He's on the computer." Nefertiti thought about why she had recently installed a second phone line, since you had to use dial up to get on the Internet, and Isaac kept the phone line busy all the time.

"I might have to send that boy to Computers Anonymous. What is he doing on the computer this early? He should be getting ready for school. Tell him I want to speak to him."

Isaac Jr., known as Ike, was the computer whiz in the family. He was more concerned with his computer games than the fact that his mother would be gone for five days.

"Ma, I was online. It's not that I don't want to talk. See, we're doing a project in science where we're watching some archaeologists dig up some old vases from a kazillion years ago. I couldn't get through the line last night, so I got up early this morning. The whole class is doing it on their computers from home. It's slamming."

"Stop using that slang with me."

"Aw, Moms. You know what I mean. Did you get my e-mail?"

"Yes, I did. I guess this cyberspace age is something for you kids growing up. The world is as small as next door now. We used to say, 'It's a small world,' but it's really one now."

"Okay, Ma, gotta go, before Savasia gets on the computer. Get your hands off of there, Mozilla!"

Nefertiti stuck her finger in her ear to stop the ringing of Ike's shouting at his sister. "All right. Love you. I'll call you back tomorrow. Be good."

Hanging up, knowing her children were safe, Nefertiti decided against taking a nap. Although she had taken the redeye flight from Los Angeles, she felt wide-awake. She had a mission to accomplish. She was thinking about contacting her girlfriend Sweet, when the phone rang. It was Ford, her husband.

"Hey, babe. You made it safely?"

"Yes."

"How's your mom and dad?"

"I haven't seen my father yet, but my mom says to tell you hello." Nefertiti knew she was lying, because her mother hadn't asked about her husband's health.

"I sure wanted to come with you this time and meet your father and the rest of the family."

Nefertiti paused. "Well, next time."

When she hung up, she felt bad for lying. How could she tell her husband of five years that she had come home to find a child she gave up for adoption, when he didn't even know about this child?

3

"What are you doing here, my man?" Unable to pretend to be civil, Isaac couldn't help the arsenic lacing each of his words, and separating them like sentinels, when he addressed Pharaoh. Isaac hadn't seen Pharaoh since his own father, Deacon Herschel Thorne, died five years earlier. After his father's funeral, on his way out of the church that afternoon, Isaac noticed Pharaoh standing over on the sidelines of mourners. Even then, he remembered thinking that the Deacon would turn in his grave if he knew the son of the man who destroyed his life was at his funeral.

Now, five years later, one glance at Pharaoh, and Isaac could see the drain of enthusiastic dissipation ravaging his stepbrother's former good looks. Pharaoh's eyes resembled red marbles, yet they held a look of cold scorn as he appraised Isaac.

"What do you mean, what am I doing here? I got just as much right to be in church as you do."

Isaac wasn't as taken back by Pharaoh's verbal facility as by his appearance. He couldn't believe his stepbrother. Pimp-walking in the church, with his old bodacious behind. Sizing him up, Isaac realized it was as if Pharaoh was caught in a time warp. He still wore his army fatigues, field jacket, and jungle boots. Under his boonie hat, he donned the same Afro he'd worn after his return from Vietnam, over twenty-three years ago.

As irreverent as ever, Pharaoh still owned that same swaggering, prancing walk. The pimp walk from their teen years. The one Isaac so envied as a teenager, when he would pass the "cool boys" standing on the corner, caressing their upside-down cone-shaped crotches like desirable women. When they were growing up, it was Pharaoh who personified the priapic black stud, who had been one of the boys who could stand on the corner as though it was built for him, play the dozens until no one would dare go up against him ("Yo' mama so black—"), and catcall to the passing girls with such finesse the others would try to imitate him later on.

Now, studying Pharaoh in the same manner one would study an amoeba under a microscope, Isaac wondered why he ever envied his step-brother. Pharaoh was dapping and throwing his hands into a high-five motion, which Isaac felt as detached from as if he were floating on the ceiling, looking down. He watched as Pharaoh's body went through a sort of twisted gyration, hand jive, dapping motion, and back-trot steps, resembling the old limbo dancers.

Just as his speech held all the cadences, inflections, and rhythms of Belize, the Central American country where he was born, Pharaoh's body kept a constant beat going on, almost like a reggae dance. Ignoring the brotherly symbol, Isaac refused to high-five Pharaoh.

"You know Rev couldn't stand yo' sorry ass," Isaac said, reverting to street talk.

Pharaoh put his hand on his chin, pulling at an invisible goatee as he pondered Isaac's words.

"Hey, watch your mouth, my brother. We in the church. Even when I was in 'Nam, the church was always said to be—what is it you call it, my man? You the writer."

"Sanctuary? And I ain't your brother."

"Yeah, that's it. Sanctuary." Pharaoh had a way of stretching his mouth over each syllable and giving the word a delectable sound.

"Well, you can at least take your hat off in the church."

Pharaoh obliged by removing his boonie hat.

"Never did have no manners, did you?"

"Hey, man. Cut the sermon. What you doing here, anyway? Bet you trying to find Nefertiti."

"That's none of your business what I'm doing here. Besides. Look, man. I met Titi before you did. I knew her when she was in pigtails. In fact, I introduced her to you." Isaac couldn't believe how childish and below-the-belt the conversation was getting.

"You a lie," Pharaoh retorted. "She was my woman first."

Isaac felt his lip twist. So Pharaoh was going to go for the jugular and remind him that he was the one who broke Titi in. He paused, letting out a breath as though the wind had been knocked out of him. When he spoke, he chose his words with care.

"She was just a kid then. Besides, she was never married to you. What you-all had was puppy love. Me and her, now, we were married for fifteen years."

Years ago, Isaac fought him over Titi, and he would again, if he had to. Just as he was ready to pull out his full arsenal of words, or maybe even fight, Calissa, who disappeared into the sacristy, rushed between the two men.

She planted herself between them.

"What are you two arguing about?" she asked. "Nefertiti Jael ain't thinking about neither one of you. Y'all think a woman is something you own like a car?"

The two men stared at Calissa with marbled, caulded eyes. She was Pharaoh's stepmother and Isaac's birth mother. But at that point, she could have been a stranger to either one.

Shrouded in the white altar cloth, Calissa's arm pointed at the two men like a loaded shotgun. Yet, they were oblivious to her weapon. Her body formed a barricade between them.

Calissa went on. "That girl barely set foot off the plane this morning, and y'all carrying on like two dogs over a bone. I don't know, but the two of you need to straighten up. She is a grown woman now, and in case you've forgotten, she's another man's wife at that."

"Mama," Pharaoh said, "this nigger in here trying to start something back up with Nefertiti. I know him. He crawled around like a snake on its belly the whole time I was away in the war. That's how he got her away from me in the first place."

Isaac could only stare at Pharaoh. Here his

stepbrother called his mother "Mama," when he, himself, her only biological child, called her by her first name.

For a moment, no one spoke. Silence hung like a Molotov cocktail in the air. Calissa spoke first. "All that is water under the bridge y'all talking about. Whether y'all know it or not, a woman is not your toy. She ain't like a car you trade in when you get tired of her. Furthermore, this the house of the Lord. This ain't no place to be arguing, anyway."

Isaac was silent. He was always quiet in the presence of his mother. He was a middle-aged man, yet he could never quite find the right words to speak whenever he was around his mother. He couldn't help himself.

Knowing his words, as quickly as they stumbled across the threshold of his mouth, labeled him a liar, Isaac directed his words to Pharaoh. "Our marriage would have lasted if it hadn't been for you. You just wouldn't leave us alone."

Then Pharaoh did it. Twisted the knife in the gaping wound that pumped Isaac's blood, almost knocking him to his knees. "You a lie, man. She was my woman first. Hey, ain't my fault she left you for a white man."

"I—" Isaac's voice faltered. He started to say something, sputtered midway through his grappling, then fell silent. The only way Pharaoh and Calissa could see his internal dialogue was through the twitching of his jaws. The round curves in both jaws were so swollen they looked as if they had rocks in them.

Without knowing it, Isaac began to ball his fists

up, making half-moons with his nails into his sweat-coated palms. His nostrils almost deflated, he inhaled so much air in an angry gasp.

Calissa ran in between the two men, putting her palms into Isaac's chest, slightly pushing him out of Pharaoh's radius of vision and line of attack.

"Look, you two. Don't start that. Y'all not boys fighting anymore. You both forty-something years old. Fully grown men. Leave the past be. Let sleeping dogs lie. Anyway, Nefertiti's already been to the church to bring those flowers and she's gone on her way. She won't be back until the dinner on Saturday."

The tension swelling the church walls threatened to explode that moment into tiny shards of hatred. Isaac was so huffed up, the only sound one could hear was the rising and falling of Pharaoh's chest, accompanied by the wind racing through his flared nostrils.

Finally, like a dying man, Isaac exhaled. "Well, she was some woman."

Although he didn't say anything, Pharaoh's shoulders relaxed, as though in this one point of undeniable agreement, there was a bond between the two men.

Suddenly Isaac's pager went off. He looked into the beeper hooked on the side of his pants.

"Damn." His home telephone number flashed in the beeper's screen. It was Roshanne.

After Isaac left the church, Pharaoh sat in a pew, hands folded in a steeple as though he were praying. For the longest time, he sat quietly, not thinking about much of anything, just being still. Without knowing it, he was waiting for Calissa.

"I'm getting ready to lock up now." Her purse in her hand, Calissa let him know she'd finished her work. Pharaoh resented the fact that Calissa's voice took on the patronizing tone that one would use with a child.

Rankled, he decided not to give voice to his hurt feelings. "You going to visit Sister Betty again?" he asked. Pharaoh knew the different church members, because, as a rule, he talked to his stepmother on the phone almost every week. Sister Betty, one of the church members, had been dying from cancer for over ten years.

"No, I don't think I'll be going again."

"Why not? I thought she liked for you to come sit with her and read the Bible."

"Well, not anymore," Calissa said, reaching for her trench coat on the rack in the church's atrium. Pharaoh jumped up from the pew and ran to Calissa's side to help her ease into her coat. He noticed the weary sound in Calissa's voice.

"What's the matter?"

Calissa paused. She drew in her breath as if each spoken word pained her.

"Sister Betty told Sister Magnolia that I'm just coming down there trying to get old bald-headed Willie Luke from her. She doesn't know. I don't want her husband. She even told Magnolia that I said that she had nine lives like a cat, and I'm just waiting for her to die. That isn't how I said it. One night, when she was feeling low sick, I told Betty that she *wasn't* going to die.

That she had nine lives like a cat. I meant it to cheer her up."

Pharaoh restrained an urge to laugh. Trying to be comforting, he said, "Well, that's too bad, Mama. I don't believe Miss Magg believed that mess. She knows how lies get started. Still, I feel bad for how this town treats you. I don't see how you even came back to this church."

"Well, the Bible says 'God forgives in a large way.' But man—he never forgives and forgets nothing."

"I heard that." Thinking of the tangled wilderness of his life, Pharaoh looked over at his stepmother.

She had been a rock for him when he was a teenager. A flash of memory slipped into his mind, where he'd found Calissa crying over Isaac, her son, because as a teenager, he refused to speak to her at all. Ironically, it was Calissa who'd taken Pharaoh in at age thirteen when his mother died down in Belize—called British Honduras at the time. His father had been only a phantom his grandparents occasionally mentioned before his mother's death.

"Do you ever regret it?" Pharaoh asked suddenly.

Calissa knew what he was talking about. Neither one needed to say a word about "it."

"If I had it to do over, I would do the same thing again." Calissa's chin jutted out in defiance.

Without warning, Pharaoh felt one of those spells coming over him, so he turned to leave. He recognized the gingery voice, the one people used when they thought that you were crazy. It was the voice that, after his return from Vietnam, had run him into the arms of the Ghost Lady, the Riderless Horse, heroin. It was also the same voice that had helped him steal from Pay Dirt's small bank account with impunity. As far as he was concerned, he wasn't the crazy one. No, they were. If they had run through the emerald Vietnam jungles, they would know what he felt. Or what he heard.

He was used to the loud voices. He adjusted and learned to live with them. Auditory/visual hallucinations, his doctor called them. Although it had been years since he kicked his heroin addiction, or since he saw visions, he still heard the voices. His doctor thought it might have come from the Agent Orange. At any rate, Pharaoh just wouldn't let Nefertiti know about them this time, when he saw her.

Before, when she'd seen him seven years earlier, she'd gotten that same frightened look, the same patronizing look Calissa would get sometimes. The only thing that occasionally calmed the voices was when Pharaoh held a paintbrush. Over the years, he'd painted wall murals, frescoes, all over his apartment. Pharaoh often viewed the world in colors and pictures. But now, Memory Rose, his landlord of ten years, was threatening to evict him if he put another "iota of paint on my walls."

Pulling away in his car, Pharaoh was thinking about how his deflowering of Nefertiti would always remain the summit of his love life. After the dry run, he'd broken her in—gotten her cherry.

The prize. He wondered why they called it that. Other than in a male's blustery ego, it was hardly ever that memorable, especially for the woman. Amen.

If he was to paint his life in song, the bluesy part would be the beats and chords that talked about his experiences with Vietnamese women, and the array of rainbow women in between that he'd slept with while he was in the service. Weaving through it all, the main melody would be Nefertiti. For the memory of Nefertiti eclipsed any other woman he'd ever had. It had only been one summer in his life, but he'd held on to it like a diamond. Something he'd take out and look at when it would rain ten days in a row, or when his disability check would be late.

Now the whole thing—the joke that had been called his life—was a coda to what might have been. For the past ten years, sex had merely been a mechanical act, a charade, wherein he just went through the motions with whomever his faceless partner was. God forbid that whoever she was would start cooing and making nesting sounds. He literally would take the first thing smoking, or do everything in his power to destroy whatever connection the unfortunate woman was mistakenly calling "love."

Pharaoh often found himself obsessing over the first time with Nefertiti. Their rendezvous usually took place at "their spot," down past the meadow, in the sunken valley behind her father's church.

Never mattered that their spot was in the cemetery. The coupling had been as bittersweet as it had been inept. Although she hadn't been his first experience, he had been her first man. The ultimate thrill. As old, yet as new, as desire. Outside of turning a bad girl into a good girl, nothing could beat making a good girl turn into a bad girl. Not that Nefertiti ever changed in his eyes. In his mind, he still kept her up on a pedestal. She'd always be "the Preacher's Gal."

After several months of enticing, kissing her neck (once, he'd left so many monkey bites on her neck, she had to wear a turtleneck to school to keep Rev from seeing them), seducing her into the forbidden pleasures of lust, she finally agreed. It reminded him of yo-yoing, how he had drawn her in, after slow walking her down.

They say you never forget your first. Would Nefertiti always remember him? Did she remember how they had hid beneath the large pine tree at the cemetery's edge, using a bed of pine needles and honeysuckle for a mattress? Or, on a spring day, could she still conjure up the cool resinous smell of pine swishing over their heads, encircling the two young lovers as they lay there tentatively tasting each other's kisses, drinking in the strawberry tightness of each other's youth? Or could she still hear him whispering those sweet words she loved to hear? Or remember him watching the fluttering of her eyelids, until she yielded to him like a cocoon cracking open its new larvae? Did she know that he felt the pine needles piercing his hands at the same time he pierced what would always remind him of the pistil of a prized tulip? Once he entered into the cave of warmth, he saw colors as beautiful as those on a monarch butterfly. Did she remember how they both melted into the earth beneath them? It had been springtime. Honeysuckle, butterflies, and pine needles would always make him think of Nefertiti and that golden spring. . . .

Anyway, he'd gotten the short end of the stick out of the whole deal. It was some lame mess. Just like the throw of dice with Vietnam. Here, he hadn't even been born in this country, and he'd had to go fight a war for it. When it came time for fighting in the war, he was no longer a foreigner who barely had his citizenship papers. When it came time for war, he was just another nigger. The killing part about it was that Isaac, who'd been born in America, was never drafted because of his childhood cerebral palsy, which, to this day, left him with a limp. But for healthy young black men (as Pharaoh had once been), it seemed as if Uncle Sam kept a special place reserved on the front lines for them. Ain't that some buzzard luck?

But before the week was out, Pharaoh was going to even up the score. He'd have some money. He had it all figured out. Then, maybe he and Nefertiti would have a chance. For they would always be bound by the daughter they conceived and who was born in 1967.

4

Later, that afternoon, after returning from the church, Nefertiti wandered down the oak-paneled staircase, past the hand-carved wainscoting, past the grandfather clock carved from tulipwood—"Big Ben," her father's one-and-only family heirloom—and into the wood-beamed kitchen, where the pungent smell of onions and gravy pulled her on an invisible string. Nefertiti found her mother standing over the six-eye antique stove, stirring a large iron skillet, calling up more pictures from her childhood. A solid size eight, Miss Magg sure looked good for a woman of sixty-five. As far as her face, her vitiligo seemed to have arrested some, Nefertiti noticed.

"Smells good, Miss Magg. What's cooking?"

"Just some liver."

"Ooh, good! You know how I love your liver!"

Her mother didn't answer, but Nefertiti knew that she was pleased. Sometimes she wondered how her mother had lived her life. Such a docile, boring life. The onus of their smoothly run congregation had fallen mainly on Miss Magg's shoulders. Her mother was the one who visited the sick, organized the social events, and formed the groups for seniors, youth, and young mothers. In fact, she was the one who started the working mother's day care at the church.

It seemed as if her mother's entire adult life had been centered around pleasing her family and the church members. Nevertheless, it had always seemed to make her happy. And she especially loved people to eat her food. Seemed to love cooking to please the Rev, as Nefertiti called her father behind his back.

But Nefertiti had to admit, no one could fry a chicken like her mother, and, in fact, she was slightly disappointed they weren't having fried chicken tonight. Her mother had been raised in a small town called Eunice, Louisiana. Miss Magg could make a crawfish etouffee that made you squirm in your chair.

"I have some boudin in the freezer," her mother said.

"Good. I can't wait to eat some. Like I was telling Ford, you ain't lived until you've eaten Miss Magg's boudin."

"Little Josh and Cleo will want some, too."

Nefertiti didn't comment. Here, she'd hoped this reconciliation would recement the family bond, but things were starting off on the wrong foot already.

Little Josh and Cleo, the subjects of her mother's comment, were her siblings, who bore resemblances to strange, distant relatives, their affinity to her was so strained. Nefertiti often felt like her brother, her sister, and herself were all strangers, stranded through the misfortune of shipwreck on the same boat, yet fighting for the last raft to safety. Maybe it was due to their age differences, since Josh was three years older than Nefertiti and Cleo was nearly sixteen years younger. Nefertiti didn't know what it was, and she'd never figured it out. But they were more rivals than siblings.

She really wanted—in fact, needed—more time alone with her parents. Changing the subject, in an effort to hide her disappointment, Nefertiti asked, "How is Daddy getting along?"

She didn't know which thing upset her more. Not having fried chicken, or knowing that her little time alone with her parents would be interrupted by morning when her brother and sister arrived. She had issues that she felt needed to be confronted with both her father and her mother. For the first time in her life, she felt strong enough to face these concerns.

"Pretty good. His blood count is still kinda low. I try to get him to take my blackstrap molasses, but he says that's for women. That's why I give him plenty of beef. They say calf's liver is supposed to be good."

"You sure he isn't pushing too hard? Getting involved in Councilman Huttleson's campaign and all." Nefertiti thought about the newspaper articles her mother had sent about Rev was campaigning for Councilman Huttleson, how he had endorsed the campaign, and how he was even using the church for a campaign headquarters.

"You know your father doesn't know anything about retirement. He's even supposed to preach this Sunday to kick off Revival Week. I try to tell your father to slow down, but he says, as long as he ain't dead, he ain't gon' lie down and die before his time."

"Yeah, he always was something else."

"Anyway, this birthday dinner is going to be a big to-do." Her mother began fingering the box of herbs on the windowsill, which she grew inside the kitchen during the winter. The wafting aroma of the sarsaparilla, basil, garlic, gingerroot, and thyme encircled Nefertiti's shoulders like an old friend.

Home. This was one of the good things about being home. She had to remember to take some herbs back with her. Thinking of Big Mama Lily's castor oil and sheep sorrel tea, she frowned.

She eased into a kitchen chair and kicked her shoes off, absently asking, "What do you mean, a big to-do?"

"Well, they are even going to combine the dinner with announcing Councilman Huttleson's bid for mayor. There was a photographer who was supposed to come by and take some pictures of your father this afternoon before he left. They're going to put the whole affair in the colored newspaper. I hope I didn't miss her when I ran out to the airport to pick you up. Anyway, I was to page your father if she came by before he got back. I don't think that woman ever showed up. Had some unusual name, too. Supposed to have been some college friend of Cleo's. I don't know. Ahhh, well, I can't remember. Hmmmm. Wonder what's keeping your father."

Nefertiti wondered, too. Since he'd told Miss

Magg that Nefertiti was welcome to come back home, why was Rev trying to avoid seeing her?

Nefertiti had grown up in Shallow's Corner, a small enclave of Detroit, where the Bible Belt was as strong as in the South. For those who did not comply with the tight strictures of the sanctified church, there was censor, ostracism, and stigma. How well she had learned. . . .

But thinking of the name "Shallow's Corner," it described the terrain perfectly. It was just that. A little sleepy river town pushed off in the corner of Detroit by the river. It was so small, it wasn't even on the map.

Many of its residents, former sharecroppers from the South, settled there after World War II, looking for the better life offered in the city. At some prehistoric time, a glacier had inched over the land, leaving an indent on the earth's face like a crater in the moon. The city was founded upon the sunken basin where the river had once flowed. This empty riverbed was away from the whites who lived on the higher land in Dearborn, Bloomfield Hills, and Palmer Heights, Michigan.

Nefertiti's street, Black Stone Drive, a cul-de-sac, was home to a collection of brick houses in a variety of styles from Cape Cod to ranch to bungalow, which ironically had Gothic, Baroque, or Greek touches among the hodgepodge architecture. Gargoyles and turrets lifted above the other roofs on the street. Her parents' house was surrounded by a high wrought-iron fence, which often reminded her of a cage.

She stared out the kitchen window at the new apartment building constructed where the old funeral parlor—also her ex-husband's childhood home—used to stand next door. It covered the lot that their first church had been built on. At one time, the minister's house, the funeral home, and the First Solid Rock Baptist Church had stood side by side in a somber row, with the cemetery behind the meadow not far below it.

When Nefertiti was growing up, the town used to call their street "Tombstone Territory," instead of Black Stone Drive.

As a little girl, Nefertiti used to be so afraid of the ghosts from all the cadavers next door, Big Mama Lily had placed a mirror under her bed for protection. "Ghosts don't like to see themselves," she would tell Nefertiti. "I would make you a bottle tree, but Reverend say that we are Christians and we can't keep with the old ways," Big Mama Lily would add. Nefertiti had never understood what her great-grandmother meant by that.

Well, now she had new ghosts from the past to contend with. And she didn't have Big Mama Lily to help fend them off for her, either. She would have to do it for herself.

It had been seven years since she last stepped foot in this room. Seven years. Since her last fall from grace. It had taken her nearly twenty years to earn her father's forgiveness for a mistake in her youth, and in just one act of will, she had been banished from the Garden of Eden of her father's love, spurned once again.

And whenever her family, which included her father, one older brother, and one younger sister, closed ranks against her, she went teetotaling crazy. Only Miss Magg had continued to talk to her during this period of exile. Over the years, without ever uttering a word, her family had a way of disfellowshipping her, if she disagreed with them. She was the apostate.

In the most recent exclusion, her father had stopped speaking to her when she married Nigel Ford, a former classmate from her one year of college at USC. Ford had also been the lawyer who helped her get connections to arrange her divorce from Isaac. There was only one problem with Ford—he was biracial, part white. In earlier times, he would be called a quadroon.

From the onset of her divorce from Isaac, her father's beloved former son-in-law, Nefertiti felt as if she were some type of pestilence to be avoided. She became like what Rev would preach against suspected dissidents, "the leaven in the congregation." Only Miss Magg stayed in touch with her during those seven years of exile.

But ever since her father's heart attack last spring, when she'd sent money to help pay for part of his hospital bill, from what Miss Magg said in her letters, Nefertiti was welcome back home. They were giving her father a seventy-fifth birthday party at Solid Rock Baptist Church. At first, she had declined the offer.

At the last minute, in a moment of unexplained rashness, she purchased a plane ticket, and the Prodigal Daughter had come home.

Nefertiti felt like she would come apart if she

didn't get back home and take care of what was bothering her. So although she was happy about the tentative reconciliation, there was something else. Something deeper. So deep, she almost couldn't face it in her soul. She could no longer recognize the woman she saw in the mirror. There was a sense of shame, a cowardice, that she did not particularly like when she saw her reflection.

This was her first visit home in seven years. She had come alone, convinced she needed to work out so many things. It was also because of the dreams. She couldn't shake the dreams she'd been having about Big Mama Lily and about Desiree:

> *It's me, it's me, it's me, oh Lord,*
> *Standing in the need of prayer.*

Perhaps that was why she had to come back east, both physically and mentally, to the *daylean*—the Gullah word Big Mama Lily used to use for dawn. Clean to the beginning, where day and all things began.

5

If he could open up a school for all the married
men who had lost their good wives to these "outside" women in the street, he would. *Humph.* He'd
probably become a millionaire. When Isaac married Titi, he'd never felt sure that she was over
Pharaoh. Because of this, he used to be jealous
and possessive, making her account for every
moment she was out of his sight. But with the birth
of his children, he began to feel her love surround-
ing him like a well-worn, comfortable bathrobe.

And that was when he began to take her for
granted. Why did it have to be this way? What did
the old folks say about never missing your water
till your well run dry? Well, maybe that was what
still excited him. The challenge. The chase. Now
that she was gone, he wanted her back. When he
had her in his life, he'd lost interest. But not at
first, though.

At first, she'd had his nose wide open. She had
been his first woman. Or had he simply been
whipped, because Titi surely knew how to whip it
on him? So what had gone wrong? The thing he'd

always loved-hated about her was that she never let him penetrate her center. She simply would not give up who she was, to be with him. Unlike many women, she was unmalleable. You couldn't tell her nothing. Then there was that baby she'd had as a teenager, too—that, in the height of his affair, he decided he had a right to do what he wanted to, and even went so far as to feel justified in his affair. After all, he felt he could get even, since he secretly held her past against her.

So when Roshanne had promised him the moon, he had believed that Titi was the problem. She wouldn't listen to him. But now, the paradox was that he wondered what had been so mesmerizing about Roshanne in the first place.

His second wife reminded him of a hollow nutshell. You get your mouth all tooted up for a meaty center and find nothing inside. There he went again. Thinking in metaphors. Maybe that was his problem. Isaac often thought in images, icons, and symbols. At times, he wondered if he confused what was real with what he imagined. It was like living a double life—that "double consciousness"— even more so than what W.E.B. Du Bois had described for the Negro in America at the turn of the century. Although he didn't see himself as deep— in fact, he was obtuse when it came to women—he wished his mind would just rest sometimes.

Suddenly Isaac's car phone rang. He grabbed it on the third ring.

"Hey, Isaac." It was his agent, Robert Winthrop.

"Any news?" Isaac went straight to the point.

"No bites yet, but I mailed back your last version

for you to work on your revisions. You should get it in the mail by tomorrow."

"Cool."

"If we can get a book deal, your plays can be published in hardback, like August Wilson's plays. You'll reach a much wider audience that way. Might even get more crossover."

Isaac's mood lifted. "That's what I'm talking about. I'm really getting tired of waiting."

"Don't worry. I've got a good feeling about this independent publisher, Harmony Reads."

"I hope so."

"Don't worry. Keep your chin up."

That's the one thing Isaac liked about his agent. Robert was his bona fide cheerleader. He'd kept Isaac going during this dry spell.

As he turned the curve into the Palmer Heights area where he lived, a sense of sadness overwhelmed him. How long would he have to keep beating himself over the head? Even now, he couldn't get over how blind he'd been. He wouldn't be the successful playwright he had become, had Titi not stuck by him through those lean years.

After all, during their twelve-year marriage, she had been the one who had always held a steady job. Titi had told him that he had a calling. His first obligation was to fulfill his calling, she'd said. So that was what he had done throughout their marriage. Pounded away on his old typewriter.

Moreover, he never would have believed in himself, had it not been for Titi. Not after the childhood he had suffered. She was the one who helped him get to where he was today. But what did he have to go and do? Destroy everything. Why?

To this day, he didn't know. But maybe he could make sense of the *how.* As he had become more of a public figure, a household name, enticing women began hanging around like insects around a flowering tree. Women were suddenly everywhere. And they had started looking really good, especially after he began resenting the day-to-day burdens of being tied down with a wife and family. How could he have known that achieving success at thirty would also become anathema?

He was one of many firsts in his generation. First from Shallow's Corner to receive a Guggenheim Fellowship and a National Endowment of the Arts Award. First from Shallow's Corner to make more than enough money to get by and support a family. First to really make close to six figures. First to make money doing what he really loved. Being a writer. And it had gone to his head.

Now he couldn't help but wonder. Had the women only been using him? Oh, sure it had felt the other way around at the time, like he was the one getting over on them, but had it been that way? If only he could turn back the hands of time. How had he been so stupid? Even though he knew all along that he was the same plain old Isaac with the inset-eyes, he had begun to believe his own press.

His success, coupled with having a wife and family, had rendered him a handsome man. He'd gotten even more "fine" when his money started rolling in; so much so, he'd gotten the big head. Forgotten how he'd gotten his start. Who had been in his corner when he was a nobody. Talked a lot of head, too.

"I did everything for myself. Didn't nobody do nothing for me," he used to preach whenever he got tired of paying bills. Tired of baby diapers. Tired of the "dull" doldrums, which begin as a gangrene in every marriage.

Now here he was, seven years later. Déjà vu. He really didn't like being married to Roshanne. He didn't know if it was marriage or Roshanne, but he definitely knew that he'd made a mistake when he lost Titi for this woman.

"Did you pick up the ice cream I told you to get?" Roshanne asked as soon as he opened the door, interrupting his reverie.

Isaac frowned. Now, she knew he wasn't supposed to eat ice cream with his recently diagnosed diabetes, but she kept all types of sweets in the house. It was as though she wanted him to die. He shivered at the thought.

"No, I forgot. Here's some Chinese food for dinner."

That was another thing he didn't like about Roshanne. She never cooked since they'd gotten married six years ago. Oh, she had cooked all the time—things like lasagna and shrimp Creole and jambalaya in red sauce—when he was sneaking around with her before Titi left.

Now he was painfully reminded that Titi could cook. Boy, could Titi put foot in some food! Even after she'd work all day in an office, he'd often come home to a glass of chilled wine and coq au vin wafting from the kitchen. Nothing like this "I don't do kitchens" Roshanne. Isaac had gotten to the point where he couldn't stand the thought of eating out anymore, so he either cooked or bought takeout.

Besides, other than the trust fund his father had left him, his money was getting funnier and funnier. He was still living off the royalties from his former plays, *River of Blood* and *Blues River.* He hadn't had a hit in several years now. He wondered if having tasted success at the young age of thirty had, like a flashing star, burned him out, and if he would ever have a hit again. He hated to admit it, but maybe Roshanne was right. He was washed-up. Through. Finished.

When he saw his old family album opened on the sofa, he asked, "What did you do today?"

Roshanne slipped something from the album into her silk robe pocket. He started to ask her what it was, but she always accused him of prying too much.

"Oh, I was just straightening out these old pictures."

"Where did you get those from?" Isaac recognized the album's gold-printed cover—the one that he and Titi had once had. "I thought I had put my old pictures away."

"Oh, they were out in the den. Don't worry. I don't want to throw out your pictures of your precious past."

"Did you get the job?" Isaac asked. Roshanne had supposedly gone on one of her many half-hearted interviews earlier that afternoon.

"No." Roshanne turned away and got busy setting out paper plates for the Chinese food.

* * *

That was another thing he disliked about Roshanne. She hated to work, and that meant he had to concern himself with keeping his job at the junior college, where he taught creative writing. He'd found that since they'd been married, Roshanne never worked steadily on any job. Even her acting career had soured. That, coupled with her excessive weight gain, had killed his desire for her.

Occasionally she'd get a secretarial job, then quit, saying she couldn't be confined all day. She had things to do. What things? Isaac wondered. Like watch her soap operas and talk shows? Heaven forbid, if she missed those, then they had to be taped for her. And the worst thing was that he found out recently she had gone on a sleazy shock-drama talk show. When he confronted her, Roshanne shot back, "So what?"

When he asked her why she couldn't keep a job, she would retaliate, "That's what I married you for."

"Did you get to see Her Highness?"

Isaac jumped. He hadn't seen Roshanne walk up on him. He turned and looked at her buttermilk face.

Jealousy had transmogrified her once-attractive features into a muddy alignment. Her eyes looked as though they were ringed with green moss—there was so much hatred lying at the bottom of their empty pools. Isaac shook his head to make sure he wasn't seeing things. Roshanne had turned back into herself.

"What are you talking about, woman?" Isaac twisted off his camel-colored cashmere coat and tossed it on the Duncan Phyfe sofa. He'd had this sofa when he was married to Titi. Roshanne didn't argue with him to hang his coat up, but neither did she pick it up.

Nefertiti had left everything behind, and it seemed as though nothing Roshanne bought, no matter how much money she'd spend on it, ever had the impeccable taste or the class of the furniture that Titi had picked.

The room, which had once been a subtle marriage between soft eggshell colors, elegant antiques, and live plant foliage, was now a harsh blend of blues, purples, and blacks in glass and leather. The Duncan Phyfe sofa was the only antique left in the living room, and it looked out of place in the lagoon of junk Roshanne had picked.

When Isaac didn't respond, Roshanne begin to heckle him.

"Hey, I know you didn't get sanctified all of a sudden."

For the first time, Isaac really looked at Roshanne's elongated features, which resembled a jackass more and more each day. He didn't like what he saw—pure, unmitigated evil. How had he been so blind? Further, how could he correct this mistake?

Something in her face called to mind what his father had said—rather indicated, since he could no longer talk at that point—about Roshanne.

Following his father's first stroke, the Deacon had come to live with Isaac and Titi for the last five years of their twelve-year marriage. Regardless of how rocky their marriage had gotten, Titi had been good to his father. Even after she'd left Isaac, she'd made arrangements for Herschel Thorne to go stay with another relative.

After Roshanne moved in with Isaac (under the condition that he promised to marry her once his divorce from Titi was final), she agreed to take care of his father. Through their honeymoon period, his wife had seemed like a devoted, loyal woman whenever Isaac was around. But within six months of moving in with Isaac and his new wife, his father had died. It was as if the Deacon had given up the will to live.

And it was during those six months before his father's death, Isaac had to admit to himself, he had never seen his father look so depressed. Not even when his father's first wife, Isaac's mother, Calissa, had walked out on him. Not even when his second wife, Beulah, had died suddenly, leaving him a widower in his early sixties. Not even when the funeral home had been burned down in the 1967 riots, and his father had been too old to rebuild the business.

Near the end of his father's seventy-year life, he stopped speaking, he had weakened so, following a second stroke. Silently he would look at Isaac, then look at Roshanne off in another room, and shake his head. The day before he died, Isaac had sat with his father, trying to reach him.

"Daddy, what is it? You've got to tell me. What's wrong?" His father held Isaac's hand and pointed to the closet.

"What is it, Daddy? Daddy, you know if I could breathe for you, I would. What is it?"

When his father pointed to the closet again, Isaac understood. He went to the closet that used to belong to Titi.

"Who, Titi?"

With great difficulty, his father nodded his head.

"She's not here anymore, Dad. She's in California." Isaac had almost swallowed those words.

His father just shook his head, tears glazing his eyes.

Just the memory made Isaac shake his head as his eyes moistened. Was his father trying to tell him before he died that this Roshanne was no good? Had she been mistreating his father in his absence? The more Isaac thought about it, the more riled he became. He knew exactly what he had to do.

Now, remembering this day, Isaac wondered if the thought had been planted in his mind ever since then to try to win Titi back. What was he going to do about Roshanne? What would Titi do about her husband?

He'd have to work out those details, but he was on a mission. Like a fruit fly, knowing he only had a short time to live, he was acutely aware of the shortage of time. He'd learned Titi's plane would be leaving on Sunday, and it was already Wednesday evening.

"Do you hear me?"

"What?" Isaac said, coming back to the present.

"Did you hear what I said, man? Are you deaf or dumb? Did she bring the kids with her?"

Roshanne's question failed to hide the sneer stamped all over her face. Even a blind man could see Roshanne's dislike for his children from his former marriage.

And children being children, they sensed Roshanne's dislike for them, and now Isaac noticed that they were beginning to spend less and less time at his home during their summer visits. Their last visit had only lasted a week.

Isaac stopped dead in his tracks. That's it. He would use the kids for an excuse to go visit her parents' house. He could pinch himself for this fortunate twist of fate. He wished he'd thought of it himself. He would go later that evening.

6

Transfixed, Nefertiti stared at Miss Magg as she chopped liver and onions. Miss Magg's light-brown-fading-to-white fingers, where the vitiligo was spreading, moved in and out of the raw liver with the butcher knife. The onions made Nefertiti's eyes tear. Between the two sensations, Nefertiti imagined that the bloodred meat was her heart being chopped, stabbed, and desiccated into a red dust. It reminded her of the bloodiness, the afterbirth, and the pain of her first child's birth.

"Why are you wearing African clothes, Titi?" Miss Magg leaned over and gathered several of Nefertiti's dreadlocks in her hand and fingered them with interest. Usually reticent about asking questions of her adult children, her mother shocked her. Her words were so abrupt, they hit her like karate chops, shaking Nefertiti out of her dead stare.

"You mean you never saw African garb before?" Nefertiti lifted her eyebrow, both to ward off her mother's criticism and to act oblivious to it. Still, when she sat down in a chair, she found herself twisting her widow's peak, a nervous habit carried over from her childhood. "Miss Magg, this is a caftan. Usually, I have a head wrap to go with it." Nefertiti took another bite out of her apple, looking away.

"It reminds me of that dashiki you used to wear."

That had been her year of rebellion, when she was a senior in high school during 1969.

Nefertiti smiled.

Exhibiting another habit carried over from childhood, Nefertiti opened the refrigerator door, stared into space, trying to remember what she was looking for. She couldn't quite recall, stared blankly at the carton of milk and neatly packed bacon, eggs, and wrapped leftovers, then closed the door.

Nefertiti picked another bright apple from the straw cornucopia on the butcher-block table and took a crunchy bite from the center. She decided not to follow up this motherly carping remark.

"Why did you stop pressing your hair?"

There Miss Magg went again, chipping away. Nefertiti imagined that if her mother chipped long enough, hard enough even, maybe one day, she, Nefertiti, would emerge as the sculpture of "The Perfect Fine-Fine Daughter."

Nefertiti didn't answer her.

After a while, Miss Magg had a new question. "How's your store doing?" Her mother knew how to change directions in midstream of conversation.

"Great." Nefertiti felt her cheek muscles assembling into a smile as she considered The Treasure Chest, her African boutique. Her store was just reaching its second anniversary. She also specialized in memorabilia, such as old scrub boards and washtubs, African statues, artifacts, relics, and paintings. In one corner, she had first editions of early African-American writers, such as Zora Neale Hurston, Wallace Thurman, and Richard Wright gracing her bookshelves.

Her Los Angeles store was situated across the street from a park that housed a tic-tac-toe variety of transient men. Because she gave out coffee, some had begun to frequent her store to get a warm cup of brew in their stomachs.

The homeless men were a loyal group, she discovered. In exchange for her kindness, they often washed her store windows and watched out for burglars. Nefertiti had even spearheaded a literacy class for them, conducting lessons on Booker T. Washington's *Up from Slavery*. Recently she'd brought in a partner, Phyllis, who was running the store while she was on vacation.

Because of her store, Nefertiti had catapulted into an arena where she was open to things that had never occurred to her while she was working for someone else.

For one, she had discovered an interest in genealogy. She was amazed at the amount of research she was able to find in the cyberspace of her computer. That brought her back to one of her reasons for returning home. Because of her curiosity, she'd packed her tape recorder. If she could find time alone with her father, she planned to ask him some questions about his side of the family.

Nefertiti had heard that Rev had Cherokee Indian on his side of the family, but that was about all she knew. She hoped that in doing this project together, she and her father could heal some of the distance between them.

On the other hand, Nefertiti knew a lot about her mother's side of the family through Big Mama Lily, her maternal great-grandmother, who had raised Miss Magg. Throughout her growing-up years, she'd never heard her father tell anyone anything about his family or his childhood. It was as if he came here like Adam, a fully realized man. Through Big Mama Lily, she only knew his mother had been known as "Bertie," and his father had had an unusual Indian name, but they called him "Pretty."

"I sure worry about you. Giving up that good job and all." Miss Magg tried to soften her criticism.

Nefertiti thought of her fifteen-year tenure at the government's housing division with distaste. She had become a second-level supervisor, a fairly high level in the government, before she resigned. She thought of all the Chanel and Yves Saint Laurent suits she used to wear and had given up in the past two years.

Expensive straitjackets, she thought, *that's all they were.* Now that she didn't have to work for mainstream America, she was becoming more and more Afrocentric, anyhow.

"Look, Miss Magg. That 'good job' was about to put me in the nuthouse. Besides, Ford makes good money. His practice is really growing with this welfare reform. You know panel attorneys are in demand in California. As long as there is—and I hate to say this—child abuse, he'll always have a job. At least I don't have to keep working at something I hate, like when I was married to Isaac."

Nefertiti knew how her mother had always favored her first husband, Isaac. Although her mother was polite to Nigel, she didn't think her mother really liked her new husband. Her mother could only see the brand-new tri-level ranch that Nefertiti had walked off and left behind in Palmer Heights. Miss Magg apparently had selective amnesia and had forgotten the six-day workweek Nefertiti used to put in to build and keep that house, while Isaac sat on his butt at the typewriter.

"You think Daddy will ever be able to fly to California and see me? I'd like him to see my new house." Nefertiti began talking as if she had never stopped. Miss Magg didn't answer.

Nefertiti decided to overlook her mother's evasion. She really did want her father to come see her English Tudor home, with its winding staircase, high-beamed ceilings, and skylights throughout the upper level.

She knew it was stupid, but she wanted him to see how well she was faring. Even better than his namesake, Joshua II. But just as her father would probably never come see her home in Palos Verdes Estates, he would never admit that she was doing better than her brother, Joshua. Her father couldn't see anything she did that was good in her life. In his eyes, she'd always be the black sheep of the family.

Her mother began rinsing her rice over the sink. With her back facing Nefertiti, Miss Magg asked, "Where are my grandchildren?"

Nefertiti took a deep breath to keep her voice from trembling, she was becoming so angry. She didn't even know how to put her mixed emotions into words. She loved her mother, but she resented her for not taking a stand years ago, and although it had nothing to do with today, it kept bubbling up inside her.

"Savasia and Ike are staying with Yolan. You remember Ford's sister, don't you? You know she's married to an Ethiopian. The kids love it over at her house. Besides, Buffy and Tyler are about the same ages."

"I remember," Miss Magg began. "Maybe I am old-fashioned, but I am of the mind—" She stopped, as if she had already said too much.

"Go ahead and say it, Miss Magg." Nefertiti felt her temper registering on the Richter scale of her slowly building rage. "You just can't get used to the idea of me being married to Ford."

"I didn't say that."

"You might as well have said it. But I'm going to tell you something. As far as I'm concerned, Ford is black. It's his mother who is white. But you met his mother. Mother Leah is cool people—for a white woman."

"No, that's not it. I—I just wanted to see my grandchildren."

"Well, I have a lot of unfinished business to take care of during this trip."

"All the other grandchildren will be here."

"I know. But it's just one of those hard-core choices mothers have to make, isn't that right, Miss Magg? Besides, all of the grandchildren won't be here. Have you forgotten your first one?" Miss Magg didn't answer. Her face had the stricken look of someone who'd had an ice cube suddenly dropped down her back.

Nefertiti finally broached the subject on her mind. Her main reason for coming back to Shallow's Corner. Her mother was very astute. She began to move around the kitchen, acting as if she were in a hurry to complete her chores, and couldn't be bothered.

"Miss Magg, I'm going to try to find Desiree. She just turned twenty-six this year."

The moment tasted laden with fear. Fear of the unspoken. Fear of the past. Desiree was the child whom Nefertiti, at age fifteen, had given up for adoption. Her child was born March 17, 1967, and three months later, Nefertiti turned sixteen. Before anyone could speak again, the phone rang.

It was "Tiger," her father's youngest brother, her favorite uncle. The uncle she favored so much, having the same set of deep dimples, the same skin coloring.

Ever since she was a little girl, looking for the hidden quarter in his hands and ears, Nefertiti had loved Uncle Tiger. Seven years earlier, when she was going through her divorce, it was Uncle Tiger who'd sided with her.

He told her, "You've been swimming in a little pond, Little Bit. But there's a big sea out there. As long as you swim in a little pond, you'll get men with little-pond ideas. They'll either have a little bit or no success, but with little-pond ideas, they'll never go anywhere in life."

"Well, Isaac is successful, but that's not the reason I'm leaving him."

"I know, Lil' Bit. I think you've outgrown him."

To this day, Nefertiti wondered if Uncle Tiger had seen Isaac when he was running around in the streets with his other women. As much of a lady's man as her uncle was, he would not have abided seeing his favorite niece hurt.

"Hey. What's going on, Lil' Bit?" Her uncle's voice brought a smile to her face, lifting her mood.

"You've got it. What you know good, Uncle Tiger?"

Nefertiti was always happy to talk to her uncle Tiger. He was the only living brother her father still had. "Silo," an older brother, had died before Nefertiti was born.

Uncle Tiger was the one who always reminded Nefertiti that whenever he looked in the face of death, he decided to eat, drink, and be merry as long as he lived. You couldn't take nothing with you. There were no pockets in a shroud. *Carpe diem*. Seize the day.

What amazed Nefertiti about Uncle Tiger and Reverend was the fact that they were full-blooded brothers. At first glance, they didn't even physically resemble each other. True enough, Reverend had more of the burnished-amber color of the Cherokee Indian blood that flowed in his veins, whereas Tiger manifested more of the ebony in his complexion from the family's African blood.

But it was something else. It was in the two men's temperaments that they reminded her of salt and sugar. One had the vinegary disposition of salt, and one had the temperament to sweeten life's pains.

Yes, it was in Uncle Tiger—the wayfarer wanderer—the drifter—the one whom they might not hear from for two years at a time, but who would always show up living in some new country, such as Japan, or some different state—the latest being Mississippi—whom Nefertiti had always seen as lightness.

Oddly, in Reverend, the pompous, God-fearing family man, she'd always sensed a darkness. She wondered what made her think this. Even so, she wanted him to visit so she could show him how well she was faring, in spite of how he'd treated her as a child. Had he treated her differently because she was the darkest of her siblings? she wondered.

After a few more pleasantries were exchanged, Nefertiti handed the phone to Miss Magg.

Thinking of her Uncle Tiger, Nefertiti walked over to the kitchen table to take a seat as she listened to her mother greet her uncle. To her astonishment, her father, Rev—despite his pacemaker—not to mention an old bullet wound, which he'd suffered in the leg during the '67 riots—burst into the kitchen, dashed across the ceramic tile floor with the alacrity of a much younger man, and snatched the phone. Although shocked, Nefertiti wondered if and how long had her father been listening outside the kitchen door to their conversation.

"This is my people, Miss Magg, and I'd appreciate it if you let me talk to them!"

Her father's words felt like a glass of water in the face. Nefertiti wanted to speak up to her father on her mother's behalf, but her tongue felt as tied as it had when she was a young girl. Thinking of how Reverend chopped her up at this first meeting in seven years, Nefertiti felt her tongue do a somersault in her head, reminding her of the time she forgot a Sunday school piece for Easter as the whole family looked on.

She'd never forget the look of disapproval on her father's face. Reverend hadn't spoken to her for a week behind that one. Looking back, she realized Reverend had seemed cold and disapproving even when she was just a little girl.

Looking crushed, Miss Magg put her fingers to her mouth, warning Nefertiti not to say anything. How had her mother ever put up with her father all of these years? The omnipotent Reverend Godbolt.

Gazing over at her mother, Nefertiti realized how fragile and old her mother was beginning to look. How come Miss Magg had never spoken up to Rev over the years? Nefertiti kind of felt sorry for her mother, but she simultaneously was feeling a slow burning rage building within her.

When her father got off the phone, he spoke to her mother first, as though Nefertiti weren't even in the room.

"Where is the checkbook, Miss Magg?" Rev's words seemed to lance her mother.

Miss Magg frowned, but she didn't say anything. After letting out a snort through her nose, she asked, "How much he need this time?"

"Look, Miss Magg. I'm all Tiger got in the world. He is my people, and if I want to help him, that's what kinfolk is for. Did I ever deny your people anything all those years? I want Tiger to be able to make it to the dinner Saturday night. I plan to get him a plane ticket."

Miss Magg gave Nefertiti a conspiratorial glance, then spun around and left the kitchen.

Nefertiti knew that in spite of her mother's halfhearted effort at defiance, Miss Magg was going to hand over the checkbook to Rev. Her father, with his briny ways, knew how to intimidate people and get what he wanted. Her mother was a woman groomed in the art of deep silences, secrets, submission.

When her mother left the kitchen, Nefertiti reached up and hugged Rev. She was still the little girl seeking his approval. She felt him stiffen under her daughterly embrace. She cringed. What? Here, her father had been out all afternoon while she ran chores for her mother, and this was the best he could do? Wasn't she trying to bury the hatchet and make up after their seven-year estrangement? Well, this was not getting off to a good start.

"Where is your hair?"

It took Nefertiti a second to get the nitty-gritty of what Reverend was saying.

"Oh, this is so simple and easy to keep up." Nefertiti hoped to convey a breeziness she didn't feel.

"Do something with it. And take off that African mess. Didn't you bring some decent clothes with you that you can wear? The colored newspaper will be at my party Saturday. I don't want any more scandals. Haven't you disgraced this family enough?"

Without waiting for a reply, Reverend turned away and stalked out of the kitchen.

Some welcome home. Would anyone ever forgive her teen pregnancy before she got married?

Or would Rev ever get over her second marriage to Ford? Rev had always been brutally outspoken. He didn't just say his words; he rode them bareback. Unless you had a strong ego, he could break you down to sawdust. Like he'd successfully done with his son, his namesake, Joshua II.

Rev was a savage good man. He had to have the hubris, Nefertiti imagined, some ancient African chief had possessed, the genetic strain finding its way down through the years to his descendant.

His words left Nefertiti feeling shorn, naked, like a bald egg. As if she had betrayed the family once more. Why did he hate—or maybe "dislike" was the better word—her so? Her happiness over her mother's cooking, and her excitement over talking to Uncle Tiger, had lifted up her spirit, making her glad to be at home, but now she felt her mood plummet like a mockingbird shot down in midflight.

Before she could pick herself off the floor of her mind, the doorbell rang. Too speechless to worry about it, she went to answer the door, trying to get a grip on her hurt. But by the time she got to the front hallway, no one was at the door. Absently, she wondered who it could have been.

After she returned to the kitchen, Nefertiti found Miss Magg was back at the stove, cutting down the fire to let the liver and onions simmer.

"Miss Magg, did you hear what I said before—"

7

Something about watching Miss Magg's back brace, then buckle under the weight of her question, made Nefertiti halt in midsentence. The words hung between them in the air. Was she, herself, innocent of the crime because she had been under age? Was hers the crime of omission? Should she have not agreed to sign the adoption papers and give her firstborn child away to total strangers?

The kitchen was silent. Save for the two women's breathing, it felt like the space between sleeping and waking. Sort of like a twilight sleep. This sleeping repression, this wordlessness, had stood between them for nearly thirty years. Although she and her mother had grown very close over the past ten years—they could talk about *almost* anything—they couldn't discuss the past.

Miss Magg broke the silence. "My daffodils are beginning to push up through the dirt·in my flower box. I always did love spring. Makes me think of what Mama Lily said when I was a little girl. Said spring was the time of the year to start everything all over again. Winter has buried its dead, and spring was giving birth to new life."

Nefertiti had heard the story so many times about how her mother came to be called "Magnolia," she could almost quote it verbatim.

That was what she thought her mother was going to say: How one Easter, when Miss Magg was about five years old, with long thick braids swinging down her back, she'd had on an orchid-colored taffeta dress. An older lady from her church had said that the little girl looked as pretty as a magnolia. From that day forth, "Magnolia" had stuck. Later, when she'd married Reverend, he always called her "Miss Magg," and the congregation followed suit. Eventually their three children had done so, imitating all the grown-ups. The way Shallow's Corner had of pronouncing words, it sounded as if her name was "Miss Mack," like in the song, "Old Mary Mack (All dressed in black)."

"I never heard you tell that story about Big Mama Lily before. I thought you were going to tell me the story of how they started calling you Magnolia."

"I don't know why you kids never called me 'Mama,' like everybody else's child."

"Ford asked me that once. That's all I remember ever calling you was Miss Magg. Maybe because we called Big Mama Lily, 'Mama,' with her living with us, and all. I don't know. . . . What time is the dinner Saturday? I thought it was going to be on Friday evening."

"They changed it to six o'clock. Friday night was not a good evening, since that is choir rehearsal and usher board meeting night. It's a good thing the tickets hadn't gone to the printer yet. We're having a family dinner here at the house Friday night, though. I was just thinking of my daffodils, though. Sort of remind me of myself. How I used to sing all the time. Might could've gone somewhere as a gospel singer."

"I never knew you sang."

"I know. I stopped after I got married."

"Why?"

"I don't know. . . ."

No more words passed between the two women as Miss Magg began to dish up the food into serving bowls.

At last, Nefertiti found her voice. "Miss Magg? Did you hear what I said about Desiree?"

"I just think it would be best if she sought you out. I don't know." Miss Magg's voice faltered. Her mother's eyes, sunk in her diamond-shaped brow, blinked. Her face closed in on itself like an old-fashioned icebox. She probably would say no more on the subject.

Nefertiti was surprised when Miss Magg's speech took on a staccato cadence. She seemed to be circling around what she wanted to say.

"It's sort of like my mother, Betty Lee. I don't know if she is alive or dead. I don't think I would even know her if I passed her on the streets. But I don't think I would like her to come bursting into my life, either, after all this time."

Nefertiti had accepted, without question, that her maternal great-grandparents, Big Mama Lily and Grandpa Bullocks, had raised her mother. She had never thought about this unknown stranger, Betty Lee, who actually would have been her maternal grandmother. She only recognized Big Mama Lily and Grandpa Bullocks, who had lived with Nefertiti's family since her early childhood, as grandparents.

"Don't you ever wonder about her?" Nefertiti asked. Her mother shrugged and didn't reply.

Nefertiti decided to get to the point. She could already see her mother shadowboxing with her.

"Well, I do wonder about what ever happened to my child. I have dreams about her all the time now. Do you know where the birth certificate is? I plan to go to the agency."

After a long silence, Miss Magg answered. "It's in my trunk. In the attic . . . in the family Bible."

"I'll get it myself. You don't have to give it to me."

"Well, just don't let your father know what you're planning to do."

Nefertiti nodded, although she was at a do-or-die stage, and she really didn't care what her father thought. She decided she would wait for her parents to go to bed and then go up to the attic. Even so, just the thought of taking this step toward trying to right a wrong from her past made her shudder.

8

Later that evening, from the window of her old bedroom, Nefertiti stared out at the gloaming. Her old bedroom was situated on the second story of her parents' house. An old-fashioned saltbox house, complete with a verandah and swing. She hadn't realized how much she'd missed home. She watched the silvery birch trees, quivering in the scud, moving like lightning rods all up and down Black Stone Drive. She was back home. Home to Shallow's Corner.

Nefertiti's thoughts wandered to her mother. Miss Magg still looked good for her age, she decided. She just wished her mother would stand up to Rev, but some things never changed. But overall, Nefertiti was happy to be at home. Even if home meant hidden secrets, half-truths.

Now it brought up for her what her father had said when she told him she was marrying Ford.

"Girl, don't you know that they used to have laws against miscegenation?"

Ooh, how she hated that word! Its harshness. Its dissonance. Following her marriage to Ford, five years earlier, her father had stopped speaking to Nefertiti. This breach had come at a time when Nefertiti was planning her first visit back to Michigan after a two-year stay in Los Angeles. Although she had sent her parents plane tickets, and her mother had visited last winter, her father still refused to come.

Because her mother had written, *Your daddy wants to see you,* Nefertiti had been hopeful. In light of this, she didn't want to risk tearing the thin membrane of peace in the family.

But still, she couldn't get over Reverend. *Power is a funny thing,* Nefertiti thought. For instance, take Rev. He was seventy-five years old, but spry as any fifty-year-old man. He still had that same pompous, supercilious air about him. It wasn't just that Rev was still a good-looking mango-colored man, but it was that indefinable something. In a word, it was *power.* Power made an old man swagger. In fact, it made an old black man bebop when he walked. Yes, even her father, who'd had a mild heart attack and now wore a pacemaker, had the stride of a much younger man. Hadn't officiated at his church in over five years, yet the church was still giving him this big dinner bash for his birthday.

She could still see his august head, leading the group of elders at their church. She had learned long ago, it didn't matter who had the titles. It was who had the power. The influence. It was sort of like the hamstring in a pot of greens. It didn't look like much, but it had the power to flavor the whole pot.

Her father had always been like that. Able to

back and give support to the first African-American mayor. The nod of Reverend's head could make or break an African-American politician's career in Detroit. *What is that saying,* Nefertiti mused, *about absolute power corrupting? What will you sell your soul for, Reverend?*

To make matters worse, her father was like cilantro in her life. He had the ability to overpower her and flavor her decisions, making Nefertiti elect choices that she wondered if she would have made of her own volition. Her choice to marry Nigel Ford was the second choice she had made independently of her father. The first one was to divorce Isaac.

But had her father influenced her decision to marry Ford? Even if only perversely. Had she married him to defy her father? To show him? Yet, in a funny way, Ford was beginning to remind her of her father. Recently her husband had begun dabbling in politics, too. He was thinking about running for the city council.

When they first made it home, her mother had hinted, in that conspiratorial way of hers, that Rev was downtown talking to Councilman Huttleson. She'd gone on to say that her father was planning on endorsing the latter's campaign for mayor in November's city election. As far back as the late 1960s, Rev had been involved in local politics, so this did not come as a surprise to Nefertiti.

She felt unsettled by her memories, and only the handmade quilt on her bed made her smile lovingly in remembrance of Big Mama Lily, who had been a great raconteur. In fact, she had told

the little girl Nefertiti so many stories, Nefertiti
sometimes felt closer to her than she had to Miss
Magg. Now Nefertiti found herself wondering if
Big Mama Lily had made some of these stories
up. According to what Big Mama Lily had told
her, each patch in their quilt told some bit of
family history on her mother's side. Some of
these stories went back into slavery. One thing
Big Mama Lily used to say was that she had been
one of seven daughters, and that she was a "two-
headed woman." When Nefertiti asked her what
that meant, all Big Mama Lily had said was that
she'd been raised in New Orleans. What had she
meant by that?

Boy, Big Mama Lily had been a quirky grandmother. The day before she died, she had cursed
Miss Magg out for a cigarette.

When Miss Magg told her, "The doctor said
you don't need no cigarettes, Mama Lily," the old
woman sat up in her bed—she refused to stay in
the hospital—and announced, "I'm gonna meet
my Maker with a smile on my face. Dammit, give
me a cigarette."

Big Mama Lily had also been the only one in
their neighborhood who still had a henhouse. Said
she had to have something of the country with her.
Every morning, her favorite rooster, Mannish,
would crow, waking up the entire neighborhood.
Mannish must have been old as Methuselah when
he died. . . . Seemed like he died right after Big
Mama Lily, too.

But it was her father's side of the family that Nefertiti knew the least about. The only thing she
knew about her father was that her uncle Tiger was

his only living relative. The one tangible piece of the past that tied her very private, very distant father to any history was the shiny grandfather clock, which chimed in the downstairs hallway, and which, he said, was a family heirloom.

Nefertiti would never forget how Big Ben earned her the only spanking she'd ever received as a child from her father. When she was about eight years old, Rev had spanked Nefertiti soundly for breaking the glass in the cabinet of the clock. It had been her job to dust the clock every Saturday morning, and that day, she'd gotten careless with a game of ball. She wished she understood why that clock was so important to him—almost more important than her, it seemed.

9

On the drive to Titi's childhood home, Isaac thought about his new play, *House of Mourning*. So far, he had beaten the bushes looking for investors to back its production, and had come up empty-handed. Now he wondered if anyone would ever perform this play. It was loosely based on his childhood. The main character had grown up in a funeral home next to a church. Isaac had even found a way to use the hearse—which, in real life, had doubled as their family car—as a setting.

As he reminisced about his childhood, his love for Titi had been inevitable. When he was growing up, she not only had been the minister's daughter, but the girl next door. She had also been there for him when they were children. That was one of the things that had made him fall in love with Titi way back when.

The Godbolts' house still stood on the corner of Black Stone Drive, next to where the old funeral home and the original First Solid Rock Baptist Church had stood.

He would never forgive Calissa for having

deserted him to the howling winds of life, as far as he was concerned. How she had snatched the bunting cover of her love off his back before he was strong enough to fend for himself. Maybe that's why he failed to develop enough backbone as a kid. That was one thing he could say for Titi. Even as a kid, that girl had backbone. But, as far as Isaac was concerned, it was because she'd had a mother and father to put it into her. Especially a mother. And even a great-grandmother, Big Mama Lily, who had been like the second general around Titi's home. Isaac had missed having someone say, "Boy, put some Vaseline on your ashy elbows. Comb your knotty hair. When you brush your teeth last?"

No, a mother just wasn't supposed to do what Calissa did to him. To think Calissa had named him Isaac, out of the Bible. She'd always told him that Isaac meant "laughter." What a joke! His whole life had been just one big laugh. Good God, he had only been ten years old when she left! And he wished he could say that it hadn't bothered him. But it had.

To this day, the white critics said that his writing bore witness to some unknown suffering, some deep trauma, which pounded like a clenched fist in each word he wrote. They said his writing was like a "howling." If they only knew . . . it had been like going through a death. Only he'd known his mother had still been alive.

He'd fought and been beaten up by so many kids, so many times. They had called his mother "Callie of the Alley," "whore," "streetwalker"; he could not recall his childhood without remembering the bloody noses, the black eyes, the scraped ribs. He was the one who would be chosen last when they had to side up for teams. He was already ostracized—the one that no one wanted to play with, saying he had "the cooties"— because he lived in a funeral home.

The fact that his father had been a mortician would have been a stigma by itself. But growing up on the second floor of the funeral home added to Isaac's trauma. And as if that wasn't bad enough, when his father insisted upon using the hearse as their family car—even long after he could afford a second car—Isaac was sentenced to a childhood of taunts. To top that off, he'd had the misfortune of being born with a mild case of cerebral palsy. So when he did walk at the age of two, Isaac always dragged one foot behind him. Thereafter, the neighborhood children christened him "the Mummy."

But the coup de grace—his mother's leaving, then making a public spectacle of herself by not moving out of Shallow's Corner—had ruined whatever shred of normalcy his childhood might have offered him. The only plus side of his lonely childhood was that he'd become an avid reader, which became a boon to his writing career.

The constant ridicule, combined with a lack of confidence, led to Isaac dropping out of school in the eleventh grade. It was Titi who would encourage him to go back to night school for his diploma.

The first time he recalled knowing that he loved Titi, he was about eleven years old. That particular day, a group of boys, led by Bulldog Harrington, waited for him outside the school-yard. Worked up by Bulldog, they had decided to beat Isaac up for knowing the answer in class. In fact, it was Bulldog who had started everyone calling him "Undertaker's Son" (in addition to "the Mummy"). The crime of Isaac's being well-read—meaning "smart"—had a total negative connotation in Shallow's Corner. It was just too much for his peers to handle.

As Isaac lay in the mud, shoulders rounded, head covered, as he tried to block the storm of blows, kicks, and punches, he heard a girl's voice yell, "Y'all know you wrong! Leave him be! Bullies! Go pick on somebody your size!"

He never knew where she had come from, but Titi had run up to the group of boys who were kicking and socking Isaac's balled-up body. Swinging a bat that she held in both hands, like an avenging sword, she chased the boys off, one by one.

After Isaac stumbled to his feet, Bulldog pushed him in the square of his back for good measure, then told him, "All go on with your walleyed, bubble-eyed, fish-eyed self. Mummy's boy. Sissy. Letting a girl take up for you."

Staggering away to safety, blinded by a veil of tears, Isaac stumbled into a lilac bush. It was Titi who helped lift him out of the bushes. When he discovered there were no broken bones, Isaac found out he'd not been so lucky, after all. Prickly needles and little thorns were peppered throughout his hair. It hurt just to try to dislodge them. But, one by one, Titi picked them out of his woolly hair with painstaking care. Had even spit on the edge of her plaid shirt and wiped his bloody nose, to boot. He could still feel her spit cleaning him up and smell her lavender aroma to this day. After that, they had become best friends.

As young adults, when he was taking night courses at City College, it was Titi who had encouraged him to submit one of his plays to an English professor. The professor had entered his play *River of Blood* into a citywide contest, and the rest became history. His play had even run on Broadway for a year.

What had happened to all his success? It was as if it had dried up like an empty lakebed. When had he lost the golden touch? Suddenly he knew. It had been after Titi left him. There had always been something about Titi that had made him be more than he could have ever been by himself. And like Napoleon, and many other great men before him, he was to find that the loss of that special someone—as he tripped over power and fame—had destroyed him. Roshanne had been a bad replacement. He hadn't had a big hit in over seven years—the time since he and Titi's separation, then divorce.

If it wasn't for the royalties, and the trust fund his father had left him, he would have been bankrupt. Since there were no offers for the script for *House of Mourning*, he'd written a more modern play, *The Harps Upon the Willows*, which he was hoping would turn his financial life around. It was a play centered around the diaspora of modern African-Americans and their hang-ups with materialism. It posed some of the same questions that the first manumitted slaves asked of themselves. Were they going to keep a slave mentality, or could they reclaim the proud warrior spirit of their ancestors?

"What is this mess?" Robert had red-lined on page after page of Isaac's play *House of Mourning*. Although Isaac was angry at first, now he saw that his semiautobiographical play did need an overhaul. He was typing at a frenetic speed, hoping to have the play done in time to give to Nefertiti before she left for California that upcoming Sunday.

Memory was a funny thing. As he was working on a line in his play, a smell, a melody, or a noise could trigger the remembrance. Or maybe it was the mind's way of retelling the story to itself to make sense of reality.

In the first montage, Isaac came home from school early and found his mother's brown smile missing—the brown smile that had tempered growing up in a funeral home. Next, in the corridor of his past, he pictured a scene wherein he found his father, who had already been distant, out in the yard making a bonfire out of his mother's clothes. As his father had burned up all his mother's remaining clothes with the evening trash, he cursed, vilified, and muttered oaths. (Or had he imagined it?)

"Jezebel! Slut! Fattening the frog for the snake! I'll see you on the side of the road in the gutter before this is over!"

Although Isaac never lived to see his mother, Calissa, crawling in the gutter, he experienced the pillory of his mother's disgrace. The last freeze frame was the hushed grown-up whispers, scourging him, just the same as a holler. His

father—respectable Deacon Herschel Thorne—
who had only sung church songs around the
house, began to hum and sing bluesy dirges
whenever he was in the bathtub, and whenever
he thought that Isaac wasn't listening to him:

I had me a woman, who left me all alone
Now she with another man and all I do is moan.

From then on, Shallow's Corner formed an
implacable wall of hate, scorn, and disgust
against his mother, Calissa. Later, when Isaac discovered reading, and found that he had a con-
genital love affair with words and books, he
realized his mother had become like the colored
Hester Prynne of *The Scarlet Letter.* The only difference was that Calissa didn't have to wear the
letter *A* sewed on her breast collar. That was un-
necessary. The sin was already emblazoned in all
the good Christian people's minds.

Shallow's Corner consisted of various classes of
working colored people at that time. With the exception of a few schoolteachers and nurses, all the
blacks lived together—educated and uneducated
alike—during the 1950s when Isaac was growing
up. Paradoxically, in an effort to uplift the race, the
children of Ham were more puritanical than their
white counterparts. Although the tenets were
subtle, there was classism within their race. Business owners and preachers, such as his father,
Deacon Thorne, and Reverend Godbolt, held
high positions in the community. For Calissa to go
against a pillar in the community—why, it was unforgivable. Like blasphemy.

10

"What time did you say Little Josh and Cleo's plane will be in tomorrow?" Reverend asked his wife in the privacy of their bedroom.

"Oh, I think one's plane will be in at seven in the morning, and the other at eight. I guess I'll get to the airport and just wait for the other's plane. No sense in making two trips."

"That's all right. I'll go pick them up."

"You know Little Josh and Gloria are bringing the kids with them, so I'll go. I plan to take the church van to pick them up."

Reverend coughed his concession. "I'll go with you."

Miss Magg fumbled with a piece of thread hanging loose from the afghan thrown on the Naugahyde armchair in their bedroom. After dinner, the couple had drifted there, leaving Nefertiti alone downstairs with the breathing disquiet of the house, since dinner ended up being a silent, glum affair.

As Miss Magg slipped on her robe, Reverend began pacing the well-worn Oriental rug, which covered most of the hardwood floor. Miss Magg sighed. This was what her husband usually did whenever he wanted to start an argument—rather "discussions," as he called them—when delivering his marriage sermons to the congregation's young couples.

He cracked his knuckles first. Looking on, Miss Magg gritted her teeth, steeling herself. She decided to grab the bull by the tail first. "What took you so long down at Huttleson's? Titi had been waiting to see you all afternoon."

"Is that so?" Reverend gave Miss Magg the stare that always unsettled her.

"Well, you could have called."

Reverend ignored her.

"You know Huttleson has a good lead. And we're finding out this little guy, his opponent, was just a stalking horse used by the other party to confuse the issues. He's trying to play on the burning of the black churches in the South as a platform. It doesn't take a rocket scientist to know that this country is as racially divided as it was before desegregation laws were passed. Anyhow, when that's not working, it seems as if Huttleson's opponent—this Dumas fellow—is trying to come up with a smear campaign. But we're trying to get to the bottom of it and squelch it."

"What was it?"

"I can't talk about it."

"Well, why did you bring it up?"

"I don't know anymore, Miss Magg. It seems like this generation of young Negro men had been making so much progress in the eighties, I thought things were changing. But the nineties seem hell-bent on putting them back in their place. It seems like a conspiracy against black men in power. I don't know what's going to happen if this new bill to reverse affirmative action passes."

"Well," Miss Magg said, "if you ask me, some of these young men are doing it to themselves. Between the drugs and white women, I don't know which one is undoing our young men the most."

Reverend's head snapped around on his neck. "Did you hear something on the news about Huttleson?"

"No. I was just thinking of the scandal with that other mayor." Recently the newspaper had been splattered with the malfeasance of various black public officials across the States. "Well, it's a shame. That's all I know. We've got to stop blaming the white man for everything. Some of it is our own race. It seems we can't get over the crab syndrome. Got to pull each other down into the bucket whenever we see one another trying to get ahead. Don't even need a lid on a crab bucket."

"Well, you can't believe everything you hear, Miss Magg. Anyway, just because Huttleson is a Republican, he is only going back to the old family values colored folks used to have. I don't know what's getting into young folks today, anyway."

"Well, you know this welfare-reform issue isn't going over big in the colored community."

"Colored folks used to didn't dare take a handout. Welfare is the worst thing ever happened to a colored man. Just another form of slavery. Here, we were sharecroppers and never accepted a handout."

"Speaking of handouts, Tiger doesn't seem to

worry about getting a handout from you every time you look around."

Reverend paused for a moment. "I can't believe you said that. I swear, Miss Magg. All these years I've been with you, and I didn't know you were this mean-spirited. You getting more ornery every day God sends. You know good and well I got to look out for my people. As long as they are my people, and they are black in America, I'm going to look out for them. Did you think I was going to let Tiger just lay up there in jail that time? Did I ever complain about Big Mama Lily and Grandpa Bullocks living with us all those years?"

Miss Magg didn't answer. Reverend pulled out his watch from his waistcoat.

"Yes, all these years you ain't wanted for nothing. *Nothing*. Ain't never had to work in Miss Anne's kitchen. But you ain't never appreciated it. Then gon' take up for that gal, knowing how much heartache she done caused you."

"What do you mean, 'that gal'?" Miss Magg's voice rose an octave higher. "I don't care what you say. Whatever she's done, she ain't been no hypocrite like you!"

"If I weren't a Christian man I would—" Reverend's hand shot up in the air.

"Or you would do what? You're an old man, Joshua. Like I told you when we was married, I been raised. If you even think I'll let you hit me again and get away with it, you got another think coming. I'll lay you low, you hear me? What are you looking at? Joshua, why are you looking at me like that?"

Joshua paused, his raised hand still in the air.

Miss Magg's jutting jawline exhumed a memory of his mother. Or maybe it was his father he was remembering. A sudden cold feeling spread throughout his arms and legs, reaching his toes, and he knew he was thinking of his father.

"A man ain't worth a quarter once he get his nose up under some woman's dress," his mother, Bertha, used to say when he was growing up. For that reason, Joshua Godbolt had promised himself as a young boy that he would never be ruled by the carnal desires of the flesh. And whatever twists and turns his life might take on the journey, Joshua Godbolt had vowed never to be like his father, Killsprettyenemy Godbolt. Therefore, to be unlike his father, he promised himself that he would never beat on a woman. And he'd kept that promise, too, except for that one time. . . .

From the time Joshua became saved when he was eighteen, until the time he moved north and got his first church, he'd always had a burning hunger to own his own land. He hated how the colored didn't own anything in Bessemer, Alabama, where he was from. He hated how all the bigger plantation owners had peacocks running around in their front yards. As a young boy, he'd promised himself that one day he, too, would have peacocks gracing his front lawn. When he moved north, Joshua never did get the peacocks, but he got the second-best thing to them—power.

As a young man, Reverend Godbolt had but one driving desire—to be everything that was the opposite of his father. This made anything else he pursued in life, including his wife, Miss Magg, anticlimactic. Called "Pretty" by everyone who knew him, Joshua's father had been part Cherokee Indian. His father's mother, a Cherokee, was a descendent of the Oklahoma tribes who came through the Trails of Tears March. She had passed away when Pretty was seven years old. It was Light Spirit who had insisted on giving her son an Indian name. Grandpa Bryce had obliged. Hence, his father was christened Killsprettyenemy. And like his name implied, Pretty grew up to be a lady-killer.

"Daddy, where did we get the last name Godbolt?" Joshua asked his father one day when they were coming out of the fields. At the time, Joshua was about nine years old. In a rare moment of closeness, his father had taken the time to explain a little family history to him.

"From what my daddy remembers, Great-Aunt Millie told him that during slavery the coloreds wasn't supposed to have they own last names. Most of the records didn't even give a name. We was called 'Cuffee's Sambo,' or whoever your parents was. When a name was used, we was supposed to be named after our masters. But a lot of slaves had two last names. The one their masters gave them, and the one they secretly chose that described them to theyself, or tied them to they kin.

"Take my granddaddy Shilo. He named himself Godbolt after he was hit by a thunderbolt when he was seventeen and lived to tell about it. I guess he felt God had delivered him. He became somewhat of a preacher after that. He ended up owning a lot of land, too. Eventually the white folks lynched him so they could take back the land. That's all I know.

My daddy never talked about my granddaddy too much. It was too dangerous to even talk about such back then."

Joshua never forgot that conversation. Most of the time his father was distant, angry. The only other thing he knew was that his father would always comment on how his dead grandfather's preaching career had led to him owning so much land. Joshua had learned early the ignoble quality of life that came from owning nothing.

The emotional landscape of Joshua's entire childhood had been punctuated with domestic skirmishes, like the cowboys and Indians. Only in his family's case, his father was the Indian, his mother the cowboy. To the end, it seemed that for all their battles, neither one won the war.

No matter what the weather or season, no matter whether they were in good times or bad, whenever Pretty got shot up with corn liquor, he would come home (as Bertha put it) "trying to raise the dead" with his family. More often than not, he would jump on his wife, kicking and slugging her brutally. At first, Bertha did not fight back, but as the years rolled on, she fought back as mightily as a man.

"It ain't who can dish it out, it's who can take it," Bertie would say as she'd fire up a pot of boiling water or grits, in preparation for the next battle.

Pretty seemed to take every grain of frustration over his life as a sharecropper out on his once-beautiful, little wife. Even in high heels, Bertie had barely stood five feet tall; whereas in his stockinged feet, Pretty was at least six feet six.

Where the lines of the Indian and black blood had combined in equal proportions, one could say that Pretty was a handsome man. Bertha, herself, had been a voluptuous, comely woman when the couple married.

But Bertha's face eventually became railroaded with tracks of the abuse, and her bones became angular from all the knocking-about she'd suffered.

"I see you got your Indian up," Bertha would say as soon as her husband would cross the threshold. "Pretty," his mother would preach, "God don't like ugly, and he ain't crazy about 'pretty,' either."

For all Bertha's caustic tongue, nothing stopped Pretty from jumping on his wife.

Although Pretty was laconic—even taciturn throughout the week—it was as if a clock began to wind up tighter and tighter as the week of sharecropping wore on, and, predictably, the world would blow up in a fracas of profanity, swearing, and cursing by Friday night.

Until his oldest boy, Cyrus, whom they called "Silo," after his uncle, got grown and stopped his father, their lives had been fraught with the perils of Pretty and his weekend rituals of fighting Bertha. But by then, it was too late. Their mother's looks, her health, and even some of her once-sharp mind had been destroyed.

For that reason, Reverend lowered his raised hand, not because of Miss Magg's defiant chin shoved out in his face, but because of Pretty. He just walked away.

11

"Vi-jay!"

No one could call her Christian name like Big Mama Lily. Her teachers pronounced it with an emphasis on the first syllable, but her grandmother always pronounced her name with the stress on the last. It almost sounded as if her grandmother was calling her "Vagina." It was the same way Big Mama Lily pronounced "roach" in two syllables, or "Detroit," with the stress on the "De."

This particular night, Big Mama Lily called Miss Magg in from the front porch where she had been talking to a boy nicknamed Tiger.

"Get in here, gul! You know about the scandal his family had a couple years back. I know you know there is bad blood in the family when they kill one of their own. The Good Book says the sins of the father are visited upon their children."

Miss Magg had first met Tiger when she was in the tenth grade. Her family had moved from

Eunice, Louisiana, to Bessemer, Alabama, the year before, and already one of the gossipmongers had told Big Mama Lily what Tiger had once confided to Miss Magg in private. Tiger had sworn Miss Magg to secrecy regarding this family secret. Tiger was in her homeroom class at school and had begun carrying her books home every day.

"Why do they call you Magnolia?" Tiger asked.

"None of your business." Miss Magg was being fresh.

As time went by, it was as if her indifference lit a fire in Tiger's loins, he became so captivated by her. Although they couldn't officially date, they had liked each other from afar over those next two high-school years.

But two years later, just after graduation, when Miss Magg was only seventeen, Joshua came to town on the visiting circuit of ministers. Nine years older than Tiger, Joshua was twenty-seven at the time. By then, Tiger had dropped out of high school, so Big Mama Lily had forbade Miss Magg to have any more dealings with him.

When Joshua came to call the first time, Big Mama Lily was all smiles and approval.

"Get down here, gul. Reverend Godbolt is here to see you!"

When the phone rang, Miss Magg left Reverend, who was pretending to be sleeping on his side of the bed. She knew he was upset, and that he was awake, because she didn't hear his snores. She guessed he was upset because she'd backed him down. Absently, Miss Magg answered the phone, mind still lingering on her memories.

"Miss Magg, it's Calissa. I set the altar for Satti-day. Is there anything else I can do for the dinner?"

Miss Magg paused.

"No," she finally said. She couldn't help the coldness which entered her voice.

"All right. I don't think I'll be coming to the dinner, anyway."

"Suit yourself."

I don't know why I acted that way toward Calissa. I think I'm just upset because I didn't get to bring up the baby with Reverend. The baby we never ever talk about anymore. It's so many things Rev and I have never talked about. The only difference between me and Calissa is that she acted on what was in her heart. If people only knew . . .

Nefertiti was always my fighter child. She is more like Calissa in terms of she doesn't care what people think. She got a divorce even when I told her not to get one. From the looks of things, she did the right thing.

Maybe her name is where she gets her strength from. I named Nefertiti out of one of the schoolbooks. I had a teacher, Mr. Brooks, who used to tell us all about Africa. Said there was some colored folks who were kings and queens over in Africa. Yessiree. Said Nefertiti was a queen, chief wife of Akhenaten, or somebody like that. She held as much power as the king did. Funny, I re-member that and sometimes I can't remember what my babies looked like, or things that happened when my kids were growing up.

I gave Nefertiti her middle name, Jael, out of the

Bible. She was the one who nailed the Canaanite captain's head when they were at war with the Israelites, God's Chosen People. Jael was a warrior, and she was blessed. I knew this child was going to need to be blessed in this life. . . .

Well, she got a rocky start in life, but she sure done made a good life for herself now. Rev just don't know. I got all these pictures she done sent me of what that near 'bout-white husband of hers done did for her. Trips they done took. When I went to visit her, it look like that man worship the ground she walk on.

She got this big beautiful mansion. She could have a full-length mink, but she say she don't believe in killing animals.

Only thing I don't like is all those animals they got. She got about ten doves, some big looking parrot talk-more-trash-than-the-radio, a fat turtle running all over the backyard. She even has a swimming pool. Not that I can swim. Never learned as a girl. But those kids of hers swim like fish.

I think I might be able to talk Rev into letting me go visit her next spring. I miss those birds-of-paradise flowers they grow out there. I tried to bring a cutting home, but I guess our soil don't grow that type of flower.

I get tired of the congregation sometimes. I need a rest from the friends at church. Well, I got rest at Nefertiti's house. She got a maid, too. A Mexican lady. "Hispanic" or "Latino" is what Nefertiti says they call themselves now. Then, that near 'bout-white husband of hers . . . even if she do say he got some black blood in him, he don't look like it. But who is it for me to judge? I don't know about him. But he seem to treat her good. Seem like he adore her.

Lord, I don't know about that gal, either. I wonder if

she really love him? I don't think she ever loved Isaac. That boy used to worship the ground she walked on, but Nefertiti's so . . . so different from me. She seem like the kind of woman can take or leave a man. I just can't imagine living by myself. I wonder if I coulda done it if I had been born in a different day.

Naw, I couldn't. I ain't like these young women today. I don't want to work nowhere. I don't think I would want to work in a pie factory eating pie, as much as I love sweets. I am so glad Rev's congregations have always taken good care of him. I swear, if I had to go to work somewhere, I'd starve.

But thinking of that Nefertiti. That girl always did like to work. Working almost soon as she had Isaac Jr. Now, that's one thing I think is wrong with her. She work too hard. Why can't she let her man take care of her?

But one thing for sure. She ain't selfish like Little Josh. The time when Cousin Letty Pearl's twelve-year-old granddaughter drowned, she sent money to help bury that child. And I can't forget about what she did for her daddy last spring. Here, with him not even speaking to her. Rev oughta be 'shamed of himself. Up in the pulpit preaching forgiveness every Sunday God sends, and he don't forgive or forget nothing.

And my firstborn, Little Josh, God forgive me, but it's true—he don't care about nobody. All that money he done made, with his old stuck-up wife. He barely send me a Christmas card, come Christmas, and this girl done up and sent me a mink. That child Cleo, she another one don't think about nobody but herself. She want to be more than she is. But her daddy think she the salt of the earth.

When I was courting Tiger before I met Rev, there was plenty of times I wanted to sin, but I didn't, because

*it would've killed Mama Lily and Grandpa Bullocks.
I was they pride and joy. After the way my mama, Betty
Lee, ran off and left me on them, I couldn't bring no
child into the world without a husband.*

*I remember our wedding night. Reverend jumped up
as soon as he was finished with his business and
checked the sheet. What if I hadnna bled? Would he
have left me?*

*But, Lord, I was always afraid this day would come.
Now Nefertiti wants to find my grandchild. Lord, did
I do the right thing? I thought I was doing the right
thing at the time, but now, I don't know. I don't know
anything anymore. Did I even do the right thing when
Nefertiti was born?*

Miss Magg hadn't protested when she said that
she wasn't coming to dinner, Calissa noticed. She
felt the twinge of rejection that for years she'd
learned to ignore. She had been able to ignore
her alienation from the community before Pay
Dirt had died, but this slight, coupled with her
little run-in with her son, Isaac, earlier that day,
made it impossible to ignore the pain stabbing at
her heart. How long would she have to pay? The
old recriminations began to haunt her again.
Why couldn't she have led the "good Christian
life" like Miss Magg had?

Played life safe. But, looking back, she couldn't
help herself. It hadn't just been living in the same
house with the dead, and the embalming that had
gone on all those years. It wasn't even Deacon's
dry, cold ways. It was her kitchen clock that had
done it.

Calissa remembered clearly the day she'd stood in her kitchen, staring at the clock. Her life ticking away. Deacon hadn't touched her in months. When he did, he was impotent. But it was that ticking clock that did it. That sound was the sandbar that had driven her out into the streets. It had started innocently enough. A night out with the girls. Pay Dirt had been a saxophone player down at the local blind pig—the after-hours joint.

Afterward, she didn't know which had hurt the most. Losing her son, or being turned out from the church.

You've shamed us, Calissa. You've dishonored your family, your husband, your marriage vows, yourself. But couldn't you have thought about your little boy? Now you're going to be turned out of the church.

For twenty-five years, she'd refused to set foot back in the church. Pay Dirt had been her whole life. But after his death, ten years earlier, she'd felt the need for community again and had returned to the church.

But now something else was bothering her. She could smell it. Trouble. No, it was something worse. She didn't want to give the Dark Horse a name. After years of being married to an undertaker, she was on a first-name basis with Death and knew him by name. But who, Lord? Who?

12

A few blocks away from his house, Isaac turned on his radio and heard Smokey Robinson's "Ooo Baby Baby," and almost screamed. Lord have mercy, the old artists knew how to rap to get their ladies back. These new youngsters—"rap artists," they called themselves—they didn't know what rapping was. Even though he couldn't sing, Isaac crooned along with the music.

Snapping his fingers, singing "Wo-wo-wo," Isaac was so engrossed in the song, he didn't hear the sound of the siren until it swooped down upon him like a spread-winged hawk preying on a field mouse.

"I'll be damned," Isaac muttered. He recognized the flashing red light easily. Like any of his Nubian brothers, he tensed up and placed his hands on the dashboard, where the police could see them. He knew what to expect. It was a common sight to see another African-American male pulled over by the curb, spread-eagled on the ground, at all times of day and night. The nicer the car, the more probable cause to pull them over, it seemed. He also knew better than to reach in his pocket for his license or go into his dashboard for his titles.

The two white police officers, brandishing their billy clubs, got out of their car, swaggering up to his Mercedes. The raspberry-pimple-faced one had a sneer twitching all over his face. Isaac braced himself. He decided to try the cooperative tactic, as he felt he was beyond the buffoon, shucking and jiving, stage. Perhaps if he handled this man-to-man—"I'm a black professional trying to make it, just like you" sort of thing—the matter would work out all right.

"I'll be damned," Isaac muttered to himself when both officers kicked his back and front tire's golden rims simultaneously. Still, he was going to try the cooperative strategy.

"Yes, how may I help you, sir?" Isaac spoke first.

The beefy strawberry-blond-haired cop looked like he could spit on Isaac.

"Boy, did you see that red light? What are you doing up in here?"

Isaac bit down on his upper lip, trying to contain himself about the word "boy." Here it was in the 1990s, and white police still called grown African-American men "boys." Now, he could see it if he looked as thuggish as Pharaoh, but he was clean-cut in appearance.

"I live here down the street," Isaac answered evenly, trying to maintain his temper. "I'm Isaac Thorne. Do you remember the play *Blues River*, which ran Off-Broadway? Haven't you heard of the playwright Isaac Thorne? That's me. Wait, I'll get my license."

"I don't give a damn who or what you are! Don't you reach in your pocket. Get out of your car and put your hands on the hood."

As they frisked and searched Isaac, he became livid. How long would it take before this whole thing blew up into another riot? When he had participated in the 1967 Detroit riots, he had knowingly been breaking the law. But now here he was, law-abiding, taxpaying, mortgaged to the yin-yang, and he was still treated like just another nigger.

He felt the same tears of humiliation smarting in his eyes that he'd felt as a young boy when his mother had left. What did he own—really own—besides the clothes on his back?

"So you live in Palmer Heights, huh?"

There was disbelief in the officer's voice as he handed back Isaac's wallet. "How can you afford a place like that?"

"What are you doing here so late? Don't you know it's after nine? My parents are trying to get some sleep."

It wasn't the kind of welcome he had hoped for. Not after being pulled over by the Man. Not after feeling emasculated. He had kind of wanted to get his feelings soothed. He felt his eyes scrunch up and his shoulders tighten with tension. The first thing he noticed was the scent of lavender. Feeling swaddled in her familiar smell, Isaac disregarded Nefertiti's words and looked into her face.

Hers was a face that a sailor would be glad to see

after being on the seas for days. It was a face that would remind you of all that was different, yet wonderful, in women. He was glad she wasn't wearing any shades. The last time he had seen her at a distance, she was wearing sunglasses, which had only added to her mystique. She still had that same widow's peak, breaking the smooth expanse of her high brow, placed over those same sensuous, indigo-colored full lips, and that same caustic tongue.

Hers had always been an expressive face that drew on the range of human emotions. Her dimples could dance mischievously or cut your heart to shreds when she was angry. She could move from caressing smiles to anger to tears to laughter in less than a second. And oh, could Nefertiti laugh! She could throw back her head and let out a gale of mirth that put you to shame for joy. She had what writers called an "infectious laugh."

But today, she wasn't laughing. Just like she could laugh, she could tear a man up one side and down the other. She had a deep, melodic voice, but in the heat of rage, it could go into a soprano. Hers had always been an open face, one that did not conceal her true emotions. Right now, her light brown eyes looked like detonators as she glared at him.

"I came to see my kids." Isaac knew that his cashmere coat gave him a dapper and prosperous look, but he also knew that it was five years old.

"I didn't bring the kids with me. I left them with my sister-in-law."

"You mean you left my kids with some honkies?"

He knew this incendiary remark would incite the riot act in Nefertiti.

"Run that by me again."

"You heard me. I said, 'Did you leave my kids with . . .'"

"Correct me if I am wrong. Were you worried about these kids when you were running up and down the street with Roshanne? Let Roshanne give you a baby. Matter of fact, what happened to that baby she was supposed to have been pregnant with, just before we broke up?"

Isaac cringed, just remembering how he'd been tricked into marrying Roshanne, but he tried to steel his tongue. This wasn't supposed to be happening. But once the ball started rolling, he couldn't stop the truculent sneer from forming on his face and in his words.

"Oh, yes. This is a new twist on the 'black mammy' syndrome. Now you got a white woman taking care of our children." He stood back, waiting for his verbal karate chop to land. After going through the racism displayed by the police, he felt justified in his racism against a white family he didn't even know—other than that his children seemed to love these people.

"Nigger, please. Who takes care of my children when they are in my care is none of your business. By the way, your child support hasn't showed up in the last couple of months. Who do you think is supporting your children? Are you worried about a white man supporting them when you don't send their money?"

"Look, I just sent that money off."

"Sure. Right. The check is in the mail."

"Wait a minute. Your hands are not all clean in this, either. You know you remind me of Eve. The woman tempted Adam with the apple, and was the cause of their downfall, but man had to take the fall for his woman's stupidity."

"Now you're going to twist the Bible up on me," Nefertiti said. "Don't give me that sexist crap."

"So you're blaspheming now. Did I ever mention you and Pharaoh while we were married? That nigger even had the nerve to be over at the church earlier this afternoon. So I'd suggest people who live in glass houses don't throw stones."

Isaac knew he was breaking a promise he'd made to never throw up the child Titi had before she married him, but he had to say something to bring her down. As far as he knew, Titi had never cheated on him with Pharaoh or with any man. Even so, he wanted to hurt her like he hurt at that moment.

Nefertiti was quiet for a minute.

"Be that as it may," she finally said, deciding to be civil, "you get your month in the summer with the kids."

"I ain't like you, Titi. I want to see my kids."

Nefertiti didn't reply. It was that old demon again. The past. The secret. They had made a pact when she married him to never mention her past.

"Isaac, get out of here. The kids aren't here. You and I have nothing else to say."

"Titi, I didn't come over here to argue with you."

"Good night, Isaac. Or I'll call the police and tell them you are disturbing the peace." Isaac froze.

He definitely didn't want another encounter with the Man after what he had gone through. He shook his head, pivoted on his right foot, opened the door, and left.

"Good night, Titi. We'll be talking some more." After the door shut behind him, he said under his breath, "Much more."

After she closed the door behind Isaac, Nefertiti stood, back pressed into the solid oak wood, hand still on the knob, thinking about throwing some salt after his unwanted visit. She remembered how they had gone at each other, their words deep-piercing swords. How the arguing, combined with all the other frontal insults, and all the unspoken resentments, had corroded and destroyed their marriage. She admitted to herself that being an angry black woman hadn't helped her first marriage any.

She felt as frustrated as she was on her last day at the government's housing agency. Why was it that anytime a black person spoke up, he or she was considered "a bad nigger" or—as her last superior had put it—"You have a bad attitude." This was one reason she was glad she worked for herself now, but she still had the same type of frustration from racial injustices she saw as an entrepreneur. Trying to get a loan from the bank and being denied made her blood boil.

Yet, she never wanted Ford to see that side of her personality. So far, she'd successfully hidden that angry woman from Ford, the one who could cut Isaac down with her flashing eyes and razorblade tongue. But how could you call a man who—for all practical purposes—looked white a "nigger"? How could she go all the way back home on Ford, as she usually did when she gave vent to her emotions? It didn't happen as often as when she was younger, but she could be guaranteed a blowup at least once a year now.

After months of insults at the bank, at the market, at her kids' school, fighting for their equality, she would explode like Mount St. Helens, the lava of her pain scorching all those around her. So to keep from releasing this she-devil and wreaking havoc in her new marriage, Nefertiti had learned to drive off alone and sit by the ocean until she calmed down. The ocean tended to soothe her.

She was never going to be the same person she was when she first married Isaac, but she knew, at the same time, that it was unfair to unleash all her hurt and bitterness in her new relationship. Generally, Ford was so easygoing she didn't get as angry as she used to, but she knew what she was capable of.

She didn't wish Isaac any harm for all her tongue-lashing, but she was satisfied to know Isaac's chickens had come home to roost, anyhow. From what her childhood friend Sweet had told her, Isaac's plays weren't doing as well as when the two of them were married. Nefertiti hated to gloat, but good for the two of them! Why had Roshanne thought that she could build happiness on the garbage heap of another woman's unhappiness?

This reminded her of Big Mama Lily's philosophy on alliances and misalliances between married couples.

"You can have a stupid man, but a couple can make it if the woman is smart. But take a smart man. He won't have nothing in life if he got a stupid woman."

This made her think about something Big Mama Lily had said about her paternal grandmother, Bertie, whom Nefertiti had never known. Bertie had died before Nefertiti was born.

"Bertie—may she rest in peace—was a good woman, but she was stupid."

She guessed that her grandmother was right. Roshanne was stupid, and now, no matter how smart Isaac was, he could not achieve anything with this albatross around his neck.

But, at the same time, Nefertiti was thinking how it's a dangerous thing when a woman does a Pygmalion in reverse. Maybe that had been the failure of her first marriage. Nefertiti would never forget the story Big Mama Lily told about her own sister, Great-Aunt Martha. Great-Aunt Martha had been a schoolteacher married to a railroad porter, back in the 1930s and 1940s, when that was a top-paying job for a colored man.

Everyone always said how Uncle Roy, who could not read, would sign his check over to Aunt Martha with an *x*. One day, Aunt Martha decided that she wanted to teach Uncle Roy how to read. Now, Aunt Martha was a social climber, and she wanted to fit in with the high society of the Negro community. In order to do this, she wanted to be able to say her husband was educated, like she was. Unfortunately, according to Big Mama Lily, their married life went down the drain from that point on. Once Uncle Roy learned to read, he started beating up Aunt Martha and taking back his check.

"You ain't taking all my money," he'd say.

So whenever Nefertiti looked back over the hills, valleys, and plains of her life, she knew what her mistake with Isaac had been. Similar to Aunt Martha's plight, Issac's plays, instead of being a boon, turned out to be the downfall of Nefertiti's and Isaac's marriage. When she'd seen his talent for writing, she encouraged him to take writing classes. As his teachers recognized him, she supported him as he took small paying fellowships, stipends, and grants. She backed his decision to quit his job at the Ford Motor Company plant, but actually, their happiest years had been when he worked in the plant. Once Isaac became known as a playwright, he began to change. It had started out innocently.

First, he would come home an hour late. Then it was two hours. Before she knew it, he was staying out all night. How a man ever entertained the idea that he could tip out on his wife without leaving telltale signs was beyond Nefertiti. Every woman had her own spirit, her own way in bed, her own way of being. She left it as a brand on the man. Whether he knew it or not, a cheating husband would turn—like a chameleon—into a different person before the wife's eyes as he became molded into the making of the other woman's liking. A sure telltale sign.

Nefertiti never got over the madness of it all. In the beginning, Isaac used to say that he had to stay out working long hours on his plays and helping with the directing so that he would have the money needed to support his family. As time went by, Nefertiti felt like a piece of china left up on the shelf for display, and not for everyday use. She got tired of trying to smile at the occasional family gathering when Isaac accompanied her and the children. She no longer wanted to accompany him to the opening of his plays, because she never knew which woman in the audience he might have slept with. In short, she got sick of the game of charades. Eventually she felt like she had been dragged down to the lowest rung of her life; she had hit rock bottom, emotionally and mentally.

Meantime, Isaac's father, the Deacon, became sick and stayed with them for the last five years of their marriage. Even so, Nefertiti had been good to the Deacon. Although she was in California when he died, Nefertiti had contemplated coming back to the funeral, but changed her mind, reasoning that she had done all she could for the Deacon while he was alive and could appreciate it.

Before she separated from Isaac, she had made two lists: why she should leave her marriage, or why she should stay. The Deacon's name was at the top of the "stay" list. What kept her there as long as she'd stayed was that she hadn't wanted to leave Isaac's father old, sick, and alone.

When she'd asked Miss Magg for her advice, her mother had been of no help, as she discouraged divorce.

"Gul, men been doing it for years. Remember how Cousin Letty Pearl would come stay with us sometimes for two months a year? Her husband would be done came down with the claps or something, and she'd come here to keep herself out of harm's way. You shouldn't leave about no outside woman. Is he still paying the bills?"

When Nefertiti asked if Rev ever ran around on her, Miss Magg said something strange. "Rev ain't no normal man, Titi. You can't go by him."

Suddenly Nefertiti recalled the two major things that had helped her make up her mind to divorce Isaac. One had been her quilt. When she was a little girl, she'd owned a security blanket, a piece of a quilt Big Mama Lily had made for her. She carried this blanket around until it had become so bedraggled that it disappeared when she was about four years old. Later she was convinced Miss Magg had sneaked and thrown it in the trash.

That night, when she couldn't find it to take to bed with her, Nefertiti had cried and cried. This went on for nights on end. A while later, Big Mama Lily had presented her with a new quilt—the "big-girl quilt" she'd called it—the very one that still covered her bed, but Nefertiti had adamantly refused to attach to it. She had always been a person who had a hard time letting go. Maybe that was why she collected antiques and old objects now.

Perhaps that's why she'd hung on by the strength of her fingernails to a marriage that was past resurrection. And in a moment of epiphany about herself, she admitted she was the only one holding on. If Isaac, or any man, for that matter, had wanted to leave, he would have left. No vacillation, no asking for advice, no guilt. Gone. Split the scene. Isaac only stayed because he'd wanted to have his cake and eat it, too.

But the memory of her inability to let go of her baby quilt when it was far beyond its usefulness had only been one of her reasons. The second one came from the dolls. Yes, it had been those dolls that, in the long run, finally caused Nefertiti to divorce Isaac.

Yes, it had been the two black rag dolls that were the straws that broke the camel's back. She knew a little bit about hoodoo from Big Mama Lily. Come to think of it, she could have lived with Isaac's lack of sexual interest in her. She could have even tolerated his prissy ways regarding sex, always wanting the lights out.

But it was the dolls that had ended her months of oscillation. One night, shortly after Isaac came in and gave then–four-year-old Savasia two rag dolls—from a "friend," he'd said—something woke Nefertiti up. Roshanne had recently been cast as the leading lady in Isaac's plays. As his late nights were becoming later, Nefertiti suspected that Roshanne was the reason for his absences. Now the dolls felt tainted in a way she couldn't explain, but she assumed she knew where they came from. Without knowing why, she had gone to her daughter's room, grabbed up the dolls, and jumped in her car.

As Isaac had stayed out all night, anyway, she didn't have to explain where she was going in the middle of the night when she drove two miles away and threw the dolls in a Dumpster behind a market. Afterward, she even remembered finding condoms with pitchfork faces on the tips in Isaac's wallet. (*What kind of hoodoo is this?* she'd thought.)

Within weeks of this incident, she began to itch all over. None of the allergy tests could ever explain what caused the welting and swelling. Sometimes her lips even swelled into unsightly messes. This cemented her decision to leave Isaac.

Looking back, it all began when Roshanne had been picked as one of the leading ladies in Isaac's play *Blues River*. At first, everything had seemed businesslike, on the up-and-up. But insidiously, like a black widow, Roshanne had spun a dangerous web of lies, trickery, and deceit, until she'd gotten Isaac.

Near the end of their marriage, Nefertiti just wanted to get out of the whole mess, with her sanity, and she didn't care who got her husband. Roshanne had been the siren who shipwrecked their marriage.

Maybe the old folks were right. If it ain't broke, then why fix it? She should have never pushed Isaac to reach beyond his furthest dreams.

So after going through the valley of indecision, Nefertiti had finally concluded that she was not married to the Deacon. She called a distant relative of Isaac's to let his father live with their family, and she made her plans to move to California. Later, when she'd heard that Isaac had taken his father to live with him and his new wife, Roshanne, and the Deacon had died within six months, she couldn't help but feel guilty.

When Nefertiti had left Isaac and moved to California seven years ago, she exited Shallow's Corner with four trunks that contained her and her children's clothes, a potential job transfer, her severance pay, and Nigel Ford's phone number, which he'd given her the year before when he came through town for a law conference.

Ford had looked up her parents in the phone book—how many Godbolts would you expect to find, anyhow?—obtained Nefertiti's phone number, and gave her a call. With Nefertiti being lonely, as she had not left Isaac yet, she didn't see any harm in meeting an old college friend for lunch. Although the lunch went innocently as they caught up on old times, Nefertiti felt an attraction to Nigel. He seemed so warm and open that she kept his number and they chitchatted occasionally on the phone over the next year. Still, the relationship remained platonic. They never slept together until her divorce was final from Isaac.

Looking back, she'd been afraid, more afraid than she'd ever been in her life, when she moved to California. But she'd made it. Look how far she'd come in those seven years.

Her divorce and moving away from Shallow's Corner had given her the strength to face the past and look for her daughter now.

13

The first time Nefertiti met Nigel Ford in the fall of 1969, she had only been eighteen years old. She was living on USC's campus in Los Angeles. At the time, Ford was handing out flyers regarding the Vietnam War.

"Down with the establishment."

"Get our troops out of Vietnam."

He was fourteen years older than Nefertiti. At thirty-two, Ford was an army veteran, who had already served a stint in Vietnam, and had been married twelve years. He'd gotten an early discharge when he'd been hit with shrapnel. He still bore the scars on his face. As an older student, he was attending school on the GI Bill.

Although not a serious student, Nefertiti had made good enough grades. She'd won a scholarship and was planning on returning to USC for her sophomore year. Somehow, that summer when she returned home, under the influence of Reverend, she'd wound up engaged to Isaac. As a result, Nefertiti never returned to USC's campus as a student.

The only thing Nefertiti knew for sure was that she had loved Isaac like a brother since they were children. But she'd never planned on marrying him. The marriage happened more out of convenience and gratitude. She knew she never would have to explain about Desiree, and she made a pact with him to never mention the past.

Over the years, in her own way, she'd grown to love Isaac while they were married. That's what had made getting a divorce so painful.

Without any design on her part, before her divorce from Isaac, Nefertiti's and Ford's paths had crossed again. Ford was in Detroit for a law conference and had looked her up. Several years earlier, he had been divorced from his wife, but he didn't tell Nefertiti the details. All Nefertiti could remember of him was that he was a young white man who used to love to touch her Afro at the different rallies. During this visit, they'd exchanged numbers.

Two years later, when she'd left Isaac, Nefertiti looked Ford up after she moved to California, since she knew no one else in Los Angeles. Ford referred her to a friend of his who had a reputation for being the best divorce lawyer in town. Although Nefertiti didn't get her child support payments on a regular basis, and alimony was out of the question, she was happy just to have her sanity.

Ford once told Nefertiti that in an old wives' tale, whites could tell if other people were full-blooded white by the presence of half-moons under a person's fingernails. If someone black was just passing for white, the imposter would not have half-moons under his nails.

But Ford had never known this little test, until after he found out he had black blood in him. He had lived over thirty-five years of his life as a white man. His father had died from an aneurysm when he was only four years old, so he had been raised in Glendale, California, with his mother and her side of the family.

While on a business trip to the South, he looked up his father's family in the phone book. It was then, through an old great-aunt Lisette, he learned of his heritage—he had black blood in him. He was a quadroon, having three white grandparents.

His paternal grandmother, Colette, had done the unforgivable *and* unpardonable. She had married a black man, Lance Carmier, although he had been Creole. Colette's family had had the marriage annulled, but not before his father, Lance Carmier, had been conceived. Colette refused to place the baby up for adoption, and fortunately, he remained fair enough to pass. Colette's family created a myth that Lance's father had been killed in World War I.

As a socially acceptable widow, Colette eventually married back into white society, and this earlier marriage was never mentioned by anyone. Lance, Ford's father, had been raised as the white son of Nigel Ford II, the alleged paternal grandfather whom Nigel Ford III—himself—had been named after. Looking back, Nigel realized that his father, Lance, had been only slightly tanned, with a kind of French look. Ford never found out if his father had learned the truth of his origins before he died. Nigel, himself, had sandy brown hair.

Once he found out the truth about his birth origins, he knew that he could not continue living out the lie.

When Nefertiti came back into his life, Ford felt that it was Providence. His first marriage of twenty-odd years had broken up over the discovery of the truth of his birth, among other things that had eroded the union. He had never been more attracted to a woman than he had been to Nefertiti. After assisting her with her divorce and being a friend while she got settled, Ford continued to call and be available to show her around Los Angeles.

The first time Ford asked Nefertiti out on a date, she'd simply said, "I don't do swirl."

"What do you mean?"

"I don't date white men."

This was one time Ford was glad to disclose his deep family secret that had come out.

Talking about serendipity. What had started out as a casual friendship eventually grew into a love affair. Their relationship had a depth that she had never experienced in her first marriage. They both loved community affairs and believed in putting back into the community.

Although Nefertiti never loved as passionately as when she was younger, she cared deeply for Ford. She was not head over heels in love, yet there was a constancy. A companionship. Once she'd read somewhere, that men only had so many ejaculations in them. Maybe—she decided—that was how it was with women, too, only emotionally. Just as women had a finite number of eggs, perhaps they only had a limited capacity to fall in love. It was as if they were emptied out after each time they fell in love. She no longer loved Pharaoh or Isaac, but she did not have that same boundless ability to give of herself, either. Now she would always hold some back for herself. She wondered if Ford knew that he was married to a woman who would never love in the way storybooks narrated. Or was it the loss of Desiree that had impaired her ability to love? She didn't know.

The only other problem that still bugged her with Ford had been his color. In California, she saw interracial relationships all the time. It was just that Shallow's Corner found it so repulsive. Although she no longer lived there, it still had an influence on her.

It was during her marriage to Ford that she re-membered marrying Isaac for all the wrong rea-sons. Because he was acceptable to her family. Because he was of the same religion. Because he knew about her "sin," and still wanted her.

Sometimes Nefertiti remembered feeling "grate-ful" that Isaac had given her babies she could hold and take care of. But as she evolved through her thirties, and Isaac's philandering was getting more and more obvious, she just knew she had to get away from him. And she had grown since she left Isaac. It was in her relocation that she began to look back into her life and think about finding her daughter. Desiree. Desired life. As young as she was, what had made her choose that name?

* * *

"I always knew that there was something different about me. My family just didn't seem natural. It was all about prestige and appearances with them. I wasn't surprised when my first wife, Linda, divorced me after she found out.

"She hadn't spoken to her own mother and sister in twenty years. My children didn't even know who their maternal grandparents were, she held a grudge so. When her mother would write letters to her, Linda would give them to me and tell me to read them. She said she didn't want to know what was in the letters unless someone had died.

"I used to wonder why I was attracted to black women, why I always felt so at home with black people. Now I know what it was. It's not Grand-mère's fault. She was just a victim of the times. I think she's handled it well since I just straight came out and told her, 'I have to be who I am. I can't deny my heritage.' I guess I felt like Moses. I'd rather suffer with my people."

But still, there were things he told her that let her know that he really had been raised like a white man. Sometimes, in their most intimate moments, he'd sniff on her, bathe her in kisses, and tell her, "You smell so good, honey. I don't know why they used to say black girls smell. Now I see what they meant by that song 'A Taste of Honey.'"

Nefertiti would duck her head, and if she wasn't so dark, she would swear she was blushing.

When Nefertiti found out that Ford was telling the truth about his background, she thought about it. Why did she have to be so loyal to the brothers? They married white women all the time. Still, that was just how she felt. It had made a difference to her that Ford was black.

"Are you prejudiced, Ford?" Nefertiti didn't know why that conversation haunted her.

"Are you prejudiced, Ford?"

Nefertiti was thinking of a conversation she'd had with her husband just before she left Los Angeles.

"What do you mean? Am I prejudiced? I married you, didn't I?"

Now, it was times like this that Nefertiti actually hated Ford. His patronizing attitude. What was she supposed to be? A symbol of his open-mindedness? His liberalism?

Nefertiti had hardly spoken three words to Ford since he'd made that insensitive remark a week before she left. And who did he think he was? A white man? Even if he looked like one. Even if he had been raised as one. With how angry she felt toward him now, she wondered if this could be the same man she had worried about nearly a year ago during the LA riots. She remembered how she and Ned, the local homeless man, had sat at her shop, scared into a deathly silence. They looked on in shock as they watched her city of Los Angeles burn on the TV news, during the 1992 LA riots, which had been renamed "the LA Uprising" by some of the denizens.

That particular night, Ford had been late coming home from court. Nefertiti and Ned had watched helplessly as whites were torn from their cars and beaten by the mobs of angry looters.

There she sat, wondering, worrying if Ford would be the next person pulled from his car, because he would be mistaken for white. Now here she was wondering if she even wanted to return to Palos Verdes. She almost picked up the phone to call Ford and say as much when a sharp twinge in her back—one of many dull thuds that she'd experienced all day long—stopped her. With relief, she let out a sigh. Once again, she was grateful that she was not pregnant. *Thank you, sweet Jesus.*

She thought of Ford's last serious words to her—before their argument.

"You're young enough to have another baby, Nefertiti. You know, I didn't really get a chance to enjoy my older children, I was so busy climbing the corporate ladder. You are such a good mother. You know I won't treat our baby any differently from our other children. Why won't you have a baby for me?"

For the first time in her five-year marriage, she was thinking of separation or divorce. She wanted a fifty-fifty love, like the one Teddy Pendergrass described in the song, but she'd never had it. With Pharaoh, she'd been too young to really know the give-and-take of love. With Isaac, she'd been so eager for love, so eager to hold her own babies, unlike the one whom she'd been denied even to touch. She'd been careless with Isaac, giving it too bountifully, until he was oversated with it. Took her kindness for weakness. But with Ford, she'd been stingy. She only fed him teeny teaspoons of love, and he seemed as if he couldn't get enough of her. Perhaps because she'd always

held back with Ford, now she felt like she was
missing out on something.

"You are one of the sexiest women alive," Ford
would tell her in their intimate moments. Did he
mean it, or was he fascinated by her skin color?
Its satiny, midnight texture?

By far, Ford was a more considerate lover than
Isaac, so it wasn't any problem in the bedroom
that was beginning to bug her. He was even more
polished and experienced in terms of lovemaking. Isaac had had so many hang-ups. He didn't
like her to walk around braless. He didn't like to
have sex with all their clothes off. Only a lifted
gown would do. He always wanted the lights out
whenever they made love.

So what was bothering Nefertiti about Ford?
He'd been a good husband to her. He treated
her children like they were his own. Was it his
whiteness she was beginning to resent? Or was it
the stares from other couples that were wearing
her down? Nefertiti remembered how she used
to roll her eyes whenever she saw a black man
with a white woman. Now African-American men
were doing that to her.

She often wanted to turn around and say, "He's
not white. He's got some black blood in him."

But right now, she was so angry at her husband, she almost didn't feel like going back to
her beautiful home. What was that remark he
made about her dreads? She couldn't recall. She
just felt angry.

Nefertiti's thoughts turned to her wedding to

Ford. Up on a bluff in Carmel, California, overlooking the Pacific Ocean, around the Monterey Peninsula. *"With this troth, I thee wed. . . ."* It had been so breathtaking as they looked over the ocean, seeing the surf crash on the white sandy shores for miles and miles. Standing high upon a cliff before God and everybody. Everybody except her father—the almighty Reverend Godbolt. The wind had whipped up everyone's hair and their weaves. She still remembered how the waves licked at the beach's crescent on the horizon.

Because every piece of reality was always connected to another piece of reality, Nefertiti found herself thinking of Roshanne, who, she'd found out, wore a weave. So they were having problems now. Yes, buddy. What goes around comes around.

When she felt another twinge in her back, she went to the bathroom, saw her monthly had really started, and could have cried for joy. She didn't know what she would have done, had her period not come. Men just didn't know what women went through.

Just last month, she'd had a scare. She was going to have to have that operation—that tubal ligation—if that was the last thing she did. Although her doctor had taken her off the pill due to her age, she definitely did not want any more children. Ford thought she wanted to get pregnant, but she was using the rhythm method, and she also wore a diaphragm, which he wasn't aware of.

She remembered the first time she'd missed her period since her marriage to Ford. That was six months earlier. She'd felt as panicked as when she was a pregnant teen, because she knew what the deal was—sleepless nights, endless diapers, colic, the whole shebang. Unlike in 1967, when she was whisked away and hid for five months in a maternity home as the only solution, abortion was now legal, and she had seriously considered exercising her option. Later she was relieved she hadn't been put to the test.

Even so, Nefertiti wondered if she could live with herself if she had done anything, having been raised as a minister's daughter. *Thou shall not kill.* Still, she didn't know what she would have done if her period had not come.

She thought of their wedding again: *"For better or for worse. In sickness and in health."*

She still wasn't ready to talk to Ford, because she wasn't even sure what she was feeling, but she wanted to hear her children's voices. It was eleven o'clock in Michigan, but only eight o'clock in California, so she picked up the phone and called her children at Yolan's.

"Hi, Mom." Savasia sounded upbeat. "We went to Medieval Times tonight. I told you we're going to Disneyland this weekend. I can hardly wait."

"Did you get my e-mail?" was all Ike asked.

Nefertiti hung up, hoping her children's lives would be problem-free. She hoped they wouldn't make choices when they were young that would affect the rest of their lives, such as in her case.

What's the matter with me? Nefertiti thought about it. She'd never followed the rules. That's how she'd gone through all that scandal and disgrace when she was young. When you couldn't attend public schools and "show." That's why she was cloistered in a maternity home for more than half her pregnancy. Back when you were talked about like you had grown a tail. Back when it was a whisper in back alleys. *Knocked up. P.G. Left holding the bag.* That's how she was the only black girl she ever knew about in her area, at that time, to put her baby up for adoption.

Shallow's Corner had a skewed way of looking at the world. True, back in the 1960s, everyone talked about you. But when the baby came, everyone fussed over it. To go against this norm made her an iconoclast. Even if it wasn't her decision, people held her responsible. What was wrong with her? Why couldn't she be like everybody else? Never did follow anyone else's rules. Why did she have sex in the first place, when her church preached against premarital sex? Is this why she ended up in the space she was now in her life?

Is that how she wound up married to a man who looked white?

Suddenly she remembered Ford's little snide remark about her dreadlocks. "When are you going to get a perm again?"

When donkeys fly, you hear me, Ford?

The issue of the hair was just a surface matter. They seemed to be growing apart since she started her business, and he started to run for political office.

Suddenly she was beginning to question her marriage. Did she ever love Ford? Why did she worry about what people thought when it came to his appearance? Should it make a difference?

When she married him, she'd thought she loved him. He'd surely shown her love.

But most of all, given the changes in her marriage since she went into business, could their marriage stand the Pandora's box Nefertiti was about to open?

Even if it cost her her marriage, she could not turn back from her search for Desiree. She felt so confused. She didn't know if Ford loved her enough to forgive her for birthing a child he never knew about.

And, at the same time, since they were growing apart, she wondered if she even wanted to go back to him? She knew she would go back because her children were there and because they weren't his children, but she loved living in California. What could she do?

14

After Isaac had left, Nefertiti had sat up late that night, pondering her current marital situation, waiting for the cadence of her parents' argument to die, then listening for the silence and the creaks of the house, which would tell her that her parents were sleeping.

She was glad that her brother, Little Josh, and sister, Cleo, were to arrive home in the morning, and were not there sitting up late, reminiscing. This would be her only time alone to do what she needed to do. She knew where she had to start. After she could hear her parents snoring, she went to the end of the hall with a flashlight. Opening the cedar closet, she climbed up the stairs into the attic.

This was what she'd liked about this house when she was a little girl. The cedar closet was like a hidden trapdoor. Although it had shelves on one wall, there was a wall that pushed back and led to a steep stairwell.

Casting the dim flashlight she'd found under the kitchen sink before her, she stumbled on the last step. Bringing her fingers to her lip as if to shush herself, she smiled. Nefertiti found the single lightbulb string dangling in the center of the room and switched it on. The attic held the heat of the preceding day. Tilted roof beams and shadowy webbed crevasses housed crowded memories, old bicycles, baby paraphernalia, old-fashioned ice-cream machines, toys, boxes with Reverend's old sermons in them, even an old butter churn Big Mama Lily had brought from the South. She saw some of the rusted tools from Reverend's cabinetmaking days, and she saw his old Shriner robes from when he was an active member. For a moment, her eyes fell upon one of Rev's sermons. It was entitled, "To Thine Own Self Be True."

Finally she found Miss Magg's antique-looking wooden trunk, where her mother kept her old letters and her family Bible. As she opened the trunk, Nefertiti's nose was assaulted by the smell of mothballs, age, and dampness. At first, her curiosity was aroused by a faded sepia-toned daguerreotype of a stern-faced couple whose picture had been glued to an old mahogany music box. Who were they? Was this a progenitor on her mother or father's side of the family?

But looking closely, she noticed that this atavistic ancestor looked like a prototype of Uncle Tiger. She deduced that this picture was of someone from her father's side of the family. And, as she thought about it, the man, with his dark coloring and face shape, could have been a doppelganger for herself. The woman looked like a

dark-skinned Indian. Her raven-black hair hung
down her back.

Nefertiti next saw a pile of yellowed letters held
together by a faded ribbon, addressed to Lily
Sterns. She opened them and found they were all
from Grandpa Bullocks, back in 1908.

My Dearest Lily of the Valley, most of them began.
In looking at these love letters, she recalled that
her great-grandmother Lily (so named because
she had been so white as a baby, she could have
later passed for a white woman, if she had wanted)
and Grandpa Bullocks had married in 1910. The
only thing Nefertiti had always wondered about
Big Mama Lily was why she had hated white
people so. But one thing she could say for sure—
Big Mama Lily had loved her some Grandpa Bullocks, who was as sable brown as sealskin. She'd
always say, "Grandpa Bullocks is more man than
most. He's just perfectionate."

Finally Nefertiti found her mother's old family
Bible, with rubber bands holding it together. Nefertiti took a deep breath. It was as if she were
walking on sacred ground, holding Miss Magg's
Bible. This Bible had been in the family for years.
When Nefertiti was a child, no decent Christian
colored family was without the family Bible.

After taking it apart, she flipped through the
yellowed pages and came across two pages that
were stuck together. She struggled for a moment
to get the pages apart. She was between Leviticus
and Numbers.

To her surprise, a bulging yellowed paper,
folded in two creases, fell out. Opening the paper,
she discovered it was a letter. Nefertiti jumped

when a medallion, shaped like a bull's head, fell out of the letter.

The penmanship was neat, but labored-looking. The letter was from "Great-Aunt Millie." It was the date that shocked Nefertiti: *December 5, 1889.*

Nefertiti recalled overhearing Big Mama Lily mention a great-aunt Millie, on her daddy's side of the family, who lived to be 110. The two matriarchs used to attend the same church. Big Mama Lily had been the type to try to dig into people's family background so she knew a little more about both of Nefertiti's parents' ancestry.

The letter was written to someone named Bryce. She wondered who this progenitor, Bryce, could have been. Had this been a relative of her father's?

Nefertiti had always taken it for granted that she knew so much more about her mother's side of the family. Now she realized it had been a blessing that Big Mama Lily, who had lived with her family from the time Nefertiti was about two years old, had shared so much history. She had been the griot of the family.

From what Nefertiti had gathered, her maternal grandparents, Mordecai Bullocks and Big Mama Lily, had raised Miss Magg. Betty Lee had gotten pregnant with Miss Magg, had the baby at seventeen, and ran off, leaving her. No one had ever heard from Betty Lee again, nor did anyone seem to know what became of her.

Looking back, Nefertiti remembered Big Mama Lily telling her that the loss of Betty Lee had been the "big sorrow" of her life. Lily had been blessed with a good husband, but her only child had gone bad.

In fact, as close as Nefertiti was to Uncle Tiger, she'd noticed that he seldom mentioned their father, either, nor called this strange grandfather by name. Nefertiti only knew that Reverend's mother, Bertie, had died when he was a young man, long before Nefertiti was even born. But who was this Bryce? She read the letter in hopes of finding the answer.

December 5, 1889

Dear Bryce,

I hope this fines you well. I be tolerable well for an eighty-seven-year-old woman. They calls me Mother Millie at the church now, since I be one of the oldest living members, although when I was born, I was named Sunday. I never learned to read and write so I'm telling this to the new school-teacher at the freedom school. I done told her this is family business and secret and don't tell nobody.

I know I'm not long for this world, so I thought I'd tell you the story of your grandfather on your father's side. You know about what the white folks did to your daddy, Shilo, and how they sent you to Birmingham to live with Cousin Lila after that. But you never knew about your daddy's father, Samson. Samson was my baby brother.

And I want to give you this amulet, this little African-looking thing, that is the only thing I got of him in this world. If he was still living, he would be about eighty now.

You know they didn't give us birth dates or last

*names back in slavery, so we tried to name each
other our own different last names. We named our-
self different parts of the week or different parts of
the seasons or months to know when we was born
and who we was kin to. I think Samson was born
during hog killing time. We named him January,
but he was called Samson by the master. And just
like his biblical name, Samson grew up to be a
strong young buck. He had a way with horses, so
naturally, they made him a blacksmith.*

*And he was more than just a blacksmith. He
could work with the horses, especially the untamed
ones, calming them down, shoeing them when no
one else could touch a wild horse. They always
used him to break wild horses. Because of this, he
was always able to get a good job. I believe he's one
of the Douglasses who owned all that timberland
after we was freed, 'cause he was smart like that.
That's why his son, Shilo, was like that, too.
Could make something out of nothing. But I'm
getting ahead of myself in the story.*

*Like I say, your grandfather, Samson, was a
horse trainer and a blacksmith. Your oldest boy,
Theo, looks just like what I recollect of him.*

*Anyway, Samson had jumped the broom with
Violet back in the slavery days, and when she was
pregnant with their second child, that's when the
misery come. They already had your father, Shilo.
He was only a baby, just walking himself.*

*It all started with how Samson loved him some
corn bread. Violet, who was a full-blooded African,
come to the plantation when she was a young girl
about twelve. She worked in the big house as a
cook. Everyone called her Violet because she was*

one of them blue-black coloreds. The master and them always told the colored not to steal food out of the big house. Now you know that ain't human. To expect somebody to wring your chicken's neck, stew it for you, and you ain't supposed to touch it. Y'all young folks don't know how good y'all got it. Eat up from your own crops. Like the Bible says, has your own fig tree from your own vineyard.

Anyhows, as I recollect, Violet could really cook. But she could make corn bread melt in your mouth like a snowflake.

Well, if the truth be known, Violet had always sneaked food out of the big house to Samson and Shilo. This particular night she sneaked Samson a piece of corn bread, since he loved that corn bread. Even when he was a little boy, he loved him some corn bread. They say she had the corn bread split down the middle with a big glob of butter melting on it, just like he liked it. She usually sneaked things in her apron, and with her being big with they baby, she didn't think anyone would notice it.

Well, like I was saying, I think Violet was about eight months big with they second baby at that time. Master had said they could keep they baby, and they was sho' happy about that. Besides, they knew the more babies they had, the less likely they was to be sold, because each baby represented money for the master.

Somebody—I hate to say it, but they say it was one of us slaves—must've seen Violet steal that corn bread to give to Samson, because come nightfall, the overseer come to the cabin just when they were bout to go to sleep and dragged her out. I believes the other slaves were jealous because Samson had so

much freedom and they didn't. Samson and Violet
kept one of the nicest cabins in slave row, if I must
say so myself. Even had it whitewashed.

Well, to get on with my story, they tied Violet up
and put her in the barn that night. It was a
custom, whenever a slave woman was with child
and was beaten, they had to dig a hole to put the
woman's belly inside to keep from damaging they
property, the unborn child. They did this with
Violet the next day at high noon. Two overseers
held Samson at gunpoint and made him watch
what they done.

They wanted all the other slaves and the white
folks to watch. This was to be an example to the
other slaves about stealing from the master.

Samson cried as he watched them beat Violet,
and the white people laughed and laughed. She
was to get fifty lashes.

To this day, I don't know what ran through
Samson's mind. What made him do what he did.
But later on, whenever I ponder on it, I think it
was this. There was another woman, Sidney, who
they beat while she was expecting, and she'd lost
her mind afterward. That's right. She was never
right in the head after that. Maybe that's what
Samson feared.

I don't know what it was. But long as I live, I
will never understand it. Do Jesus help us?

Anyways, I think Violet's cries was too much
for him to bear, along with the white folks' laughter, and his mind just snapped. I remember he was
crying. I guess he was mad with grief and shock
over what they were doing, and I know in my
heart he loved Violet, so I think it was he just

couldn't stand to see his wife suffer like that or he couldn't take any more of her cries.

Samson, small man that he was, grabbed the gun out of the overseer's hand, shot his wife's already half-dead body, knocked the overseer off the horse, jumped on the horse, shot into the crowd of white people, and rode off toward the Alabama River. Oh, you should've seen the hullabaloo when the dust settled. After the white folks got over cussin' over losing two slaves, Violet and her unborn, they sent a posse after Samson. Weren't no sense in losing three, but probably they woulda killed him, if they had caught him. Because later, one of the field overseers, a white man, that he'd shot, died.

The main thing that saved Samson was that he did not have a brand on him. He had never worn a shackle, and that's why what I'm about to tell you happened.

Maybe the white folks had underestimated Samson when they never branded him. They had never chained or shackled him, and he had never run. So I figure they thought he didn't mind being a slave. Big mistake. Nobody colored like being a slave. It ain't human. But they thought we coloreds was animals. They must don't know. Even animals will die when they caged up.

They say they finally caught up to Samson's horse by the river. When they saw the horse going across the river with no one on its back, they assumed he had drowned. But all the time, Samson was laying under the water, breathing through the reeds. When they left, he called the horse Brutus back, and he was able to get away over to the Tennessee side. He probably took the Alabama River to the Tombigbee River where they join together. Then we figured once he reached the Tensaw River, he headed north into the Tennessee River. They never did find him.

After Samson rode off, me and the other slave women took Violet's body to the cabin and dressed it in a shroud for burial. The baby was dead inside of her. We couldn't save it. I found this amulet around her neck. Samson had made it on the master's anvil. It was supposed to be a lucky charm to protect her. I don't know. It was shaped like a bull's head. I think I heard Violet call it an ankh one time. They say it means the female parts and it come out of Africa.

I know this was old slave talk, but after that, many a slave said they seen Violet's ghost wandering in the woods at night, crying for her baby and for Samson. It was too sad for words.

Next thing you know, the crops started failing on the master's plantation. Things got so bad, all of us slaves had to be sold for taxes. It was as if Violet's spirit cursed all his prosperity, and they lost everything.

I guess I'm just getting old. I don't like the bitterness I feels in my soul when I thinks about how that young couple had so much to live for.

I finished raising they baby boy, Shilo, your daddy, right long with my children at our new master's farm. The Butlers was our new owners. They, too, had heard the story of the fall of our old master's farm. The coloreds would whisper it on the wind, sort of like High John de Conqueror, but no one would come out and tell it in the daylight.

We never told Shilo what happened until he got

grown, for fear he'd seek revenge and wind up killed, too. The funny thing was he ended up with so much land after slavery, that the white folks killed him, anyway, so that they could take his land. Maybe it ain't a good thing to have too much until we reach the Promised Land.

Anyhow, Samson was never caught and returned to our plantation. They say he prob'ly changed his name. I can only figure he done what he did out of love. The way some slave women killed they babies. Years later, I heard tell that he married again and had five more sons, who would be your uncles. Maybe you'll be able to find him or his family before we all go on to glory. I'm too old to travel anymore. After freedom come, I heard Samson had been living as a freedman for twenty years or better, anyhow. When he was sure he was really free, I believes he tried to find his family. What was left of his sisters and brothers. And I know in my heart, he looked for his baby, Shilo. But I guess he could never find us.

The last I heard a Winslow had married into a Douglass family, which sounded like it might have been Samson's grandson. What make me think this is they tell a mighty story how the grandfather escaped from slavery and became a rich blacksmith in Memphis, Tennessee. I sure hope you be able to find him or his new family. I heard Samson mighta went to Memphis and changed his name.

I don't know. I still feel like it's a curse on your family when you don't know where your kinfolk is in this life.

Love,
Great-Aunt Millie

For a long time, Nefertiti stood holding the letter and the ankh in her hand. She was so ensconced in pain, loss, and love for Violet, her distant ancestor, she could not move. The next thing she remembered, she was tasting salt in her mouth from the tears sluicing down her face. A baby who had died in his mother's womb, because the mother was almost beaten to death, and her husband chose to shoot her, rather than see her suffer a living death. She didn't know how long she stood there, weeping quietly.

When she looked down, her tears had spotted the paper, causing the painstakingly written letters to run together. She tried to wipe the wet tears away, causing the letters to smear, and the aged yellowed paper to tear. She folded the letter and stuck it in her bra, as if it were something precious that she wanted to keep near her heart. Now she understood what Rev meant when he had sounded so solicitous about Uncle Tiger. *These are my people, even if they are distant ancestors.* Maybe this related to all the disconnection in her family down to this day.

Absently she kneaded the amulet, which she had already known, from her experiences in collecting antiques, was an ankh. She remembered that ankhs were talismans for fertility and protection. She flipped back through her memory.

Nefertiti looked to the back of the Bible and found the family tree. From what she saw, this was her father's side of the family. Killsprettyenemy, the youngest son, had been Reverend's father. Bryce had been Rev's and Tiger's paternal grandfather, and Theo was one of his older sons. She took her finger and traced the family tree. If Bryce was the grandfather to her father and Uncle Tiger, he would have been her great-grandfather. Shilo would have been her great-great-grandfather. Samson would have been her great-great-great-grandfather.

Nefertiti's hands trembled and an electrical current coursed through her blood. It was too mind-boggling to absorb all at once! This was a page from a piece of her unknown history. A piece of her ancestors.

Then Nefertiti began to dig some more. Underneath the bottom layer of the trunk was a quilt. Patterns of horses had been stitched on it. Nefertiti lifted the quilt in her hand, feeling herself tied to something valuable, something of the past. The material was so old some of the rotting threads began to fray in her hand.

She now knew the taste of victory the archaeologists from Ike's Internet assignment must have felt when they discovered a fossil. This was even better. This letter was a fossil from her bloodline. Nefertiti returned to digging through the trunk. Finally she found what she had been looking for when a folded piece of paper fell out of the Bible. Nefertiti unfolded it.

She was thinking of the "great secret," which Isaac had alluded to, and now here it was. It was just a piece of paper, but its power made her fall to her knees.

It was the original birth certificate for her little girl. The certificate did not name the father of the Negro baby girl. Because she was underage at the time, and the laws for statutory rape were more strictly enforced, Nefertiti remembered never naming the father. Yet, Rev and them had known. During those days, the baby was called "illegitimate," and the father's name was not put on the birth certificate if you were not married. Other than the first name Desiree, her daughter had no name.

Nefertiti was surprised she did not cry anymore. She didn't know what she felt. Still, the years came rushing back to her with a sharp jab. The "secret" she'd harbored all these years, until she sometimes didn't even speak of it in her most inward parts. And the horror of her choice began to sink in like an underground river.

Besides being her baby, this wasn't just any baby she'd given away. This was a baby of African descent. Born in America. A baby with a legacy of children being sold away from their mothers. A baby with a history of an ancestor being beaten to death while her infant was still in the thick harbor of her womb. A baby who had a deep connection to her ancestors. She had to find Desiree, no matter what happened. Even if Desiree spit in her face. Nefertiti knew she had to try. She knew then that she was about to embark on the deepest journey of her life.

The words *"It's a curse on your family when you don't know where your kinfolk is"* seared an indelible brand into her brain.

15

Nefertiti dreamed she was being pursued all night long. She was running, running, running, for her life, trying to get away. But from whom? She couldn't see the faces of her pursuers. Her hands had nearly clawed the skin off the dream itself—she had pulled on so many limbs in a thicket of trees. It was as though she had taken on her great-great-great-grandfather's spirit and was a runaway slave being pursued. At the same time, she was still a woman, and in her heart, she knew she was herself. Yet, she was being pursued, and it was a matter of life or death.

The next thing she knew, she was trying to escape by water as Samson had. She could hear bloodhounds barking behind her. The rivers were columns of water chopping, coursing, and rushing through her old bedroom. She was lost in a fog. Her children, Isaac Jr. and Savasia, were standing on the other side of the river, calling her. A baby was lost in the veil of the fog, crying on the other side of the river. Pharaoh and Isaac were chasing her. She knew to heal herself, she had to get to the crying baby on the other side of the river. To heal them all. She finally climbed up on top of an old barge—some kind of boat. Then she remembered—Little Josh had called her "ho" and "slut" when she was a teenager. Wouldn't speak to her because she was pregnant out of wedlock. To this day, he still had an accusing attitude of "I've got something on you. I look down on you."

Nefertiti shot straight up in her old bed at the same time that the phone rang. Still a little unsettled by her dream, she listened to her mother answer the phone in the hallway, then call out, "Nefertiti, it's Ford."

Nefertiti wondered why she did not want to talk to Ford until she sorted out her feelings. She didn't know if it was because she was under her father's roof, but it almost felt sacrilegious. Although she didn't know which room of the house her father was in, she could smell Rev's disapproval in the air.

"Hi, honey."

"Hey."

"How was your flight?"

"All right. Didn't get airsick this time."

"Did you get to the doctor before you left?"

"No, I didn't have time. I'm all right."

Silence on the other end. Without her elaborating, he knew that she meant her monthly had come down. It seemed as though Ford was the one keeping charts and temperatures these days.

"Nefertiti, you know how much I want a baby. Now, you know I love children. I'll help, Nefertiti."

Nefertiti was quiet. Things were getting shaky enough between them. Why would he think a baby would help matters any? He shouldn't even be thinking of a baby at his age. Fifty-five. *Let me enjoy my menopause in peace!*

Ford finally spoke to fill in the space of Nefertiti's silence. "We had a little problem with Isaac at school yesterday."

"I talked to Isaac last night. He didn't tell me anything. What happened?"

"Don't worry, I'll take care of it. I'm taking him back to school tomorrow, Friday. He's been suspended for a day."

"What do you mean, 'Don't worry'?" The soprano in her voice raised the alarm. "What happened?"

"Just a little fight. Not to worry."

"What do you mean? He is the only black boy in that school, and you're telling me not to worry. I knew I shouldn't have sent him out to that prep school. He told me they had a lot of skinheads at the school."

"I think you're blowing this out of proportion, Nefertiti."

"With all this hazing going on. I swear, if any of those boys hurt my son—"

"That's on college campuses. This is high school, Nefertiti. Why are you so upset?"

"What do you mean, why am I so upset? That's my son!" Nefertiti felt her voice rising, something she seldom did with Ford. "Are you sure he wasn't hurt?"

"Yes, I heard the other kid is the one with the black eye. But that's not fair, Nefertiti. You know I love the children and wouldn't let anything happen to them."

Nefertiti was quiet. How could she explain her fears as an African-American mother to Ford? For all practical purposes, his other two children had been raised as white children. Their mother was white; all their friends were white. But her children had always had a strong racial pride, choosing black friends over white ones.

As far as she was concerned, Ford could straddle the fence. It wasn't like he discussed his black blood with everyone he met. He could choose to be black when he wanted to be. Perhaps that was why he didn't understand her panic every time she heard a siren when she came to the Los Angeles area where her store was located.

Her fears about gangbangers, black-on-black crime, drugs, street violence. Whenever she went downtown to the garment district to buy fabric, she saw all the derelict men of color lying around and holding up the walls of hopelessness in "Skid Row." Sometimes she would think, *A wrong turn in Ike's life and that could be my son one day. Oh, God, protect him! These men had been someone's baby boy at one time. These men who are happy to be able to get a free night and free meal at the mission. A handout.* No, she didn't want that for her son. Ford thought that Nefertiti was just too paranoid.

But not too paranoid to have another baby? And what kind of sense did that make, when she was just beginning to give birth to her dream, The Treasure Chest? She had wanted her own little boutique for the past ten years. No, she did not want to start over with a baby. Not a black one, not a biracial one. Period.

"Well, Ford, call me back once you go up to the

school with him. I'll be back Sunday afternoon. Or you can wait until I get home and I'll take him back to school Monday." Now it was decided. She knew she had to go back, in spite of her ambivalent feelings regarding their relationship.

"No, I'll take him back. No sense in him missing any more school than necessary. Is that okay?"

"Sure. Thanks. I'll talk to you later."

"Bye, babe. Love you."

Nefertiti paused. "Love you, too." When she hung up, she held her head in her hands. Did she still love Ford?

Nefertiti started moving around when she heard the hustle and bustle of her parents going to pick up her sister and brother from the airport. After reading Great-Aunt Millie's letter the night before, Nefertiti had wanted to spend some time alone with her father so that she could ask him what he remembered about his family. Also, she was curious as to how Rev got this letter from his grandfather. But she was to have no such uninterrupted time. By the time she had gone back to her room to pray and meditate before talking to her father, her parents were gone.

The day before, she had borrowed her parents' second car, the Lincoln Brougham. Today, she decided, she would rent a compact-sized car so she could get around and conduct her adoption search without being hindered. She picked up the phone to catch a cab to the car rental place, but decided she'd catch a jitney, instead. In Shallow's Corner, jitneys ran better than the cab companies, since many white cabdrivers did not like to frequent the black neighborhoods. Plus, she knew that Pharaoh drove a cab. He was the last person she wanted to see right now. But the truth of it was, she would do anything rather than ride out to the airport with her parents to get a car and be there to meet her sister and brother's planes. She just wanted to be alone with her thoughts to sort through what she had to do.

She was staring at Big Ben, thinking of her efforts at dinner to make conversation with her father.

"Daddy, you've never told me the story of Big Ben. I mean how you inherited it."

"Girl, leave the past be" was all Reverend said as he ate the rest of his meal in silence.

Nefertiti continued eating, feeling downhearted. Why had she ever thought her father would answer her questions about a great-aunt Millie, if he wouldn't even talk about the family heirloom?

Suddenly the phone rang again. It was a young woman's voice.

"Hi, my name is Zora Fairchild. I'm a college classmate of Cleo's. Anyhow, she had set it up for me to photograph your father's seventy-fifth birthday dinner over at Solid Rock Baptist Church on Saturday? I just wanted to meet the family before I do the job, so I'll know all the particulars. I came by last night, but no one ever answered the door. I rang the doorbell and no one answered."

Nefertiti felt a twinge of guilt, remembering the knock that had come following the first thing—her icy welcome from her father—which had gotten on her nerves during this visit home.

She'd been too upset to get to the door in time. Nonetheless, afterward, her parents had eaten dinner like nothing had ever happened. But that had been the first hint of a fissure, of dissension between her parents, but she couldn't put her finger on what had started it. Then it hit her. It all had started with Uncle Tiger's call.

"I'm sorry, what did you say your name was?"

"Zora."

"Could you call back later and speak to my mother, Mrs. Godbolt, or to Reverend Godbolt. They're not here right now."

When Nefertiti hung up, her mind wandered back to the fact that something was going on between her parents. What could it be? she wondered.

16

When the front door opened, Nefertiti literally felt like she did during her first experience of an LA earthquake. *Dismayed.* She knew her parents couldn't be back from the airport that soon. So no one was more surprised than Nefertiti to see her brother, Little Josh, letting himself in the house with his own personal key. His pale-skinned, crème-de-menthe wife, Gloria, and his two daughters, Megan and Heather—"the light-skinned gremlins," as her darker children, Savasia and Ike, called their cousins—dovetailed him.

"Thought I'd surprise Moms and Pops and come in my camper. We had made our reservations on Delta, but we said we'd be spontaneous and take the scenic route. We plan to stop back through New York before we return to Atlanta. In fact, we're running to Niagara Falls tonight and staying until Saturday morning, but we just wanted Dad to know we're here." Little Josh dropped his Louis Vuitton suitcases in the middle of the floor. From the window, Nefertiti could see their recreational vehicle blocking the driveway.

"Well, they're not here. Miss Magg went to pick you up from the airport—which you could've called and told her you weren't flying in. I don't know where Rev—I mean, Daddy is. I was just looking for him and didn't find him in the house. I guess he must've gone to the airport with Miss Magg."

"Oh, well. I can't wait to see the look on Dad's face when he sees my new RV."

Nefertiti looked at her brother. He had always clothed himself in an unctuous spirituality she knew he didn't live. His Armani suit, his métier for the meticulous and the provincial, were his trademark. There was something else that Josh was draped in. Nefertiti could almost smell the odor of greed and acceptance as a natural right. He was his father's firstborn, and only, son. His anointed. For a minute, when he shook her hand, Nefertiti thought she saw a skeleton holding her palm. She had to shake her head before the image left.

"Hi," Nefertiti said, perfunctorily hugging Gloria.

Gloria said, "Oh, your hair looks so ethnic."

She could feel the scorn piercing from Gloria's eyes as she appraised Nefertiti's brown-and-beige African stripes. Nefertiti could have told her that this was not an imitation print. This madras cloth had come from Ethiopia, but Nefertiti wasn't into status symbols. She knew with Gloria's designer consciousness, her sister-in-law probably would have appraised the outfit in a different light, had she informed her of its origin.

Trying not to take umbrage, and considering the source, Nefertiti decided to overlook her. It was her brother who really irked her. She hadn't spoken to him since the family reunion eight years earlier. She had been going through the hellish throes of "Should I leave?" or "Shouldn't I?" with Isaac. Thinking back, Nefertiti remembered that seeing how miserable Josh's wife looked, with her Oreo self, under all her pretensions and airs of grandeur, had also been another one of her deciding factors—even if only unconsciously.

She started a conversation with Gloria first. "How's it going?"

"I'm blessed."

Although she hadn't seen Little Josh or Gloria in eight years, they both still had the power to rankle Nefertiti. Gloria played the role of an executive's wife to the hilt. All they needed was a stage.

Nefertiti's mind began to wander, and she looked over at the family photos on the fireplace mantel. Thinking about it, Nefertiti noticed that even Little Josh's childhood pictures bespoke an air of confidence, assurance, and royalty. Then there was Cleo. In her childhood photos, her sister's Peter Pan bangs divided her smooth mocha-colored forehead with flair. Her flashing smile announced, "I'm accepted. And I know it."

Nefertiti suppressed a sense of pride at the haughty, defiant slant of her head in her childhood pictures. With two long braids on each side of her head, her pose said, "I'm the outsider, but you're not going to break my spirit."

In her family, it wasn't talent that counted, because as far as Nefertiti was concerned, Cleo, the newscaster, and Little Josh, who managed a travel agency, had little. It was only money with them. Who made the most money. Who had the most money. Who could spend the most money. They believed in doing everything top-shelf. The crème de la crème.

Well, Nefertiti had run that gamut before, and now she loved her simpler life. In spite of Nigel's money, she used her own money for her store and she didn't buy everything she could afford just to show it off. From what her mother had told her, her siblings thought that she was crazy to give up her "good" government job with its pension and benefits to run "her little store," as they called it. To them, money was everything. They could not imagine life without the brackets of a socially accepted position.

After their greetings, Gloria continued to hold a conversation. "Oh, I couldn't be better. We just came from a nice trip to Greece and Israel. We also hit a lot of little islands while we were there."

"How wonderful." Nefertiti felt her mouth stretch into a plastic smile.

"Yes, travel broadens one so."

"I see." Nefertiti almost gagged on her sister-in-law's syrupy delusions.

"We're running up to Niagara Falls while we're here. We'll probably leave this afternoon and get back in time for the dinner. Would you like to go with us? Cleo said she'd ride with us."

"Oh, I have some business to take care of. And, anyway, Miss Magg is giving a small family dinner on Friday evening. I'll take a rain check." *Get real. Do you think I would be locked up in a camper with your phony butts for even a day?*

"What do you think of those horrible Ebonics

they're trying to push in the schools?" Gloria asked. "When I was growing up, our teachers told us to enunciate and speak proper English. The other day, I was so tickled that one of my customers on the phone at work thought that I was white."

"Is that so?" Nefertiti felt her eyebrow lifting, but she cautioned herself, *Don't argue politics or religion. Stay on your program.* She didn't want to waste any energy getting riled up. She needed all of her strength for what she had to face.

"Well, then, how's your little shop? Mother Dear told me about it." Everyone called Miss Magg by her name, but this daughter-in-law had to distinguish herself to show them that they were using the wrong name.

"Fine." After what felt like hours to Nefertiti, but was actually only minutes of shuffling around in social intercourse, Nefertiti tried to politely make her exit, when Little Josh asked in a condescending manner, "So what's it like being in business for yourself, sis?"

"I wouldn't trade it for the world. Couldn't be better." Nefertiti felt her cheeks warm, knowing Joshua didn't care, and knowing to him, his bottom line was cash; so in his world, her business was not doing well.

"Oh, business at the agency has been pretty good this year. I think I'll be promoted to regional manager."

Nefertiti couldn't help herself. "Well, you wouldn't think you had a dime the way Cousin Letty Pearl told me."

"What are you talking about?"

"You know Cousin Letty Pearl is still too

through with you over not helping bury her granddaughter. It's a shame how the child went to visit her father in Texas, then drowned at a day camp swim out. It took them two weeks to get the body back to Louisiana."

Suddenly *all* of the starch dropped out of Little Josh's speech.

"I'm not thinking about Letty Pearl 'n them. I'm sick of anytime somebody black got somethin', they family think they just a money tree to come runnin' up to beggin'. Letty Pearl is a distant cousin on Mama's side. I don't know nothing about her people. Now, take white folks. When somebody in their family got some money, they don't think anybody got to owe them something. We the only race of people ain't got nothing, yet always trying to help somebody. That's why we can't get ahead."

He stopped for a moment, then started using his fingers to enumerate his points. "Look, I helped on Big Mama Lily's funeral and Grandpa Bullocks's. I got a family, too, now. And from what I remember, they still leaving food out for their dead after they die down there. And they takes the shovel and everybody helps bury their dead. Now, if that ain't as backwater as you can get, I don't know what is. I ain't got no money to be putting in all that old superstitious bull. What y'all think I'm runnin' around here—Union Bank? I'm not putting no mo' money in the ground."

"Well, 'scuse us niggers." Nefertiti could feel herself ready to go off. "You're just a selfish pig. You always were. I see you don't feel that way about sharing when it comes to Rev's land. You know you are beyond ignorant, if you think you can make it like a fly in the buttermilk. What with all this outsourcing and affirmative action reversal, we are all going to need each other."

"Well, my job is secure. That's not what this is about. I know you. Let's face it. Dad always said that I would get the largest portion of his will, being as I am the oldest and his namesake. Are you jealous of that, Nefertiti? Isn't being married to a white man enough for you? I heard about that big house you have out in California."

Before she could retaliate, the front door opened and her parents and Cleo came walking in. Nefertiti gasped. Cleo had a zillion small braids on her head, which looked like snakes on Medusa. A regular Gorgon. Rev was grinning from ear to ear, though.

Next he reached out and gave Little Josh a manly handshake, and then, one by one, hugged Gloria, Megan, and Heather.

"I'll see you later," Nefertiti called over her shoulder. "This is crapola, and I have had enough of it. One thing I know for sure. I'm not waiting for Rev to die so I can get that land of his down South."

"You know that is heir property. Whoever Rev wants to leave it to, he can." Little Josh's voice followed her down the steps.

"Well, I'm not counting on it, don't want no parts of it, but I'm not going to let you think I don't know what you're up to." In her anger, as she turned on her heel and ran down the porch stairs, Nefertiti noticed out of the corner of her eye Miss Magg's tight smile.

* * *

Nefertiti started out walking, with no destination in mind; she was so angry. She didn't even know where she was headed, at first. She had always been the chocolate drop in the family, whereas her light-skinned brother and sister had been her father's pets. The black sheep. She wondered who had coined that term. Only Miss Magg, Big Mama Lily, and Grandpa Bullocks had ever made a fuss over her, and that made her feel special.

With their exceptions, there had always been a silent division in the home. *Them* versus Nefertiti. The ties that bind and gag. It hadn't helped matters that her mother had Cleo when Nefertiti was a sophomore in high school—in fact, at the same time she was pregnant with Desiree—so it was almost like another generation, they were so far removed from one another. The sins in the name of love. No one made her crazier than her loved ones. Even family reunions blew up into big nasty fights— emotions, which crested like the lava of a volcano from old childhood rivalries, running pus, like a picked scab on a scraped knee. Unresolved conflicts festering like boils just waiting to erupt under the thin skin of time.

As she reflected on it, even when her father had greeted Little Josh and his family, the welcome had been like night and day in comparison to his performance the night before. And this time, Rev was sincere. Nefertiti had always noticed the difference her father made in his other two children. As if her reunion with her brother weren't bad enough, especially him showing up early, before she could get out the door, Cleo had to waltz through it. Nefertiti knew that it was all over; it was no sense staying around and fighting some more.

One of the main things that had struck Nefertiti was that although Cleo was wearing a zillion braids on her head and her father seemed nonplussed by them, he was still happy to see her. He was even hugging Cleo to him as they walked up the stairs. She could also still see the warmth in the manly handshake Rev had given Little Josh.

Nefertiti had a thought. Little Josh hadn't always been the way he was. There was a time when they were children, that she and her brother had been somewhat close. The two used to play around and cook up concoctions in the kitchen. It had been Little Josh who had liked to cook the most. Had even thought of opening up his own kitchen. Becoming a chef. But when Rev found out, he had said that cooking was a woman's job. The kitchen was a woman's place. Hence, Little Josh had gone into business administration, and no one was prouder of him than Reverend. Yet anyone who came within ten feet of Little Josh would always encounter the unsettled anger of his spirit. And, anyway, why would they still call a forty-four-year-old man "Little Josh"?

Nefertiti resolved not to think of her family anymore. She trudged up the street, not sure where she was headed. She decided that she would seek solace in the house of her oldest, lifelong friend, Sharon, better known as "Baby Too Sweet." Nefertiti was still about five miles away from her friend's home, so she flagged down a jitney and climbed in, deciding to focus her thoughts on Sweet.

Originally, Baby Too Sweet had been nicknamed such as a child, because she'd so loved Alaga syrup sandwiches. Because she had been raised by a divorced mother, long before being a single mother was either acceptable or commonplace, Sweet had been labeled "fast." Everyone had sworn she would wind up pregnant before she got out of her teens (according to some, *before* she even got into them) and would be on welfare with a houseful of babies.

As things turned out, Sweet had never had any children, although she was godparent to Nefertiti's children. Yes, Baby Too Sweet had fooled them all in Shallow's Corner. Now Sweet was a court stenographer for a well-known black female judge, was single, owned her own home, and was childless. All the old "biddies," as Sweet called them, would drop their eyes whenever Sweet would come strutting into church on Sundays, often tithing large donations.

Nefertiti and Sweet met when they were eight years old. Miss Dyan, Sweet's mother, had been Miss Magg's hairdresser. Until the day she had died from emphysema, five years ago, Miss Dyan had pressed hair, standing on her bunioned feet, making sure she took care of herself and Sweet. She had never been on welfare with Sweet.

When Sweet started making decent money, she tried to get her mother to sit down. Even bought her a home, but Miss Dyan refused to stop moving. Now Sweet had this extra piece of property rented out.

Before Miss Dyan's death, Nefertiti had always marveled at Sweet and her mother's relationship. From the time Sweet was a teenager, Miss Dyan had told her about the mechanics of love-making, birth control, and the mystery of men. When Sweet was in her twenties, her mother had even told her the best lovemaking positions.

The only downfall in Sweet's life—if that was what you wanted to call it—was that she had been dating a married man for the past ten years. However, Sweet seemed satisfied with her life. She would always say, "Look, I can send Harry home after we have gone on trips. His wife is the one who has to do his dirty laundry and cook his meals and raise his babies. Thanks, but no thanks."

And she never went out of her way to try to break up Harry's home, either. In the past ten years, Sweet and Harry's relationship had settled into the routine of an old married couple's.

Although Nefertiti didn't agree with Sweet having an affair with a married man—knowing the pain Roshanne had caused her—she still needed to go to Sweet for healing. Sweet had always been there for her, even back when they were teenagers, when she had gotten pregnant with Desiree.

17

As Nefertiti climbed out of the jitney, she was disappointed when she didn't see Sweet's Jaguar in the driveway. Nefertiti noticed a new coat of fuchsia paint on the wood trim of the yellow-bricked bungalow. She went and knocked on the door, anyway, thinking that's what friends are for. She looked under the flowerpot on the porch and found the extra key. As soon as she opened the front door, the strong smell of paint, which pervaded the air outside, nearly overwhelmed her once she crossed the threshold.

When she strolled into the entrance hallway, she heard Sweet holler out, "Is that you, Harry? I'm back in the family room painting."

"No, it's me. I thought you weren't home. It's Nefertiti."

Nefertiti heard Sweet's scream before she saw her.

When Sweet saw Nefertiti, she threw her roller down, and began to jump up and down. She stomped her feet, then finally came and threw her arms around her.

"Hey, girl! Titi! You're looking good."

"Hey, girl! You too!"

"Why didn't you tell me you were coming to town? I would have had something cooked for you and planned to take you out on the town."

"Well, I just wanted to surprise you. Where is your car?"

"In the shop. I should have it out around three."

"Well, would you mind taking me to the car rental agency when you get it back?"

"Sure. But you can drive Harry's extra car."

"No way. His wife will never blow me up, thinking I'm his mistress driving it."

"Girl, you still crazy. How's the kids?"

"Fine. Growing."

"Let me clean up and get out of these digs." Sweet looked at her. "How's Nigel? How come he didn't come with you?" Sweet eyed Nefertitit suspiciously.

"He had a conference to attend this weekend. Besides, I needed to do this by myself."

"What's the matter, chicken head? I know you ain't thinking about a divorce, and here I ain't had my first husband yet."

"No, everything's okay."

"Well, I know you. I can see that look in your eye. Something's wrong."

Sweet knew her so well, but Nefertiti didn't want to discuss what was on her mind—not just yet.

Sweet changed the subject. "Girl, have you heard about that crazy heifer Roshanne?"

"What has she done now?"

"Had the nerve, no—the unmitigated, gally, brass-monkey nerve—to go on a talk show, talking all her business."

"You lying?"

"If I'm lying, I'm flying." Sweet kissed her right pointer finger and placed her hand up to God, as they'd done when they were young girls. "Well, anyway, Roshanne was supposed to be telling her girlfriend about going with a two-timing man. She got her nerve. All the silver pins and grave-yard dust she used to get Isaac away from you."

"Look, let's don't even waste breath talking about that lowlife."

"I just wanted to say this. I still believe she worked some roots on Isaac. He was too nice a person before she got her hands on him. He does his mama so bad now, I can't believe it."

"Well, good riddance. She's going to have to keep on using those roots to keep him. I just didn't want the mess around me. I don't believe in that hoodoo, anyway." Nefertiti paused, re-membering the dolls. Although she wanted to believe there was no such thing as voodoo, in her heart she did believe it, but this was something she'd never shared with Sweet.

"Anyhow, Ford was telling me that Ike had some little scuffle at school. You think his teachers would call and tell me anything? Had me so upset, but I'm cool now. It's nothing I can do about it until I get home."

Sweet perked up. " Girl, do you remember Mrs. Jackson, our home ec teacher in junior high? She was the first black teacher, other than our music teacher, Mr. Carrington. I wonder what ever hap-pened to her?"

"Yeah. Come to think of it, I remember the time she saw us smoking, over by the railroad

tracks. With those bifocals she wore—I don't see
how she even saw us over a block-and-a-half away.
How old were we then? Thirteen?"

"Yes. My goodness. They don't make teachers
like that anymore. I wonder if she is still living?
But it's what Mrs. Jackson said that tickles me
now. 'I saw you Sharon. Knee-high to a bullfrog,
with that cigarette hanging out of your mouth.'"

"Oh, the lecture she gave us," Sweet added.
"Said we were too impudent. But she never turned
us in."

"I remember Mrs. Jackson was the first one to
talk to us about feminine hygiene. She made me
think that pubic hair was a jungle of odor pockets. And about periods. She made it sound like
you would get pregnant if you kissed a boy."

"Maybe they need to go back to those scare
tactics," Sweet observed.

"Like the film they showed us on drugs. One
drag on a marijuana cigarette and you were
strung out, eyes popping out your head like that
old monster Gorgo, going through sweats and
withdrawal."

"Well, it worked for most of our generation.
Maybe they need to pull back out that old black-
and-white film," Sweet mused.

"I heard that. I remember, Mrs. Jackson once
called me in her office to talk about Little Josh
and his bad attitude. She told me, 'Tell your
mother that your brother dresses nice, but he acts
'ugly.'" Nefertiti, an inveterate mimic, used the
same crisp new-dollar-bill voice Mrs. Jackson used
to speak in.

Simultaneously the two women quoted the

aphorisms they were raised on: "Pretty is as pretty does, but ugly is to the bone. God don't like ugly, and he ain't crazy about pretty, neither."

They both fell down to the floor. After they repeated the story several times to get their laugh's worth, Nefertiti had another reminiscence.

"Remember how we used to sneak out to the quarter parties?" Quarter parties were basement parties where you paid a quarter to get in.

"Weren't we a mess?"

"Well, I was always the one to get caught."

"Lady Godiva."

"You know that's right."

They both bent over, holding their sides, remembering the year Nefertiti used to sneak out with Pharaoh. They had been playing strip poker with Sweet's boyfriend, Fadel, and Nefertiti's about-to-go-together boyfriend, Pharaoh. That particular night, when Miss Dyan had gone out on a date, they had the house to themselves. Sweet was down to her bra and pants, while Nefertiti still had her blouse and pants on. Two more losses and Nefertiti reluctantly eased her bra off, but put her white blouse over her chest. Before she knew what was happening, Sweet had grabbed her blouse and run with it, while Nefertiti ran at her heels in an embarrassing, screaming pursuit. Although the whole game had taken place when both girls were still virgins, they were just beginning the foray across the moat into that mysterious country of womanhood. It was like a slow tease, that year of foreplay.

Sweet walked over to the étagère, where she had various pictures encased in crystal frames.

"Look. I have a picture taken of us at fourteen. We were in one of those dime-store booths together."

The two women stared down at the faded black-and-white picture of them with their eyes crossed, tongues stuck out, and arms locked around each other's shoulders. It seemed like eons ago. With so much that had happened throughout the years, they felt as if they were looking at strangers at the bottom of a deep well.

"Girl, Nigel doesn't know how much fun you used to be."

"Seriously, I hope he never finds out."

"What's the matter?"

"No, that's not it. Can we talk?" Nefertiti paused before she went on. "You know, Nigel is thinking of running for office. And you know how the opposing camps can dig up so much dirt on you."

"What dirt? Those sit-ins you staged? That little bud you used to smoke? Girl, you been straight for twenty years. Now, take me. I'm still down for a little smoke every now and then, myself. But besides that, from what I saw when I was out there, that man loves your dirty drawers. He won't hold it against you."

Nefertiti laughed. "So that's why you flew out to see me. To check Ford out. Girl, you too much. But I am worried he'll be mad because I never told him the truth about Desiree."

"Everything will work out." Sweet rubbed Nefertiti's shoulders in a comforting way.

"Thanks." Nefertiti began browsing through some of Sweet's latest issues of *Essence,* which were lined up on her glass coffee table.

"What ever happened to Fadel?"

"In and out of jail. A crackhead when he's out. He had so much potential when he was young. To think I gave that nigger my cherry," Sweet replied.

"You know I haven't heard that term in a long time. Brings back memories."

"But seriously. It's too sad for words. It seems like we, as black women, fare a lot better than our men do in this society. I remember the time Fadel went with that war-on-poverty program to Washington. It was right after the riots, when they were trying to see why the natives were restless," Sweet recalled.

"Yeah, he loved to brag how he shook President Lyndon B. Johnson's hand. Always said that the president had on white gloves."

"That Fadel was crazy."

"I sure do miss the people him and Pharaoh used to be. They were a part of our youth," Nefertiti mourned.

"Well, you know, Pharaoh can't help his craziness. They say he was a prisoner of war over there in Vietnam. No telling what all happened to him."

"I know, girl, I know. I guess that's what this trip is about, too. I'm trying to put the pieces of my life back together. I'm going to find Desiree."

Nefertiti went back and told the story of how she'd found the birth certificate. She didn't tell Sweet about the letter she'd found in the trunk, though. Nefertiti was still trying to absorb all the slave history information.

Sweet was quiet for a while. "You know, before my mother died, she had once said to me that you would live to regret letting your parents push you into that decision. As black folks, we don't have much—but our children, whether they're born in wedlock or not, are about all we have."

Nefertiti nodded. She thought of the story of how, back in 1952, Miss Dyan had hid in the attic with newborn Sweet, in order to get away from her physically abusive husband. Sweet's maternal aunts helped her escape after her husband left. Miss Dyan had been a single mother long before there was such a name for it, and she'd lived an independent lifestyle.

"But it wasn't all my parents' fault. I went along with them, because I thought it was the best decision at the time."

"How do you feel about it now?"

"Oh, I regret it with all my heart. That's why I'm trying to find her now."

"How will this affect Nigel's campaign?"

"I don't know, girl. All I know is that I want to find her. I dream about her all the time. She is calling me in my dreams."

"Oh, well. You made the best decision at the time. Can you imagine that child growing up in Reverend's house? Not to mention, him having his own little Princess Cleopatra."

"That was always the hardest part to take. Having given away a child when you had a sister the same age as that child. I used to be tripping. One minute I pretended Cleo was my baby, then the next, I hated her. I think that Pharaoh has always thought that Cleo was his baby."

"Well, that was some strange shit. Both you and Miss Magg being pregnant at the same time. One was too old, and one was too young."

"Well, this morning, I just couldn't take any

more of their nonsense. Now, here, Rev got the nerve to tell me I can't wear my dreadlocks to his dinner, and Cleo comes sailing in there with braids—which are beautiful, I'll give the Devil his due—and it's fine-fine. Long as it's his baby Cleo, it's wonderful."

"Girl, look. Don't worry about your hair. My hairdresser, Rasheeda, will hook you up. She specializes in natural hair, too. She can pull it up in a ball to make it look more European."

After Sweet cleaned up her paints and drop cloths, then picked her car up from the shop, she took Nefertiti to a new restaurant down by the Detroit River. The Riverfront reminded her of a restaurant in the Monterey Bay area, where she'd spent her honeymoon with Ford. Inside the lobby, soft lighting and subdued Spanish touches soothed Nefertiti's senses. The outside of the building looked like a Spanish villa, with its red-tiled roofing. Flowerbeds with artificial bougainvillea, birds-of-paradise, and palm trees made her think of Los Angeles. Mexican tiles rimmed the steps of a curving staircase at one side, with carriage lamps glowing here and there on the walls. A wide stone fireplace, with sofas grouped before it, invited one to linger and sit. A baby grand piano played by a blind man made her think of Ray Charles as he played a soulful rendition of John Coltrane's "In a Sentimental Mood." Nefertiti paused to savor each note before she sat down.

The window the two women sat in front of was framed in white fretwork, where they could watch the yachts in the Detroit River. The circular, well-spaced tables were set with red-and-black napkins and starched white tablecloths. Their table also looked out on a grassy knoll and a beautiful, lacy gazebo in which several people were sipping cocktails.

They both ordered Jamaican food. Jerk chicken. Rice and peas. Cabbage. Plantains.

"Do you remember the night in the cemetery— that night of the riot?" Sweet almost whispered the question, as if she were afraid that someone would overhear her.

"Girl, how could I ever forget? Let's don't talk about it. I still get chills when I remember that night. Maybe we didn't see what we thought we saw, after all."

The two women ate in silence. After a while, Sweet looked at Nefertiti.

"What's the matter, chicken head? You're doing all you can to see about your daughter. You've got the birth certificate. You have a plan to go to the agency. So what's wrong?"

"I guess it's not only that. It has been bothering me all night. I just don't understand why Rev treats me like he does."

"Forget it, girl."

As close as she was to Sweet, Nefertiti could not bring herself to tell her friend what she was beginning to suspect.

18

That afternoon, following their luncheon, Sweet drove Nefertiti to a Hertz lot to rent a car. After she located and rented a small Ford, Nefertiti drove her rental car, trailed by Sweet's Jaguar, to Rasheeda's beauty shop, Head Turners. Sweet went inside and asked Rasheeda if one of the operators could work Nefertiti in. Rasheeda nodded.

As she prepared to leave, Sweet gave Nefertiti a hug, then whispered in her ear, "Good luck." Since Sweet had a date with Harry, Nefertiti didn't think she'd see her again that day, but their visit had served its purpose. It had bolstered up her confidence.

As she sat under the hair dyer, Nefertiti's mind was in a turmoil. How important was the past? Should she have listened to the social workers from the maternity home she had stayed at while pregnant and just forgotten that unfortunate chapter of her life? Just gone on with her life, as though it had never happened? Then why did she still hurt? Why was she still waiting to forget?

Before she knew it, she was drawn into all of

the conversations floating around the beauty shop, the black woman's safe haven for letting down her hair.

"Rasheeda, make sure you lock this door. Did you hear how they robbed that beauty shop down on Woodward? Girl, took everybody's jewelry, money, and credit cards at gunpoint. It ain't worth it. You can't be too careful these days. People stealing the sweet out of sugar."

"Ain't it the truth!"

"Did y'all hear on the news yesterday about these white cemetery owners who want to dig up a dead baby because they found out the father was black?"

"You lying?"

"Girl, it was on the national news. Channel Seven."

"Hmm, mmm, mmm. Here we are, about to enter the twenty-first century, and racism is just as bad as ever."

"This white-black thing is never going to end."

"Ummm, ummm, ummm."

"That's a shame."

Everyone shook their head in resignation.

"Well, this book I'm reading here is something else, too. It's talking about a love triangle between a man, his wife, and the husband's male lover."

"Sister girl, let me see that book."

The hairdresser Rasheeda had to have the last say on this matter.

"I don't care if your ass is gay. But at least tell my ass before you start trying to go with me. Those men you have to watch. The double-o-sevens."

"What's that, Rasheeda?"

"The ones leading a double life."

"I heard that."

"Girl, that's some scary stuff. 'Specially with all this AIDS out here."

"Yeah, you've got to be careful."

"Ain't it the truth."

"My mother's cousin was married for thirty years to her husband. One day, he just announced he didn't want to be married anymore. He wanted to go with men."

"And what happened?"

"He left. He did claim, at least, that he had never been with any men while he was with her, but she was devastated."

"I know that's right."

"Girl, my mother's cousin hasn't been right in the head since."

"I guess it's something to wake up and find out your whole life has been a lie."

Was she living a lie? Nefertiti pondered her situation. Here she was, married to what appeared to be a successful man. But what was wrong with this picture? Hadn't she been told to forget the past? Now she even wondered about that lost link in her family. Her father had forgotten the past so successfully that she—his daughter—hadn't even known her paternal great-grandfather's name. And look at Miss Magg. She acted as though she never wanted to find her mother, Betty Lee. Well, that was them. Those were their parents. People they never chose for their parents. But this was her child. Who hadn't asked to be born. She had to do something.

But where would she begin her own search?

Would she be able to find her daughter? Initially Nefertiti had only planned a cursory search. Now she was determined that she would find her. *Oh, God, let her be all right.*

When Nefertiti was through having her hair done, she smiled into the mirror. Pulled up into an upsweep, the dreads looked more like braids. While looking in the mirror, Nefertiti felt someone staring at her. She looked around the shop. There were only four other women waiting now. Nefertiti could swear this one girl, a young woman in her early twenties, had been staring at her. When Nefertiti gained eye contact, the woman dropped her eyes, as if she were reading a magazine. Maybe she'd thought she knew Nefertiti from somewhere. Nefertiti often had that happen to her. Whenever Nefertiti would approach the stranger, and find out that she had been mistaken, she would apologize and say, "Well, you have a twin somewhere in this world."

As she left the beauty shop, Nefertiti noticed Pharaoh standing across the street in front of a liquor store. She jumped in her car and pulled away. When she thought she saw a yellow taxicab following her, she made a sharp U-turn, then jumped on the freeway.

19

When Nefertiti was a little girl, Calissa had left her husband, Deacon Thorne, with all of his respectable proppings. At the time, she only knew Calissa as Isaac's mother, as well as a member of the church. From what Nefertiti later gleaned, Calissa, who had come from a questionable background in Texarkana, Arkansas, had been determined initially to social climb and enter the middle-class Negro ranks. And for years, she had conformed. Just when she had been accepted as one of the inner circle—"the Elites"—Calissa outraged everyone with this defection.

Perhaps it wouldn't have been so bad if Calissa had only left the Deacon. But the fact that she left her child to live with Pay Dirt, a musician and gambler, had been strike number one. Strike number two was that she refused to move from town. Not only did Pay Dirt own virtually nothing of earthly value, he had no claims on anything of heavenly worth, either. Quiet as it's kept, they said he hadn't been in church since the flood. Strike number three was that Pay Dirt was said to be one of those Geechies. To Shallow's Corner, he sounded like he talked Gullah. Rumor also had it that he came from one of those Jamaican islands, which was foreign, and not the same as being an American-born colored. In Shallow's Corner, no one understood that British Honduras was not a Jamaican island. To them, anyone who spoke with a Jamaican accent came from "one of those Jamaican islands."

Whatever the case, in Shallow's Corner, nice women just didn't do that sort of thing. The year was 1958. Although good men left their "God-fearing" women all the time without so much as a titter of gossip being whispered against them, this scandal created a tsunami wave of tongue-lashing against Calissa. From that day forth, "Callie of the Alley," as she was renamed, had become a pariah in the black community.

Even when she was older, Nefertiti never understood it. When a man left his wife, everyone said, "She didn't know how to hold on to her man." But when a woman—which was largely unheard of in those days—left her husband, it was an abomination against nature. After all, women were the nesters. If women started leaving their husbands, what would become of the family? The family was the foundation of the church. So, in essence, Calissa had rocked the very foundation of the church.

"Nasty," the church women whispered. "That's all it is. Too nasty for good women to even talk about."

When requests from the mourning bench went unheeded, and the former faithful sister appeared impervious to the implacable wall of scorn Shallow's Corner had erected—as well as unrepentant and recalcitrant as the Pharisees—Calissa had been turned out of the church.

A flood of sympathy baptized the wronged husband, Deacon Thorne, who was left behind with the care of his young son, Isaac. It was no small wonder that within the next year, the Deacon and Widow Beulah Windham married.

To this day, Nefertiti remembered overhearing Miss Magg tell a friend, Sister Odessa, "I don't understand it. A good woman will love a no-good man, and vice versa. But how a woman will leave a house and plenty of money for a man who has no security, just makes me think. There has to be something to it. If it's not love, I don't know what you call it."

Odessa leaned over and whispered something into Miss Magg's ear. The two women had blushed and laughed.

Nefertiti was fifteen years old before she ever knew what it was.

Nefertiti had been raised to stay away from men like Pharaoh. But at the time, Nefertiti had forgotten all those admonitions. She became like the kamikaze Japanese pilot. Later, looking back, she was reminded how she learned that sin was like the gingerbread house in Hansel and Gretel—alluring to look at, enticing to taste, but a snare for the innocent. A cage once you got into it.

For Nefertiti, sin had taken a casual, unassuming course, with her subversion starting out innocently. Before the year was out, she had been leading a double life. Schoolgirl by day, grown woman by night.

First, it started with a movie. She had been raised to think that the movies were the devil's workshop. Sitting in the darkened theaters with Pharaoh, she was torn between watching the white lovers on the silver screen and worrying if one of the deacons would see her there with a boy. Her next foray into worldliness was roller-skating. Rev would not allow her to go skating, because he said too many hoodlums hung out at the skating rink. Under the guise of going to choir rehearsal, Nefertiti had gotten out with Sweet.

She'd never forgotten that first trip across town when she and Sweet had caught the bus to Ecorse and met Fadel and Pharaoh at the skating rink. After the boys mounted the bus at their transfer point, the bus driver had gotten lost and made a wrong turn. Through the whole trip, both boys had heckled the driver, even taken out cigarettes to show how sophisticated they were. Nefertiti had been excited by their "coolness."

As the weeks rolled by, she began to sneak out the window after everyone's bedtime and go to quarter parties and dances. She learned how to do "the Jerk" and "the Twine," a dance where she and Pharaoh rubbed up against each other, starting the fire beneath her belly to burning.

And, oh, could Pharaoh dance! He could move so smooth and silky, it made you think of an un-rippled pond. Then, the next thing you knew, he'd break into fast dancing to put some of the women to shame. But he would only dance with

Nefertiti. He said they called his dance "the Calypso" in Belize.

Since Sweet went to church with her, the Rev finally had relented and allowed Nefertiti to spend her first night away from home. That was the time she and Sweet sneaked out to the after-hours joint with Pharaoh and Fadel. Sweet's mother, Miss Dyan, had gone out on a date. That night, Nefertiti drank her first taste of wine and smoked her first joint. That was also the night that, later, their little group—Fadel, Pharaoh, Sweet, and herself—had played strip poker, and Sweet had run off with her blouse.

Both girls were so high, Nefertiti felt as if she had been running in slow motion as she chased Sweet. She'd never forget the look in Pharaoh's eyes as he stared at her mulberry-purple nipples before she put her blouse back on.

Sometimes, now, she couldn't even remember what had been so exciting about Pharaoh. Perhaps she was becoming too sophisticated—she didn't know. But the Pharaoh she'd loved had been a different sort of young man. Not the run-down-at-the-heels kind of man he was now.

She'd get the same sad feeling whenever she saw homeless men. Why did they remind her of Pharaoh? Had they once had girlfriends who'd loved them?

A chill ran through Nefertiti whenever she thought of Pharaoh and their rendezvous in the cemetery. It made her think of something Big Mama Lily used to say: "Somebody just walked over my grave."

Lily used to say that whenever a chill would

course through her. Little did her great-grandmother know that two months from the last time Nefertiti heard her utter those words, her great-granddaughter, Nefertiti—her beloved—would literally be racing over the former's grave, through the cemetery behind their church, as she ran on feet bent toward badness, heart pounding in excitement, night shadows and night echoes everywhere, to meet her lover, Pharaoh, on the other side of the cemetery.

And, oh, could Pharaoh sweet-talk a woman in his Jamaican-sounding accent! "We were meant to be together," he'd whisper in her ear as they lay together. "I'm your Pharaoh—your black king, and you're Nefertiti, my black queen."

Pharaoh would take a rose (he'd probably swiped from Calissa's garden) and take the petals and spill them all over her. "A rose for my beautiful black rose." His voice would be hypnotic. Telling her how she was his. All his. How her thighs were so shapely even in a long skirt. How he wanted her mulberry lips from the first time he saw them. How her dimples drove him crazy. How her rounded hips were shaped like a butterfly.

Within three months, Nefertiti had learned all the secrets of desire, lust, and sensuality. The first time Nefertiti missed her period, she'd prayed. "Dear Lord, just let my period come down and, I swear, I'll never do it again, until I get married." But, of course, she failed to keep her word. And the Lord failed to keep his, too. None of the herbs or the turpentine provided by Sweet (whose mother had taught her all the ropes) worked on Nefertiti. Which was why she was so confused now, twenty-six years later. She thought of Pharaoh who was now forty-five and wondered if Desiree's adoption was why he was so screwed up.

That year would always be a watershed in her life. Nothing would ever seem as bright—as pure—as the splendor of that day she'd met Pharaoh.

Although she hadn't seen Pharaoh in over seven years, the last time she caught a glimpse of him, she almost cried. She hadn't loved him in years. Still, she had never hated him for what had happened. Nor had she felt taken advantage of, with him having been almost nineteen when she was fifteen. At the time, she had been willing. Now, she found, she felt pity for him. She felt sad whenever she thought of how life had dealt with him. It seemed like ever since he'd come home from Vietnam, Pharaoh hadn't been right in the head. It was just so unfair.

So many young black brothers had been sent on the front lines of the Vietnam War. That was the war that had separated Pharaoh and Nefertiti. Or maybe their separation had been inevitable, when Pharaoh went to Vietnam the summer after Desiree's birth.

Still, like most young love, theirs had been whimsical, yet it had imprinted a mark on her soul. Strangely, her most passionate love, her most ardent lover, had been Pharaoh. She knew from him that the memories of first love never passed. They lingered, influenced, and guided long after the source of the experience had faded.

She thought of the love she'd once had for

Isaac. Isaac had been her savior. He'd rescued her from being a woman of sin when he married her, when she was nineteen years of age. Being her best friend (besides Sweet), he had known of her pregnancy. As he was so infatuated with Nefertiti, Isaac had even offered to marry her when she was fifteen, but she'd turned him down, knowing that was out of the question at her age. Being married was not something she wanted to do.

Four years later, though, Reverend had sanctioned the marriage; in fact, he had pushed Nefertiti into it, knowing it would cause her to leave her scholarship at USC and bring her back to Shallow's Corner. Once again, Nefertiti went along with the rules, went against her heart, hoping this would win her father's love, so she followed Reverend's bidding. Consequently, she ended up finishing school at City College, and later landed an accounting job with the Department of Housing and Urban Development (HUD).

Still, at the time, she'd only felt grateful to Isaac. When she'd had her two babies that she could keep, she'd grown to love Isaac. Conversely, it seemed as if when her love began to increase, his faded in direct proportion. After a while, Isaac's running around became so obvious, the sight of him began to turn her stomach. Now, because of her present distaste for Isaac, she often wondered had she ever loved him at all.

For that matter, had she ever loved anyone? She knew that she loved her present husband. Or had loved him until she had begun questioning his motives for marrying her. But who was she? Her father's daughter? Pharaoh's ex-girlfriend?

Isaac's ex-wife? Ford's wife? Nefertiti Godbolt
Thorne Ford? And how would she tell her husband, once she found her daughter? How would
it affect their marriage, since she had never told
him in all these years?

It was all the grief of unfinished business that
bothered her the most. It was like a secret. Hidden
information coming to haunt you at any second.
Kept from public knowledge or from the knowledge of certain people. But a family secret?

Any way you look at it, a family secret is different. Everyone in the family generally knows the
secret, keeps it from the outsiders—in the name
of family loyalty—and yet holds it over the black
sheep's head like a silent threat. A family skeleton rattles around in the closet, just waiting to
have its bones exposed. A footprint of the past,
whether spoken about or not, stood between the
restive insurgent and any respect the latter might
garner from the other members of the family.

Now the past had taken on the presence of a
wraith. A family secret when it related to a female
member also used the power of words—something
that held the power to haunt you, to always be
there, beating upon you like a stick across the
head. Women were given names for sexual behav-
ior that went outside of marriage. "Slut." "Whore."
"Strumpet." Nefertiti wondered who had ever
made up these words. Men, probably. You never
heard these type of labels used in connection with
men's sexual conduct.

In her mother's day, these men were generally referred to as "roosters," "dandies," "killer-dillers."

In Nefertiti's day, they were often called "a good catch."

Although they say the past is the past, you never heard anyone say, "He's a man with a past." It was always, "She's a lady with a past." Nefertiti pondered over the double standards for men and for women.

Taking everything into account, Nefertiti knew that she was considered "a good woman" now. She was in good standing with her community. Even Shallow's Corner had begrudgingly forgiven her.

So why couldn't she forget? She knew why. It was like sweeping dirt under a rug. Just too much unfinished business, not knowing where her firstborn child was, or even if she was alive. Like murky waters that lay underneath a deceptively calm lake's surface, they had the power to drown her.

But most of all, it was because the past wouldn't let her forget. Even now, when she tried to block out its pain, it would roll out in front of her at the strangest times.

For Nefertiti, the past was like a surging river, segueing in the stream of her memory. Sometimes a smell, a song, a thought, would bring it all rushing back to her. Today, perhaps it was the whispers in the wind, the bittersweet taste of spring on her tongue, or the fresh smell of thawing mud in the air that brought the past crashing around her.

In any event, the white social workers had said

that she would forget this unfortunate incident in her life. She was never to look back, they had said.

Nefertiti now wondered if the slave mothers ever forgot their children—no matter how many were sold away from them. How could you ever forget someone you carried under your heart, inside of your womb, for nine months? Something that was as visceral a part of you as your own flesh and blood, and that she would now forever carry near her heart.

Maybe what she'd taken in her spirit as being resilient hadn't been that, after all. Maybe she was like Samson. After killing the thing she loved, or, in her case, giving it away in the name of a better life, she'd become a zombie. She went about eating, sleeping, dreaming, but she was empty. Her wound was invisible to those around her, but she knew she was dead inside. Because she'd already died, there was nothing left that could kill her now.

20

A people without knowledge of their history is like a tree without roots.

—West African proverb

"Push, young lady."

"Maybe she'll think about this the next time she gaps her legs," the one white orderly says to the other. Both men talk as if she is not in the room. As if she is not even a human being, but a monkey entrusted to their care.

"Maybe we can sew it up when we get through with her," the other white orderly says, snickering.

But she doesn't care. Pain is a barreling train of suffering bulldozing down her back. Fire does the hully-gully on her spine. She is trapped in a prison of agony. She feels like a shorn sheep getting ready for slaughter. They have shaved her pubic hair. They give her an enema, which makes her bowels rush like a broken dam inside her, churling, whirling, then running all over the white sheet and in a brown waterfall down to the floor.

All the time, a white light shines over her head. She doesn't know her name anymore. She has messed all over herself in the bed. Lightning and thunderbolts zigzag through her womb. The fist of some unknown demon racks her loins.

"Just take a gun and kill me, but don't let this pain go on like this."

She doesn't recognize the animallike voice coming out of the strange contorted body she is looking down upon. Zion. Jesus. Something smells like old blood. Like Grandpa Bullocks's slaughterhouse in Alabama. The blood heat matches the summer passion she had felt.

A fetid odor almost chokes her. She stinks and she knows it. Feces. She has messed all over herself again. She can't seem to hold her bowels anymore. But with each release, the sharp pains return.

"Something's got a hold on me. Oh, it must be the Lord!

"Big Mama! Mama!"

She never cries for Daddy—the high and mighty Reverend Godbolt. He has said she and her bastard child can never set foot in his house. This is the only way he will let her come back home.

Just two weeks ago, Miss Magg revealed that she was pregnant herself. No, Miss Magg has just delivered a girl baby about a week ago . . . named her Cleopatra.

Suddenly she sees Big Mama Lily, who died several months earlier.

Now Big Mama Lily has her hand outstretched.

"Come here, Lil' Bit."

For a moment, as she contemplates running through the white light to Big Mama Lily, the pain of the rumbling train ceases. Her eyelids flutter. She changes her mind. The pain returns.

Where is Pharaoh? Pharaoh of the darting tongue, the soft words, the rough kisses. How has she, the respectable Reverend Godbolt's daughter, slated for a cotillion next summer, gotten involved with a gangster type?

Pharaoh who has broken her in to the remorseless sweet pain of love. Pharaoh who has been her first love.

"It won't hurt," he'd promised. "I'll take care of you."

"No," she had said for the longest. It had been a gradual "I'll go easy with you" seduction. Like a canoe drifting offshore into a lake of fire.

At first, she had fought him. Scratched his face. But he was like a battering ram. In the end, she had surrendered, yielded the wall of her innocence. Opened up to the bee sting of his sweetness. She is the forbidden fruit.

Now she has tasted of the forbidden fruit.

What about Isaac? Plain, ugly, frog-eyed, snaggle-toothed Isaac, who wants to tell her father that the baby is his, that he will marry her. Marry? That is a foreign country. She doesn't want to get married. She's only fifteen. How has she gotten into this mess?

She doesn't want a baby, either—if she could only turn back the clock, change this whole scenario. She remembers how before Big Mama Lily had died—that very last time she'd seen her after her release from the hospital—she'd said, "You got a throbbing in your throat, Lil' Bit. You been out there making like a woman. Your father's going to have a fit when he finds out. I wish I was long for this world. I could take the baby."

How had Big Mama Lily known about how she was hiding her morning vomiting? Or the swelling in her stomach? The pear-shaped tenderness of her breast?

And could she ever explain to Big Mama Lily why she had done it? So she had lied, and said, "I'm all right."

How was she to have known that those soft, feathery touches would lead to heat she couldn't describe, to a hell without words, then to a bliss she could only describe as heaven? It was like a faraway music. Or like sound traveling through water. Just straining to hear the song induced images and colors before her eyes. She was a piece of heather floating through the air. She was the color of an exquisite mango. She was drowning in a sea of waves.

But, as she was to find out, she is too young to be a mother.

"He was perfectionate," Big Mama Lily used to say about her dead husband, Grandpa Bullocks.

Well, now she knows what this word means. Pharaoh had been "perfectionate," too. He had already introduced her—at fifteen—to the cataclysmic heights of ecstasy. To what she'd heard Uncle Tiger once call "drilling oil." "Canoeing," "Jelly roll." What Sister Odessa and Miss Magg meant by their whispers about "the tunnel of love."

"I'll take care of you," Pharaoh had promised. "You know, you ain't nothing but jailbait, anyway. Your father will kill both of us."

Rev might as well have killed her. Because her father has sent her away to a home for unwed mothers. Most of the girls in the home are white. There have only been a handful of Negro girls like herself during her near-five-month stay. They are all the daughters of the black working class, professionals, or ministers. Without exception, the white girls are going to place their babies up for adoption. Some of the Negro girls have mothers who are going to pretend their babies are theirs.

Nefertiti has hoped her mother will feel the same way, but now that her mother has delivered a new baby, herself, she doesn't know. If she kept the baby, her father would have to stop preaching. And that would kill him. If she brings the baby home, Rev might kill her and the baby. If she gives up the baby, she doesn't know how she'll be able to live with her decision the rest of her life. Her life is ruined either way she goes.

"I won't get you pregnant."

Pharaoh's words echo in her screams. Promises, like an old blues song, meant to be broken.

Oh, Mary, don't you weep, don't you mourn,
Pharaoh's army got drowned. . . .

Faraway voices shout, "All the delivery rooms are full."

"We'll have to deliver her in here."

"No, don't let me have it in here. Do something." Nefertiti is hysterical.

"We're going to have to do an incision."

"No, knock me out. Kill me, but not that."

They bend her legs up over her head. Dripping sweat, eyes wild, swollen body bent like the contortionist she saw in a circus when she was a little girl, able to smoke a cigar with her head coming through the back of her legs, she does a backward somersault.

Scissors, as large as a hacksaw, come at her. She hears the clattering sound on the floor. The orderly in the green shirt, with the bright bloodstain on it, has dropped the scissors.

"Stop," she cries out. She remembers the television shows she and Little Josh used to watch on Saturdays, which would end with the heroine hanging over a cliff. The movie would stop and hang in her mind until the next Saturday when the heroine would pick up where she left off. But this was real life. What was happening to her was real, inexorable, and forward-moving like the tide.

Pain, as deep as a splitting tree, reminds her of the time she saw a circus show where the man sawed the woman in half.

This is the last thing she remembers before she passes out, drowning out memories of her past, her friends from the home, this secret she's carried near her heart for the past five months of hiding in the home.

When she comes to, she sees a baby's leg, as thin as a water hose. There is a bright spot of blood on it. The baby almost looks white, there is so little color. The orderly throws a tissue over her eyes so that she can't see the baby. Nefertiti is still in the labor room. They have not had time to get her into the delivery room.

"She's not supposed to see the baby. She's one of the girls from the home."

It's as if the parting of day from night, the seas from the void, the heavens from the earth, have taken place inside of Nefertiti. With the tearing of the rubbery-feeling doll from her flesh, her girlhood has been ripped from her. A weeping, cooing woman suddenly replaces the selfish girl who had not counted the consequences of her choices.

"Oh, you poor baby!" Nefertiti moans, reaching out to the baby. "Why is my baby so white-looking?"

The colored nurse snaps, "All colored babies start out looking white."

Although there is no man by her side, Nefertiti knows she has witnessed a miracle—the birth of new life—second only to the creation of the universe. A gift. Nefertiti sees that the baby is a girl.

One orderly barks at the nurse, "Take the baby away."

All too soon, the little pale bundle is whisked away from her; then they roll her bed into the delivery room.

Nefertiti is in such a daze, she does not feel the prick of the needle where the doctor has numbed her to sew up her episiotomy.

We are soldiers, in the army,
We have to fight, and some they have to die. . . .

Nefertiti had spent most of her childhood in church. That had been her favorite song. When she was a little girl, Miss Magg had told her that life was like a war. She had been given her middle name after Jael in the Bible, who nailed the captain's head. Jael is a warrior. She is supposed to be brave, but she isn't brave. She is a coward. That's why she will go along with what her parents said.

> *We got a hold on the bloodstained banner,*
> *We got to hold it up until we die.*

"Do you want to see the baby, Joshua?" Miss Magg asks Reverend Godbolt the next day. Her father's face screws up in ripples of distaste.

"No."

"Come on, Joshua. I think we should."

Her parents head down to see the baby in the nursery.

Nefertiti holds her breath. She hopes her parents will see the baby; then maybe they'll change their minds. She wishes she could be stronger and stand up to them. But if they don't let her bring the baby home, she won't keep it. She has made up her mind before the delivery. Now, though, she has changed it, but she doesn't have the strength to speak up. She didn't know she would feel this way. But if she tries to keep the baby, how will she take care of it?

Besides, what can she give a baby? She hasn't even finished the tenth grade. She doesn't have a job. And welfare is out of the question. She has been raised to think it is anathema. The scourge on the colored race. Moreover, she has disgraced her family, and the congregation if they find out, because she doesn't have a husband.

Her parents do not change their minds when they see the baby.

The only thing Nefertiti seems to be able to give the baby was the name she put on the birth certificate. *Desiree. Desired life.*

21

June Perry, her social worker, comes to visit her on her third day in the hospital.

"Do you want to see the baby?" June asks Nefertiti.

"I thought they said we couldn't see our babies if we were giving them up for adoption?"

"Well, now they say that the girls suffer more if they never see the baby. They want to know if their babies have all ten fingers and toes. So, are you up to seeing the baby, Nefertiti?"

Nefertiti likes June Perry, who is a white girl. Only twenty-three. Nefertiti has opened up to her and told her of her adolescent confusion, her rebellion against the church. She has told her of her dreams to own a store and sell antiques, but how everyone said that was impractical. Just learn how to be a secretary. Get a good job. Until she gets married and becomes a wife and mother.

When they walk to the nursery, Nefertiti is surprised at what she feels. Emptiness. Because she knows that there is nothing that she can do. The baby is large. Eight pounds. She begins to spit up milk. "Oh, you poor baby," she croons. She doesn't know what else to say.

Her roommate is white. She's very talkative.

"Hi, I'm Margaret."

"I'm Nefertiti."

"That's an unusual name."

"I know. My mother named me that out of one of her schoolbooks. She said that it means 'the beautiful one.' She said that Nefertiti was a queen in Africa."

"I heard you screaming in there. I prayed for you. I was afraid you were going to die. Are you all right now?"

Nefertiti nods. "What are you doing here?"

"I'm five months pregnant."

Nefertiti can't believe her eyes. Margaret's stomach is flatter than hers. Nefertiti's stomach is still puffy since she has delivered her baby.

"You're lying."

"No, it's true. I've been bleeding real heavy for the last two months. I'm about to miscarry. They are trying to stop it."

"Are you married?"

"No."

"Were you planning to keep the baby?"

"No."

"Well, are you sure you want them to stop it?"

"Yes. I've thought about it. Although I've been bleeding off and on the whole five months, now that I know it's not just a period and it's a baby, I don't know if I want to lose it, either. The father and I were supposed to get married. But we broke up at Christmas."

Margaret is eighteen. She had not told her parents she was pregnant until she went into serious labor.

"They were so disappointed. My father cried.

"What did you have?" Margaret has the look that says they are both in the same boat.

Nefertiti opens up. "It was a girl. They tried not to let

me see the baby after she was born, but my social worker let me see her."

"What are you going to do? Do you plan to place your baby up for adoption?"

"I don't know. I didn't know I would feel this way after I had the baby."

Later that night, Nefertiti is awakened by moans. By the time she can ring the nurse, Margaret's cries have turned to bloodcurdling screams, matching the blood covering her sheet. The nurses burst into the room and rush Margaret out. After about an hour of incessant screams, there is one long, piercing scream, then silence. . . .

A few hours later, they wheel Margaret back into the room. The nurses act so brusque and detached, Nefertiti sits up and asks them, "What happened? Is Margaret all right?"

"Mind your own business," the white nurse snaps, pulling the green cotton curtain, which divides their room, closed.

It is three in the morning when the nurses finally leave the room.

Nefertiti whispers, "What did you have?" She can't help but be curious.

Margaret whispers back, "A girl. She was born dead."

The next morning, Nefertiti says, "I know you're glad that's over. In a way, you came out better than if you had carried the baby all the way, then had to place it up for adoption."

Margaret looks away. "No, I still feel sad. As bad as I felt about being pregnant, I feel even worse since the baby died."

Realizing she has put her foot in her mouth, Nefertiti tries to think of something comforting to say. She tries to recall all of the old wives' tales Big Mama Lily used to tell her.

"You know, before my grandmother died, she told my mother she dreamed she saw a baby girl. She used to say when a sick person dreamed of a baby, that baby was clothed in death. Meaning the baby would replace the sick person when he or she died. Now, here I've had a baby just months after my grandmother died."

"That's strange. . . . What did she say about when a baby dies?"

"I don't remember."

"Well, I guess my baby will just go to Heaven."

"Now I remember. Big Mama—I mean my grandmother—used to say when a baby died, his spirit just kept someone else living in the family longer."

"That's a strange thing to say."

"Well, my grandmother—actually, she was my great-grandmother—was kinda strange. Believed in dreams and things."

"All I know is that I just feel dead inside. I wish I were the one that died."

"Don't say that."

"I do."

"I kinda know what you mean. As bad as I felt about getting caught—being knocked up—I don't want to sign the papers to give the baby away. I didn't know I would feel this way after this."

"What are you going to do?"

"I don't know. I guess I'll do what I have to do. I don't know how to take care of a baby. Besides, my mother has had a baby, too. She would have to help me, and now I know she won't help with this baby."

"Are you going to tell anyone?"

"My friend Sweet knows and her boyfriend, Fadel. Probably people are suspicious about my parents saying that I have gone down South to stay with my mother's cousin Letty Pearl."

"No one but my family knows about me. I'll never tell anyone. Not my baby's father. Not even my husband, whoever he'll be, when I get married."

"I don't know. Everyone in Shallow's Corner talks about the young girls when they get pregnant. But usually after she has it—if she repents—she is accepted back into our church. I know they're wondering where I have been for all these months. I probably could keep the baby if my mother didn't have a baby."

"That's a hard choice to make."

"What's that you're reading?"

Margaret looked up from her booklet and held up the cover, with birds painted on the outside. "It's called 'Spring Is a New Beginning.'"

They give her a shot to dry up her milk, but she is so sore the first few days, she can hardly walk. The last day of her five-day sojourn in the hospital, when she is in the shower, she looks down at her stomach, which is still swollen as a melon.

Stretch marks zigzag up above her navel and all down her breast. Her stomach has turned black. She has gained sixty pounds. Her stretch marks look like white roads on a wrinkled landscape. She begins to cry.

What will she do? Her life is ruined. How will she go on? Life will never be the same as she has known it. No longer will she be the carefree young girl racing toward the golden lights of a spring day.

Then she hears a song sparrow chirping on her windowsill outside the bathroom. She remembers Margaret's booklet.

"Spring is a new beginning," she thinks.

22

Except for when he was in 'Nam and had been given his mojo charm, Pharaoh had always said that if he was a betting man, he would not bet anything on himself—his life had been so messed up. That afternoon, after waiting all morning for the mailman, he didn't get his letter with the Agent Orange reparation check. He was so dejected, he thought he'd cry. He had done everything the letter had instructed veterans to do. His doctor had documented that some of his health problems had come from the Agent Orange over in Vietnam. He'd sent in all the paperwork. The last letter he'd received from the VA indicated that he would get a substantial part of the class action suit. Now, instead of getting the check he had been waiting for all month, there was a new pile of paperwork that had come in the mail for him to fill out.

He had been counting on that money. He'd wanted to have something for him and Nefertiti to start out their new life with. Feeling despondent, he had gone down to the liquor store to get a taste of E & J Brandy (the "erk and jerk" variety), and had seen Nefertiti come out of Rasheeda's beauty shop. He tried to follow her in the cab, but he lost her at the freeway. When he went back to the liquor store, he saw his father's old friend, Poor Boy, standing by the store with his hands out. He looked like he could use a bath and a clean change of clothes. "Spare a dime, brother?" Poor Boy's phlegmy eyes sluiced rivers of sadness. Before he knew it, they were caught up in a familiar adagio, which went like this:

"Hey, youngblood!"

"Hey, Poor Boy! It's me. Pay Dirt's son."

"Not little Pharaoh? Man, you all growed up. What you say! You a sight for sore eyes. Look like your daddy done come back to life. I sure do miss old Pay Dirt."

"Come on. I'll do you one better. I'll buy you a taste. Why don't you slide by the crib with me so we can rap?"

Pharaoh seldom had company in his bachelor apartment. He could tell that Poor Boy was impressed with his collection of old blues on 78s and albums. B.B. King. Muddy Waters. Sarah Vaughan. Ma Rainey. Once Poor Boy got his glass and tossed down his first drink, his hands stopped trembling. He began to testify.

"Boy, didn't you know the blues started in the juke joint, then jazz came out of those blues? Rock 'n' roll is the baby of the blues. Things were really jumping back then. You see, jukes was always centered around dancin', gamblin', fightin', and women. The light-skinned woman was Miss It out in high society, but the dark-skinned woman was the queen of the juke joint. More fightin' and cuttin' and stabbin' went on over them than I even care to mention. The blacker the berry, the sweeter the juice. *Hah*. Things were really hot, too, if you know what I mean. The joint would be jumping, man. Yes, Lord. Honey, let your drawers hang low. . . ."

"Poor Boy, could you tell me about my daddy?"

"Sure, youngblood. Did I ever tell you how your daddy pulled your stepmama? Pulled her right out the church, he did. But, first, you got to understand this about your daddy. He should've been in the Hall of Fame now. Or at least he should've gone down into the Rock 'n' Roll Hall of Fame. That's your inheritance, boy.

"But it wasn't just Pay Dirt's ability with music. He had a way with the ladies. A regular sweet back, if you know what I mean. But once he got with your stepmama, he never looked at another lady. What they had, sure was something. That woman looked like she was dryin' up, sho 'nuff, married to Deacon Thorne and all, but she blossomed like a flesh flower when she got with your daddy. Other than what it did to her relationship with her boy, I don't think she ever regretted it.

"Caused the biggest stink you ever saw here in Shallow's Corner, though. Calissa Thorne left one of the richest colored men in the city, what with that mortuary. Talk has it that he left everything to Isaac. But that boy done let that new wife of his toller-waller all up in that money, and he ain't got the pot to piss in no mo', nor the window to throw it out. Don't do much good to leave these grown children nothing. More families done split up over their inheritances than the Lord allow. Well, at least Isaac was an only child. Otherwise, there would have been some mess over that insurance and the money from the mortuary.

"Yeah, they never built back up the funeral home after the riots. Too bad. Brings back sad memories when I think of some of the best funerals I been to down there at Thorne's. Why, when wino Gaylord died, we almost turned the place out with the wake, but I'm gett'n' off my story.

"The night the Detroit riots broke out, your daddy and I was playing at the Blind Pig, where the whole thing got started. Pay Dirt was playing some notes like I ain't never heard, before or since. I don't think he ever played that hard again, and I was following him up on my guitar, 'Viola.' 'Sour' White was playing on the piano. I ain't never did a set like it since. Pour me another taste, Pharaoh.

"Some say these ladies of the night got to fighting over their pimp. Now, it was four o'clock in the mo'ning, and the street people was still going strong. Nothing like a fight to get the juices flowing for that second wind of the wee hours. When the police came to try and break it up and went upside Rufus the doorman's head, it was all over. Boy, niggers was fighting back and feeling good! In numbers, we strong, man. We started burning, and the rest was history." Poor Boy began to shadowbox.

"Anyway, everyone said they thought Calissa was crazy to do what she did, but money can't hold you on a cold night. It can't love you when the world done kicked you down."

"I got one woman I love that I want to get back. Do you think it's possible?" Pharaoh asked.

"Yeah, I heard about what went down with you and the preacher's gal way back when. But I want you to remember something. Don't you forget this. When you don't love someone, you just don't love them. They can be ever so nice to you, but you can't make yourself love them. And vice versa. I been in love both ways. The kind where I didn't love someone back, and the kind where the other party was just using me. I know this is sad to say, but graveyard love done killed many people. Got more people in the cemetery than cancer."

"What kind of love is 'graveyard love,' Poor Boy?"

"That's love where they don't love you back. Love ain't something you can make yourself feel, neither. It's like that blues song where women tell men, 'They got the right key, but the wrong keyhole.' I guess the best way is when you both love each other the same. But it seems that in most couples, one always loves the other more. But I tell you, any love worth having is worth fighting for."

Hearing those words gave Pharaoh a new resolve. He was going to fight to get Titi back.

23

It was eleven o'clock in Michigan, but only eight o'clock in California, so Nefertiti picked up the phone and called her children at Yolan's.

"Hi, Mom. I was voted to be on the Student Council today." Savasia was effervescent with good news.

"Good."

"Mom, what do you mean, 'good'? Why, it's awesome!"

Savasia went to a private school, where she often sounded so "Valley Girlish" that Nefertiti sometimes regretted sending her daughter to such a place in Palos Verdes.

Perhaps still being upset over Ike, Nefertiti snapped at her daughter, "Stop being a black Barbie! You're always trying to please people, Savasia. What is it you want to do yourself?"

"Mom, would you be happier if I'd got into a fight like Isaac?" She could hear the hurt in Savasia's voice.

"Well, at least he's fighting back. I just don't want you to be such a Goody Two-shoes all the time. You'll wind up like Miss Magg. Everybody's doormat."

When Ike came to the phone, he tried to side-track her. "Did you get my e-mail?"

"Isaac, what is this about you getting into a fight at school?"

"I got the best of him, Mom."

"Now, what did I tell you about violence? Things are too dangerous to be fighting nowadays. These young people carry guns."

"Aw, Mom, this is out in Pacific Palisades. They don't have as many gang members as in South Central."

Hanging up, still dissatisfied with Ike's situation, and feeling guilty about carping at Savasia, Nefertiti could not go to sleep. What was it that had irked her about her daughter's cheeriness? Was she just tripping because it was that time of the month? And what made her say that about Miss Magg? Is that how she saw her mother? Or had she seen a mirror of herself?

Not really. She'd always been a rebel. That was—until she'd signed those adoption papers. Why had she felt so pressured? Although she couldn't say she was abused as a child herself, she remembered feeling protective of her newborn. Not wanting her to go through what she went through as a child: feeling different, unwanted. Well, not by Miss Magg, but by Rev. Yet, these words were never spoken. She couldn't say exactly what it was . . . maybe that's why she knew she had to try to find Desiree. Even if it did upset Miss Magg's and Rev's little pretense that she never had a baby before she married.

24

After Poor Boy left, Pharaoh lay down to just close his eyes and think. The next thing he knew, he saw Pay Dirt. His father was talking to him about how the rhythm black people have can be traced back to the drum. He even talked about how black women could press hair to a rhythm. He told Pharaoh, *"It's in the hands, boy. Give me your hands."* Pay Dirt once told Pharaoh how the white jazz musicians would come by the club and listen to him play. Try as they might, they could never get the rhythm down pat. They were trying to figure out the exact science of jazz and improvisation, and that's where they went wrong, Pay Dirt would say. Because there's no science to it.

"It's in the hands and in the heart, Pharaoh. Give me your hands."

"But I can't, Daddy Jonah. I can only paint."

"Well, give her your hands, if that's all you can give her."

Pharaoh turned over and shook himself. His daddy had seemed so real in his dream, he could have touched him.

Before he knew it, he dozed back off and started dreaming again. This time, he dreamed about his Vietnam buddy, Cornelius.

"Why did you do it, man?" Pharaoh asked.

"Why did I do what?"

"You know."

"No, I don't," Cornelius answered.

"Why did you take point man that night?"

"You know you had the runs, man. What was I going to do? Send you out there sick?" Cornelius countered.

"I—I just wish you hadn't done it."

"You was my road dog. Why not?"

"Because I can't live with the pain."

Pharaoh woke up in a cold sweat. He just couldn't get over the guilt. It even plagued him in his sleep.

Post-traumatic stress disorder. That was the name of his disability. Such a clinical title. It didn't do justice to the reality of the night sweats or the jungle dreams. Or to how he'd never been able—or even tried—to hold down a nine-to-five job since he'd come home from the war. He couldn't have expected Nefertiti, who grew up as the minister's daughter, to live in poverty, could he? Reverend Godbolt had been too bourgeois for him. Even if his father had once done that to a woman—taken her from a better life—he couldn't do that. Even if Nefertiti was the only woman he'd ever loved.

Well, that was the throw of the dice. Life had never been a level playing field for him. From the start, the cards had always been stacked against him. But once his part of the class action suit went through, he would have money, and if all went according to plan—maybe—he'd have a chance.

From what Pharaoh had gathered now that he was older, his mother, Milda, had given birth to him when she was thirteen, and his parents had never been married to each other. Although he had lived with his grandparents and his mother until they died, he had never missed the lack of a father, until the man whom he called "Big Papa" passed away. Without his grandfather, he began to miss a male's presence in his life.

Following the subsequent death of Pharaoh's grandmother, Milda's mind had disintegrated. She died in an asylum two months after her placement. That was when the relatives remembered his father, Jonah—the boy who had lived down the road and who had been hanging around the summer before his mother got pregnant. Jonah had gone to the States but had a relative still in Belize who could help locate him. Which is what his relatives did.

Plopped down in a strange land with an unwilling, silent father, Pharaoh found that it was his stepmother, Calissa, who had made him feel at home. When he first came to live in Shallow's Corner, he might as well have landed on Mars. Pay Dirt, whose ways were incomprehensible, was too complicated for Pharaoh. The only time his father seemed to speak to him was when he melted his soul into the metal of his saxophone.

What had happened to Pharaoh? Why couldn't he get himself together?

25

"What happened to you, Pharaoh?" Nefertiti
had asked.

Well, Vietnam had happened to him. His main
man, Cornelius, had the Ph.D. in survival in 'Nam.
He was serving his second tour of duty. He used to
preach, "Don't trust nothing that moves over here
in Vietnam, including these whores."

The VCs, Cornelius would say, were masters at
ambush. Strike and fade was the Vietcong's MO.
Farmers by day, warriors by night. Man, woman,
and child. Everyone was your enemy. Children
were said to be either thieves, beggars, or VC—or
all three. You couldn't be fooled by their innocent
appearances. "A child would kill you, just as fast as
a man," Cornelius would add. That's why children
sometimes had to be killed.

Pharaoh couldn't tell the difference between
the North Vietnamese Army and the South Vietnamese Army. They all looked the same to him.
He also learned that he became a name, rank, and
serial number. To Uncle Sam, all the brothers
looked the same. To the Vietnamese, it seemed,

they often looked stunned to see people who resembled them fighting on the white man's side.

From the time his plane landed in Da Nang, until he took the "Freedom Bird" home, he'd felt like he was in a science-fiction movie. It was worse than any nightmare, everything was so strange. He could still hear the choppers over head, and feel the heavy metal of his M-60 machine gun and M-16 strapped around his shoulders. The world had become a place of hand grenades, land mines, snipers. He had been a greenseed when he arrived. When he left, his mind had been dislodged from its axis.

"They say we all look the same," he'd tell Cornelius, "but I think they all look alike. It's still a shame. They kind of look like us, with their yellow skins. The white boys call them 'Charlie,' but I can't call them that. That's what we called the white boys back home, 'Mister Charlie.' Maybe we don't need to be over here."

"Look, if black people were as tight as the Vietcong, we could make it in America," Cornelius would say. "They believe in a cause. We just over here be-*cause*."

Because of Vietnam, Pharaoh had left Shallow's Corner. He couldn't say he had traveled, but he'd seen San Francisco, Hawaii, Guam, and Thailand. He had learned how people in the other half of the world lived. And he had learned that these yellow people were as oppressed as black people in the States. The only difference was they were willing to fight for their freedom.

For as Pharaoh was to learn, the VC could be treacherous. They worked out of caves and tunnels.

With fierce loyalty, they sometimes fought with crude instruments, such as rakes and hoes, when they couldn't steal American ammunition. But they fought down to their dying breath. They were warriors.

By the time Pharaoh arrived in Vietnam, in 1967, 58,226 were dead or missing in action.

Pharaoh sometimes had mixed feelings about the country. The countryside, bejeweled with its emerald-glass jungles, golden bamboo fields, diamond rice paddies, and glassy crystallike seas of waterfalls, looked like a paradise. A little of what Pharaoh imagined Heaven must have looked like.

At the same time, the country was an odd amalgamation of Heaven and Hell. There were beautiful mountains, streams, hills, waterfalls, but there were whores, cheap perfume, crimson lipstick, near starvation, living death if captured by the enemy, and eye-flung-open, screaming death if killed. Your best friends, your whole outfit sometimes, and your COs could be wiped out in a seemingly small skirmish. Death was the great leveler and common equalizer. You were neither white nor black when you were leveled to the ground.

He and Cornelius had gone on many missions together. Many nights, army trucks had seen them whisked to places like Vinh Long, Nha Trang, Long Binh, Pleiku, Da Nang, Saigon, and Chu Lai.

Although this was Cornelius's second tour of duty, he seemed to love Vietnam as much as he hated it. He'd lost many friends over in Vietnam and seemed to be on a mission to get any that were POWs out of the VC prisons, or avenge the deaths of the friends he had made.

From the start, Cornelius had taken Pharaoh under his wing and looked out for him. Showed him the ropes. From the dapping of the brothers, to the solidarity that the bloods had among themselves, he had initiated Pharaoh into the brotherhood.

"We can't play that Uncle Tom, house-nigger shit over here, youngblood. We got to cover each other's ass, or we ain't gon' make it. This is the closest I've ever been to another black person. I've made some good friends over here," Cornelius would school him. "And I done buried a many of them, too."

When Pharaoh met Cornelius, who was out of Tupelo, Mississippi, he learned that that was one of the luckiest days of his life. After months of Cornelius saving Pharaoh's posterior, whenever they went out on patrols, they had grown very close.

After a while, Pharaoh noticed that Cornelius always wore a funny-looking, smelly thing around his neck.

"This my mojo hand," he would tell Pharaoh. "You ain't heard of High John de Conqueror?"

When Pharaoh admitted he hadn't, Cornelius closed down on him and wouldn't say another word on the subject.

One particular evening, about seven or eight months into his Vietnam tour of duty, Pharaoh was supposed to be walking point that night. But he had dysentery so bad, he could hardly stand up. Cornelius had ceremoniously taken the mojo hand off his neck and given it to Pharaoh.

"Naw, mon. You can't do this," Pharaoh had refused. "I'll be all right."

Cornelius stared at him seriously. "I'm doing this because you my brother. You can't find one in the States like you can in this place. We more brother here than any place in the world. We got to watch each other's back."

"Well, thanks, mon."

"I'm a-tell you what I'm going to do. I'm a-take point man for you tonight. Just try to get yourself straight and stay here at the camp" was the last thing Cornelius had said to him.

When Cornelius didn't return to camp by the next day, Pharaoh and a few others went out looking for him. When they found Cornelius a day later, they only found a corpse. Cornelius had been shot in the heart, eviscerated, and impaled on a stalk in a field of bamboo. He looked like a black scarecrow, wooden stake running ramrod through his body. But the horror of horrors, the unspeakable thing, was that Cornelius had been castrated. His penis was stuffed in his mouth like a sausage. All Pharaoh could think was "Mon, that was supposed to be me. He saved my life."

Before they could remove Cornelius's body, Pharaoh and the two soldiers with him were caught in a cross fire, then captured. During his six months of captivity, Pharaoh had been tortured within an inch of his life. His cell consisted of a cage in a tree, where he could neither stand nor move about.

Over time, Pharaoh had learned enough Vietnamese to understand different words and to obey orders. When he overheard the VC soldier saying to another one that they were going to put him in a snake pit, he made his move. He had been plotting his escape, anyway. Hugging his mojo hand, he feigned an illness, which made the night guard let him out. With all the strength he had in his half-starved body, Pharaoh stabbed the guard in the head with a stone he had been sharpening into a blade for months. He escaped that night, running until the watermelon splendor of dawn. He hid in the trees by day, and traveled the jungle by night, until he made it back to Saigon, where he collapsed. By this time, he was dehydrated, emaciated, and shell-shocked.

Pharaoh was so tired of running in his dream, his limbs were sore. The jungle kept slashing at his face. He was being pursued. *Can't stop running. Run, black boy, run.*

26

Staring at the sepia-toned, bronze-framed pictures of her "coming out"—every colored girl's dream—Nefertiti succumbed to a wave of nostalgia, which lapped at her thoughts. Paradise lost. She looked at her bold, undaunted stare in her picture. How old was she then? Sixteen? This was a few months after she'd delivered Desiree. Already living out the lie. Being a debutante involved in the Negro Cotillion. Isaac, her escort, who had been her father's choice of a beau for her, stood squinting into the camera. He'd always been nearsighted. Even in the picture, Nefertiti looked much older than Isaac, as if she'd seen more. Which she had. Had she ever had a time of complete innocence in childhood? she wondered. She was too tired to try to remember.

Suddenly even her old pale pink bedroom seemed pretentious. The white eyelet curtains. The white dolls, with their unblinking clear blue eyes lining the shelves. It occurred to her that she had never had a black doll the whole time she was growing up. Her daughter, Savasia, only had black dolls. All of it seemed as pretentious as Rev's baby grand piano, which no one ever played.

She frowned when she remembered how her high-school junior year had been one of trying to make up with her parents for the first year after Desiree's birth, but after that, she'd become a rebel with a cause, with the rest of the youth culture. As she looked at her high-school graduation picture, with the big Afro, a wave of nostalgia for the good old days was resurrected. She'd always had the Promethean spirit of rebellion, and that's when she had claimed it as her own.

She could still see the clenched fists of the Black Panthers. Hear the warrior cry and drumbeat when James Brown pronounced that he was black and proud, making her feel, for the first time, like the world had caught up with her noble spirit. Like it recognized her beauty. It had been an exciting time. When rebellion was the norm. When being different was convention. When social cataclysm was the hue and cry of the day.

She wondered if this generation had ever tasted the bittersweet joy of sit-ins, which she'd experienced in high school and college? It was though her involvement in the anti-Vietnam movement at USC that her path had crossed with Ford's, during that one year on campus.

An iconoclast even in high school, she could still hear Miss Magg's lament when she helped organize a walkout during the twelfth grade. Looking back, this walkout had been instrumental in their school getting their first black-history class. Miss Magg had thrown a fit.

"Girl, you don't know how good you got it. You

are able to go to that good school. We had Jim Crow laws to worry about. We would've never walked out of a good white school, if they had let us in one back then. I don't understand you young people." Even so, her mother's voice had held a hint of awe and respect in it.

She looked at the picture of her Afro from her senior year, remembering how the Reverend had preached a sermon on young people "turning from the old ways with those revolutionary Afros." Meanwhile, his own daughter sat in the front row that Sunday, she and Sweet snickering the whole time.

Nefertiti's mixed feelings at being home caused her childhood to pass before her in montages as incandescent as candlelight. Singing in the choir. Tambourines, castanets, and hand clapping, like chattering teeth, still echoed in the nebulous skies of her memory.

> *This little light of mine,*
> *I'm gonna let it shine. . . .*

More tableaux curled around her brain. She and Sweet hiding their nickels, destined for the Sunday school collection plates, in their top braids. Dozing off at Bible study in the dining room. Those were the innocent, happy days. The days before the fall from grace. The first fall, anyhow. The days before she knew she had to be free. Now she was in the second fall of her life. And what a free fall it was. She had arrived at a time in her life when she knew—whatever the cost—that she must be free. That's why she had to find Desiree.

"You've disgraced this family before. Now you've gone too far. As far as I'm concerned, you are no daughter of mine."

The power of the unspoken word. Although her father had never said those words, she'd felt his wrath through his stony silence. That's how she knew unspoken words had power, and they were beginning to poison her marriage. The things she and Ford didn't talk about.

But she knew, in that space without words, one of her reasons: she'd never loved Ford with the reckless abandon she'd had in her youth (she could only feed love out of an itty-bitty teaspoon now), but she cared deeply enough about him.

Why didn't she want to have his baby? For one thing, she never wanted any more children. Period.

Hearing the high cry of the wind beating down on her thoughts, she became aware of something. This type of strong monsoon wind was a portentous sign. It started up a susurrous dance of the trees. Underneath this sound was the wail of a baby's cry. The auspices were not good. Her eye began to twitch. She started scratching her arms. *Oh no!* She hadn't brought her allergy pills. She remembered how the itching had started happening in her life, and shivered. That, and the fact that Big Mama Lily had often said that trouble blew in on the wind. Just before she boarded the flight from LAX, witches rode her in her sleep.

The last dream she could remember was about Big Mama Lily saying, "Go back home. Clean your house." Was it Big Mama Lily who had hagrode her awake?

Heart frozen in her chest, Nefertiti stared out as the wind began its rhythm of a low moan, until it crescendoed, lifting and rustling the dead leaves from the yard into a high wail.

Right then and there, she decided she had to move forward and not be paralyzed by the past. She picked up a piece of paper and made a list.

27

The next morning, Nefertiti got up before her parents were even out of bed. She had a list of places to go, such as the adoption agency, DMV, and also a call she wanted to make to check on her business. She was so glad that Cleo and Little Josh and his family had already left for Niagara Falls.

Seeing the Children's Home Society through grown-up eyes, Nefertiti felt like Alice in Wonderland. The ivy-covered mansion, built along Georgian lines, with its rolling lawns and azalea gardens, was still as sedate and well-manicured as she had remembered. However, it was no longer as big and intimidating as it had looked when she was a girl.

That was right, she thought. She had been a girl the last time she walked these corridors—a frightened girl caught in the oldest web in the book, unwanted pregnancy. The hardwood floors were still as austere and shiny as a convent's. The same old Victorian furniture filled the large rooms. The only thing that was different was Nefertiti.

Mrs. Beck, the social worker, went straight to the point. "Did you sign the consent form?"

"Should I have?"

"Yes. This way the adoptee can contact you if she is on the list. You see, we had no way of knowing there would be a cultural revolution, and young single girls having babies would not be the taboo it was back then. In the 1970s, young women just about stopped giving up white babies, too."

"Well, why are you still in business?" Nefertiti wondered.

"Most of the babies we get now are because the mothers have had three or four babies, and the grandparents won't put up with any more. Generally, today, with the acceptance of teenage motherhood, a first baby does not go up for adoption."

"Interesting. Tell me, what are reunions like today?"

"When we're through, I can show you photos of the reunions that I've handled. They have been interesting, to say the least."

Nefertiti had a list of questions. "Did her adoption take place in Michigan?"

"Yes."

"Did Desiree keep the same name?"

"Yes."

In the past several months, Nefertiti had gone to the library and had read up on the different adoption-liberation movements, which had been started mainly by the adoptees. The different reunions between birth parents and adoptees ranged from bittersweet to very positive. But those lost years—that alter life, which might have been—was always a vast sea that had to be bridged between the mother and child tied by blood.

"Have you heard from her?"

"No, we haven't heard from her. But I can give you nonidentifying information, such as the adoption home study."

Nefertiti left the agency, disappointed but optimistic. Although she had hit a blind alley again, at least this piece of paper was something. More info than she'd had before about her child. Child . . . woman. She was going to have to get used to the time that had elapsed. In her mind, this golden child was still the newborn she had once glimpsed. Frozen like a butterfly in amber. Nefertiti would have to let go of the image of a baby. This was a grown woman she would find. At least, she hoped she'd find Desiree.

Just reading the information, Nefertiti went as numb as she did after being given novocaine at the dentist's. So it wasn't a bad nightmare, after all. It had really happened. The social workers had told her to go home and forget it ever happened. Get on with her life. Find a good man, settle down, and get married. She would have other children. She would forget about that first one. Her mother had implied to her, too, that this was for the best.

In her mother's day, Nefertiti would have been stood up in the Chastisement Corner. According to Big Mama Lily, Betty Lee had been stood up in the church and refused to repent. To her dying day, Big Mama Lily felt this cruel act was what had cost her her child. She always felt that this was what had caused Betty Lee to leave home and never return. Big Mama Lily, herself, had stopped going to church after that happened.

During the 1960s, Reverend Godbolt, proud man that he was, would not have been able to keep preaching at his church, had she openly kept her baby and remained unmarried. This would have turned all their lives upside down. So this seemed to have been the only way possible to handle the situation.

And Lord knows, Nefertiti had tried. Tried to live out a normal teenage life. Tried to forget about the past. Went on to marry. Had other babies. And tried not to remember the first one. But try as she might, even though she had blocked out a lot of information in her head, her heart had its own memory. Its own map of the roads it had traveled. It had always been there, taunting her. But now, it was more than a specter. She was staring, face-to-face, at her past, made tangible on the crumpled sheet of paper in her hand.

Nefertiti thought back to the day that she met the young man who was to become Desiree's father. "Is it true what they say about the preacher's daughter?"

That was the first thing Pharaoh had asked her, when he followed her home from the soda shop that long-lost day. That day that still stood like a bright beacon in the corridors of her memory.

She had been so young and innocent. Well, maybe the bobby sox, brown-and-white oxfords, and long skirts had only been a simulacrum of innocence. No, looking back, she hadn't been so pure, considering the furnace boiling beneath her navel in the pit of her loins—sin just waiting like a volcano to burn her to a cinder. Within that year, it was as if there were a rift in the earth, the before and the after, in the changing from childhood to womanhood.

As soon as she started talking to Pharaoh, Nefertiti knew he was trouble. A warning bell rang in her head as her stomach churned, and sweat ran between her legs. She didn't know if it was his accent, but she was mesmerized by him.

Pharaoh personified "Sin walking in shoes." He was one of those "do-rag–wearing jitterbugs" that her Daddy preached against. A member of the class of "slick-talking, sugarcoat-tongued sinners, lying in ambush, just waiting to lead a Christian astray from the path of righteousness." Pharaoh had a golden tongue.

The way Rev preached about sinners, they were as insidious as hand grenades in a minefield, just lying in wait. Lying to take the unsuspecting to perdition. Like many young people, she never believed her father.

Yet, to Nefertiti, it was as though her and Pharaoh's meeting had been preordained.

"You one of them sanctified girls," Pharaoh had teased her. "One of them Holy Rollers."

"What are you talking about?"

"I can tell a mile away."

"How you know?"

"I can tell by that long skirt you wearing and no lipstick."

Nefertiti looked down at her pleated burgundy-plaid skirt. Because of her short stature, her bobby sox almost came up to the hem.

"Oh, I guess you prefer people like Honey Jackson and Mimi Collins, wearing all that makeup and those short skirts?"

"Naw, but at least they ain't 'fraid of they daddy."

"I ain't afraid of anybody or anything."

"Mighty spunky for a preacher's gal."

"Who told you?"

"I got my ways of finding out things. I know about sanctimonious people like your father. And I know about Goody Two-shoes like you."

Despite the girdle that Miss Magg made her wear because of her rounded hips, Nefertiti felt like Pharaoh was undressing her with his eyes. Like he could see straight through her. She didn't quite know what that meant, but she felt her face getting sweaty with heat.

Like the serpent had deceived Eve by making her think God was withholding something good from her, unless she ate from the Tree of Knowledge, Pharaoh had known how to make Nefertiti feel that she was missing out on something.

Looking back, she realized her seduction had been gradual—like a boat drifting on a sea of sin. Yet, to this day, she could never quite say that she'd felt Pharaoh had been evil. The first thing she had noticed when she looked Pharaoh in the eye was that he didn't have horns nor carried a pitchfork, like the one painted in her father's sermons. Pharaoh's eyes caught the twinkle of the sun in them, and if she had been struck like Paul on the road to Damascus, she would not have altered the course she was to take. For his smile was like a circus and cotton candy wrapped up in one.

Her mother was so reticent when it came to talking about "the birds and the bees," her only sex education had come from Big Mama Lily. She used to say, "It ain't how they look, Lil' Bit. It's what they say. 'Specially an ugly man. Now, take your great-uncle Blue, my half brother. He was the ugliest thing in shoe leather—looked like an anteater, even if I must say so myself— but, oh, how the women loved him! He really knew how to sweet-talk a woman. If a woman said he was 'too dark,' that's when he turned the fires up to try to woo them. He really knew how to charm women—to bring them under his spell.

"Before it was over, he had four women who would sit around and cry and laugh about the terrible-sweet things he did to them. One was named Bessie. She said that Blue had swung on a rope into her bedroom window while her boy-friend was in the other room—even though she didn't like him at first, she fell in love with him for being so crazy. But one of them—Irene—well, he ruint her. Before she died, she used to just sit and drink all day and say, 'I just don't give a damn.'"

Now Nefertiti pondered this story that had been sitting in the back of her mind, unbidden, all these years. What had made her think of that? Really, what was it about some men that women found so attractive? Was it that special something that a man possessed—that deep mystery, that black magic? Was it the way he held his head to one side when he said, "Baby"? Was it their charisma?

If that was the case, then Rev had charisma. Yet, that wasn't the same thing as what Big Mama Lily had described in Great-Uncle Blue. Neither was it that indefinable quality she'd seen in her uncle Tiger. And, at one time, in Pharaoh. As she thought about it, even in what she recalled of Pharaoh's father, Pay Dirt.

What did they all have in common? They were men who could not—no, *would not*—be tamed. Like her double-great-grandfather, their souls could not be branded. They could not be tied down. Did not follow the prescriptions ordinary men followed. They were freemen, long before the Emancipation Proclamation.

Maybe they were like falcons, kings of the air. Birds of prey whose regal spirits couldn't be chained, branded, or tamed. . . .

Yes, she had to find Desiree. She would do whatever it took.

28

After Nefertiti left the Children's Home Society, she went to a phone booth inside Food Fair. Using her telephone card, she called her business partner, Phyllis. She knew it was early, but Phyllis was an early bird.

Phyllis wanted to purchase lladro figurines and Tiffany lamps at wholesale prices. She believed they needed to expand their inventory beyond Afrocentric items.

"You know, 'Black Art' is getting big, Nefertiti. Do you think we might introduce a line of paintings?"

Between the two partners, Phyllis was the more progressive one. But, then again, she had less to lose than Nefertiti. Having sunk her whole life's savings and her pension from HUD into Treasure Chest's future, Nefertiti had the most at stake. But even though her profit margin had been slim so far, the psychological payoffs had more than compensated for everything.

"Don't purchase a lot of either one," Nefertiti told Phyllis. "See how—say—just the first dozen of each item sells. If it works, we'll buy a larger quantity. How's business been since I've been gone?"

"It's been pretty busy. Which is a good thing. And thanks for the go-ahead on the purchases. Hey, are you feeling okay, Nefertiti? You sound kind of down."

"No, I'm fine. It's just that home is always full of a lot of old memories. Some good. Some not so good."

"Yes, I know how trippy it gets whenever I go home and visit my family, too."

Phyllis was an only child, but she, too, had issues relating to her aging parents.

"Okay, I'll check in with you tomorrow. Thanks for keeping everything together while I'm gone."

"You bet."

The Department of Motor Vehicles had moved from its old office on Shane Street, and Nefertiti had to drive an extra hour to get to the new office. When she went inside, they didn't check her old HUD badge. She used to do background criminal checks through the Department of Justice in order to rent out Section 8 properties, so she was familiar with the ability to use her badge. She flashed her old HUD badge without anyone questioning her and was given access to the computer. She ran all of the birthdays that were the same as her daughter's, and tried to match them with the ones that had Desiree as a first name hoping to get some sort of information. She had no such luck.

Nefertiti next went to the library and looked through old newspaper microfiche of birth announcements from that year. She worked on this the rest of the morning. When her eyes got tired of looking at the tiny print, she decided to take a break. It was to no avail. It didn't make sense to go to the old hospital, because it had been torn down, and she had no idea as to where those records might be.

At a loss for what to do next, Nefertiti got into her car and started driving, without a destination. Without questioning her reason, she stopped at the same florist from which she'd picked up the flowers for the church service. She picked out a single lily.

Almost as if she were in a trance, Nefertiti drove to the cemetery where they had buried Big Mama Lily. She just wanted to talk to her.

The cemetery had grown since Nefertiti had last visited her great-grandmother's grave seven years earlier. The cemetery's piney smell almost knocked her down when she first entered. The cemetery had to be entered from a backstreet way, as it dead-ended at the hill that Nefertiti used to sneak down. Surrounded by cypresses, eucalyptuses, and pines, the air was so redolent with their aromatic fragrances, Nefertiti felt delirious.

Big Mama Lily was buried next to Grandpa Bullocks, who had died five years before his wife's passing. After silently addressing Grandpa Bullocks, Nefertiti turned to Big Mama Lily's onyx and green headstone, put the lily on top of it, and caressed it.

Other than the sounds in her head, the chattering blue jays and the robins were the only noises she could hear.

I got trouble on my mind. I know you used to say get down on your knees.

Nefertiti knelt down before the headstone.

I still can taste your rutabagas and corn bread, Big Mama Lily. I can smell the vanilla in your apron when I would bury my head in your lap. I remember you told me how the slaves used to make hoe cakes on a hoe with some coals underneath them. That your grandmother told you about it. I remember how they told me you put an egg over the door when I was a baby, and that to this day, I don't have any cavities. Why were eggs always so important to you?

Something in the wind said, *"Pray."*

Well, she hadn't done that in a long time. Was she getting too hardened to pray? What was life doing to her? She thought of one of Big Mama Lily's favorite church songs:

> *I want to be ready*
> *(I want to be ready when He calls me.)*
> *I'm trying to get my house in order. . . .*

How did the rest of it go? Is that what Big Mama Lily was telling her in the dream? What did it mean to get your house in order? Or was it clean your house? She didn't know.

It had rained the day that they buried Big Mama Lily. Nefertiti wondered why it always seemed to rain at funerals. Had it rained at Grandpa Bullocks's funeral? She couldn't remember. Big Mama Lily used to say that when it rained at funerals, God was crying, too, but crying tears of welcome, because one of His children had come home.

Nefertiti sat and tried to remember some of

the other sayings Big Mama Lily had told her.
Was it that the first baby born in a family after
the death of a member was the same individual
come back, just as they saw a young moon after
the old one was gone? And she said that sometimes the deceased came to visit in the form of
animals, or they were reborn in the family line.
Nefertiti had a thought. What if Desiree had
been Big Mama Lily reincarnated? Oh, that was
just an old wives' tale! Where had Big Mama Lily
got all that foolishness?

The smell of heather, faintly mixed with urine,
floated through the area, baptizing her in a wave
of déjà vu.

After she got off her knees and was walking
out of the cemetery, Nefertiti thought she heard
a leaf or a branch crush under someone's foot.

For each step she took, Nefertiti suddenly realized there were footsteps behind her.

"So you've returned to the scene of the crime,"
a voice spoke, directed at her.

Nefertiti jumped as though she'd seen a ghost.
It was Pharaoh standing behind her, so close she
could feel his breathing on her neck.

He was still wearing the army fatigues he'd
had on when she saw him the last time, several
years earlier. Nefertiti definitely smelled a slight
odor of urine on him.

"What are you talking about?"

"Oh, you've forgotten? The best loving I ever
had in my life, and you don't remember? I've got

my stamp on you, girl. What are you doing here, anyway?"

"Wait a minute. I know you don't think what happened between children—because that's all we were—means anything?"

"So it meant nothing?"

Nefertiti didn't answer Pharaoh.

"What are you doing, anyway? Following me? This the second time I've seen you," she challenged.

"You know what I want to talk to you about."

"What? I'm not a mind reader." Nefertiti was flip.

"I want to know where our daughter is."

Nefertiti did not reply. It aroused too many conflicting feelings of loss, guilt, and grief.

"Silence doesn't work, Nefertiti. You've been quiet for twenty-six years, and what good has it done? You're like someone trying to close the door on a house with a fire inside it. It's like a volcano just waiting to erupt."

"Leave me alone, Pharaoh."

"Did you ever find her?"

"It's none of your business."

"Look, that was—*is*—my child."

"Didn't feel like it when I was in that delivery room, Pharaoh. It was just me feeling all that pain. I was just a child myself. It's a miracle I didn't die, my labor was so hard. Where were you?"

"I was young. I was afraid of your father. I thought he was going to put me in jail for statutory rape."

"Pharaoh, Sweet knows what you did to me that night during the riot, how you hurt me.

Besides, all you would have done was ruined my life. My father was right about boys like you."

"Oh, what did he tell you about boys like me? That we were beneath you? That we were not good enough for Miss Elite? Is that why you didn't answer any of my letters from 'Nam?"

"What letters?"

After Desiree's birth, Reverend had picked her up from the hospital.

"I don't want to ever see that nigger hanging around here again. If I find out you are sneaking out, I'm a-send you away again. You hear?"

"You didn't get any of my letters?"

"Well, Reverend must have thrown them out. You know I was in school during the day."

"Well, I still believe Cleo is my daughter."

"Now, you know I told you that wasn't true."

"I don't believe it."

"Suit yourself."

Pharaoh was quiet for a while. Finally he said, "I love your hair like that. I wish I could paint a picture of you now. You know, I once did."

"You did?"

"Got it here in my car now. I want to give it to you. It's a picture I painted of you that summer we went together. I want you to keep it, lest you may forget. You did once care."

29

Perhaps if he had been considered a war hero, Nefertiti would see him in a different light. But there were no parades welcoming him back. No newspaper articles. No respect when he wore his jungle uniform or his boonie hat. It was as if everyone had developed selective amnesia. They had his name, rank, and serial number when they drafted him, but now, nobody knew his name. It was as if Vietnam were an illegitimate child everyone just wanted to forget. Just like his child had been.

Once, after his discharge, he'd gone to Solid Rock Baptist Church, which was the cornerstone of the black community. He just wanted acceptance from his people. True enough, he had worn his fatigues and combat boots, but he thought this would be a symbol of pride for having served his country. Instead, the white-gloved ushers had stopped him at the door and escorted him to the curb. Other than for Pay Dirt's and Deacon Thorne's funerals, and in his recent attempt to try to see Nefertiti, Pharaoh had not been back to church since.

After Nefertiti drove off, Pharaoh stood in the same spot, inhaling her perfume. A real light fragrance. He wondered what it was. Exhaling, he felt a tingling start in his groin. It reminded him of the songs about the love jones coming down on a person. Why didn't they write songs telling how the scent of a woman was an aphrodisiac? Women just didn't know. Now, that was the spice of life. No wonder they called it "that old black magic."

Human beings smelled that special someone the same way dogs could sniff from a three-mile radius when a bitch was in heat. The way the drones—those hapless, ill-fated soldier bees— knew when that courtesan, the queen bee, was ready to mate. *Ohhh, baby*. And he, in his mating dance, was ready to tango.

Before she left, he had just came out and said it to her, sincerely and shamelessly. "Titi, I love you. Girl, don't you know I never stopped loving you."

Nefertiti looked shocked. "No, you scared me, and if I recall, you slapped me the night of the riots. From then on, I didn't have the same feeling for you."

"I swear to God, I didn't mean to slap you. I didn't mean to pull on you that night. I wasn't trying to hurt you or rape you. Why did you refuse me?"

Detroit, Michigan, July 23–30, 1967

"People, get off the streets! We are warning you. Go into your homes. There is a seven o'clock curfew."

As far as Nefertiti could see, the National Guard wasn't playing with the native sons as they rode through the streets in their army tanks. M-60s were pointed at people's heads, "like they were just so many watermelons running attached to nigger legs," as some put it.

"We will shoot once in the air, and the next time at you. For you are criminals. You are breaking the law. We will not stand for this. We will have law and order."

The white National Guardsman's words, spoken through his bullhorn, rivaled the Rev's words in the sultry evening air.

"People, we must stop this rioting. We must have peace. We have to let the Lord take care of it." Rev was pleading with the disgruntled masses over the loudspeaker hooked up to the pulpit in his church.

"Shut up, Uncle Tom."

From her room, Nefertiti could hear the roar of the crowds. The din sounded like cymbals clanging and crashing.

The word was on the streets. The ham snatchers were running amok. She didn't care. Her world ended when the ink dried on the adoption papers she'd only just signed.

"Please, people. Dr. King does not preach violence."

"We done had enough of your preaching, hand-in-hattin'."

"Shut up, Rev."

"Step back and let real men take care of this."

"Down with whitey!"

"Burn, whitey, burn."

The world was like a carnival, except the adults were participating.

"People, this is not the way."

"To Hell with the Establishment!"

"Death to the pigs!"

From her upstairs bedroom, Nefertiti could hear the din, the clamor, the noise. The world was a war zone. She could smell the tar, soot, and ashes. From her window, she saw the destruction. It was Armageddon.

It had been going on for five days now. There had been more than forty riots that summer. In Newark, New Jersey, twenty-six had died. (Before it was over, forty-three would lie dead in Detroit.)

"People, we must stop this rioting. We must have peace. We have to let the Lord take care of it." Reverend's voice was relentless, sounding like a broken record.

The sky was orange with fire. Gunshots rang out. Glass shattered every few minutes. Some people ducked when they saw the National Guard. Others ran brazenly past them. The white National Guard soldier was on a bull horn; now he was hollering, "Go into your homes, or you will be arrested. The curfew is seven o'clock."

The police began to arrest people. Bulldog Harrington, the neighborhood bully, had been shot and killed on the first day of the riots. Mayhem ruled the streets, both day and night. "People, we must stop this rioting." Reverend continued to appeal on the loudspeaker. "We must have peace." People were brazen as they ran across TV news cameras, carrying sofas, tel-

evisions, and cases of food on their shoulders.
They ignored Reverend's pleas.

"Burn, baby, burn."

"Burn, whitey, burn."

None of the stores had set their merchandise
out for sale. Like a sudden downpour of hail-
stones, disgruntled looters had the city under
siege. An angry maelstrom of mobs destroyed
everything in its merciless trek as it set fires, destroyed property, and looted. Billboards wilted like
black dahlias. Telephone poles resembled char-
coaled lynch trees. The law was dead that week.

Such a short time ago, she'd witnessed her own
girlhood abruptly die when she gave birth. Now,
from her bedroom window, Nefertiti watched a
black sky, torn by smoke and fire, and a street split
by anarchy.

"People, we must stop this rioting." Reverend
continued to appeal on the loudspeaker. "We
must have peace." People ran by, carrying hi-fis
and speakers on their shoulders.

The cries outside the church almost drowned
out Reverend's sermon. The family lived two doors
away. From her bedroom, Nefertiti felt her heart
die. Her body was still alive, but she was a zombie.
She didn't even want to talk to Sweet. She only
wanted to lie in her bed and stare at the ceiling.
The only face she could see was that of her baby
girl's. She no longer felt like fighting. She wanted
to give up.

The first time she'd seen Pharaoh after she'd
come back from the maternity home, she was
walking to the mailbox.

"Is that my baby your mother has and is

pretending to be hers?" Pharaoh's question surprised Nefertiti. She had never considered that people would think something like that. She could only stare at him. She didn't even have the strength to talk to him anymore. A riot of loss was burning inside her. As upset as she'd been over the pregnancy, she had no idea that she would feel this way.

After Desiree's birth, Nefertiti hated going to church. She could no longer stomach the sight of Sister Maude's—and the other older women's— self-righteous curled lips. Of all the older women, Mother Catherine was the worst. She spent the whole service at church, peering like a sharp-eyed eagle. Her eyes were so piercing, it was as if she could tell who was a virgin and who was not.

The older sisters in the church hated music. They said it was the Devil's brew. Especially rock 'n' roll. Good girls were to wear no lipstick. Have no boyfriends. Wear no miniskirts.

One would think the older sisters had never been young before. All they seemed to believe that young girls should do was sing in the choir, be chaste, and kiss their old withered asses, Nefertiti thought. The church mothers spent every Sunday, and prayer meeting, fanning their big, sagging bosoms, and looking over their shoulders back at the rest of the younger members in the congregation, eyeballs peeled for any signs of impropriety or fornication. Searching for some telling sign that some young girl was being "fresh-tailed." Nefertiti didn't think for a minute that they believed she had gone down South to school. But all of them were afraid of Rev, and no one had the temerity to approach him and question him.

In Shallow's Corner, the Bible Belt girded its young girls tighter than a chastity belt topped by a corset. For those who did not comply with the church's tight strictures, there was ostracism, and stigma. Well, her chastity had been defiled.

If they only knew for a fact that the rumors about her disappearance to her cousin Letty Pearl's in the South were true, there would be scandal. She could tell from the way the church mothers were staring at her stomach what they were thinking.

Fortunately, her stomach was as flat as before she'd had the baby. When her mother walked up the aisle with baby Cleo, she knew they thought that the baby was hers. If she could only keep her heart from melting down to nothing.

They didn't know. She didn't have to wait to die and go to Hell. This was Hell right here. Having had a baby and having to pretend otherwise. What greater punishment than this? Well, if the wages of sin was death, she wanted to die.

"We're going to help you this time," Rev had said, "but the next time you're on your own."

Well, she wished this were the time. Help? Having a baby that you would never see, and having a little sister—the very same age—that you wanted or wished were your own. *Give me no help.* She hadn't expected to feel this way. She noticed the maternal feelings started after the delivery of the baby.

"You could end up being a grandmother by the time you're thirty," Miss Magg had said.

At the time, Nefertiti couldn't conceive of being thirty, let alone a grandmother, so that was all immaterial to her. Until the pregnancy and delivery, she had felt invincible. Other girls got pregnant. Not her. She had never even envisioned a future that included children. In fact, she didn't even think seriously about the future until she'd gotten pregnant.

She was about three months pregnant when Miss Magg had confirmed her suspicions by taking her to the doctor. After that, Reverend had become so cold toward her. He would look through her, as though he didn't see her anymore.

It wasn't like it hadn't been prophesied by Sister Ilene the summer before.

She remembered when Sister Ilene had come to tell her mother that Nefertiti had been sassing her in her mom-and-pop store. That had happened the summer she had turned fourteen.

"I just thought I'd tell you before she winds up pregnant."

Nefertiti could have been knocked over by a feather from Miss Magg's response to Sister Ilene. "Getting pregnant isn't the worst thing that can happen to her."

"What?" Sister Ilene was stunned, speechless.

"The worst thing could be turning out like you. Yeah, I've seen how you been running with Sister Ada's husband. If you pull that mess on me, with Rev, I'll kill you," Miss Magg concluded.

30

Later, that night, a rock hit her bedroom window. Nefertiti thought it was her imagination. When she heard a second rock, she knew that she hadn't imagined it. It was her friends Sweet and Fadel. Her father had forbidden her to run with Sweet anymore, since he figured she had to have been behind all the lies Nefertiti used to tell to get out of the house.

"'S'appening?"

"Girl, com'on out," Sweet whispered.

"I can't."

"Aw, com'on, they getting down on Twelfth Street. It's like the Mardi Gras. It all started over the police trying to break up a blind pig."

"I don't care."

"Dang, Titi. You ain't no fun no more."

"I don't want to loot anything."

"No, that's not what I'm coming for you for. It's Pharaoh. He want to see you."

"I told you I'm through with him."

"Girl, he's going to Vietnam. He's been drafted. He just wants to say good-bye. Look, Rev ain't gon' miss you, with all that singing and shouting they doing in there."

The two girls, along with Fadel, ran across the meadow, with their heads ducked, milkweed slashing at their legs.

She could hear the choir's voices fading in the background: *"Ain't gonna study war no more. . ."*

As they ran through the meadow, they saw BooBoo and Anteater Man running by with what looked like cases of liquor on their shoulders. Both boys' faces were covered with soot and smoke. They both looked drunk with the excitement of the riot.

"We got some more hidden down in the graveyard. Hey, come by the crib and grab a drink," they called out to Fadel.

Fadel waved his hand to say, "Later."

The moon looked as though it were dripping blood, it was such a crimson red. It provided an eerie backdrop to the night.

By the time they reached the wall of the cemetery, Nefertiti's and Sweet's legs were so wet from the milkweed and thistle, they both had to reach down and swipe their legs.

"Wait a minute," Nefertiti said before they climbed the cemetery's wall. "I want to talk to Sweet in private."

Fadel obliged and turned his back.

"You and Fadel doing it yet?"

Sweet nodded.

"Make sure he use a rubber or pull out."

"You should talk."

"I swear Pharaoh pulled out. I don't know how I got pregnant. But, anyway, that's some terrible mess. I just don't want it to happen to you. That had to be the most horrible pain I ever went through. It makes cramps look like schoolyard play."

"Can I ask you something, Titi? You sure you won't get mad?"

"What is it?"

"How does it feel?"

"What?"

"You know. I hope you don't get mad. But how does it feel to never see your baby? You know, Stormey had a little boy. He is so cute. Her parents are crazy about him."

Stormey was another fifteen-year-old girl in Shallow's Corner who had been pregnant at the same time.

"It don't feel good. That's all I can tell you."

Pharaoh stepped from behind the old pine tree at the edge of the cemetery, the tree beneath which their daughter had been conceived, The nearby cypress bent in the wind, as if it wanted to hear their conversation.

"Nefertiti, I've been drafted."

"I'm sorry, Pharaoh. I really am."

Before she could say another word, Pharaoh grabbed her and began to kiss her with more passion than she'd remembered. She could taste the blood-heat of the smoke and fire on his tongue, smell it in his hair. For the longest time, he held her in his arms. He began crying softly into her shoulders.

"I need you, Nefertiti."

"Pharaoh, I can't. You just don't know all I went through."

"I'll take care of you."

"Pharaoh, no. I can't. I'm not the same silly girl anymore. I'll never be the same."

"Please, baby. Don't send a man to his death without giving him some. This may be the last time I'll see you."

Although her mouth was saying "no," her lips and body began to say "yes." She'd thought it would be easy to go back to being a girl again. Now she had the typhoon desires and passions of a full-grown woman.

"I'll take care of you."

She'd heard those words before.

"I'll take care of you." The words echoed in her head, like an old blues song, promises meant to be broken. Harbinger of memories.

This was the cemetery where she'd lain with Pharaoh. Where he was supposed to have taken care of her. Like a river rising, she felt the old desire beginning to flood through her as Pharaoh continued to kiss her. Suddenly, though, the baby's face flashed in her mind.

"No!" she shouted, pushing him away. "I can't!"

"Nefertiti, please."

"I said no. Leave me alone!"

She was beginning to pull away from Pharaoh, when he slapped her. Pharaoh began to pull on her, tearing her blouse and exposing her bra strap, skeleton white against her dark breast.

"Now, look what you've done."

"I've seen them before, Nefertiti. You're mine."

A quiet voice said, "She said leave her alone."

Nefertiti turned, surprised to see Isaac.

Isaac took her by the hand and began to try to

lead her away. Pharaoh began to pull on her other arm.

"This is my woman, man. She's had my baby. You better go mind your own business."

"I wanted to marry her last year. She's the one said we were too young. You left her high and dry. But she's going to be my wife one day." Nefertiti felt the fear in Isaac's sweaty palm, but his voice was even. Was he crazy? He couldn't beat Pharaoh.

"You a-lie."

What happened next, happened so fast, Nefertiti couldn't believe it. Isaac hauled off and hit Pharaoh. The two began to kick and fight on the ground. They tore off each other's shirts in the tussle as they rolled over the graves. Sweet and Fadel came running out from their hiding place.

"Stop! What's wrong with y'all?"

"Y'all gonna kill each other."

"Get them away from each other."

"Quit fighting. Y'all brothers, man!" Fadel seemed more upset about that than their fight. "Y'all is kinfolk."

No matter how Fadel, Nefertiti, and Sweet tried to pull the fighting stepbrothers apart, they couldn't stop the fight.

Minutes of fist upon fist, blow upon blow, spit upon spit, elapsed. It seemed like the fight was going to go on forever. The young men's breathing became ragged.

Suddenly the roar of an M-60 pierced the air. The five young people screamed, they were so startled.

A bullhorn called through the darkness: "Halt! You are under arrest."

As they came to their senses, they realized it was the National Guard.

"Run!" Fadel cried out. "Beat feet!"

All Nefertiti remembered was seeing the Guards gaining on Fadel and grabbing him. She and Sweet knew they would never make it to the cemetery's wall in time, so they ran and sought shelter in the gardener's toolshed. (It would be twenty-six years later before the two ever discussed what they saw in the cemetery that night. It would be then that Nefertiti understood the significance of the apparition they saw while they were hiding.)

By the time Nefertiti and Sweet made it back to Black Stone Drive, their end of the street was engulfed in flames. Both the church and the funeral home were on fire. The street was lined with firefighters. The only reason the Godbolts' home was not on fire, as they later found out, was because the wind was blowing east, and their house sat on the west end of the street.

Perhaps Miss Magg was so relieved to see Nefertiti was safe and hadn't perished in the fire, she didn't question the soot on her face or the tear in her blouse.

"Oh," Miss Magg cried, collapsing in her daughter's arms. "Oh, Titi! I'm so glad you're all right. A bullet ricocheted and hit your daddy in the leg! The church and the funeral home are on fire. I think a cinder blew over from the stores that were on fire on the next street. Come on, we have to get down to the hospital. The ambulance already took your father there."

The sky rained a torrent of Molotov cocktails, rocks, and bottles. The police had called the fire department to pull out the hoses, not just on the fires, but on the looters.

Colored people fought with the police and the firemen. Years of oppression and frustration found their way into hurtled bricks and lighter fluid.

"All power to the people!"

Nefertiti looked up to the sky, she felt so helpless. The moon was bloodred and hung so low, it looked as if it were crying. Dazed, the remaining members of the church were standing outside, holding hands, as they watched their church burn to the ground. A mournful song broke out, with the refrain being the call. It was one that Big Mama Lily used to like.

Down on my knees,
When trouble rise,
I'm talking to my Jesus,
From the other side.

31

Whenever Ford would say to Nefertiti, "You've only had two children," she wanted to tell him, "That's a lie. I've already had three." But she'd never told him about Desiree, the child she'd delivered when she was only fifteen. He knew that she had suffered difficult pregnancies with Isaac Jr. and Savasia, almost losing both babies in her seventh month—that she'd even suffered miscarriages before their birth—but he didn't know that she'd had a child placed up for adoption. She had been married to Ford, and known him off and on for more than twenty years, yet she had never told him her secret.

The power of the unspoken word. It had held the power to make her question as a child if her father loved her. It now held the power to destroy her new marriage, just as it held the power to have kept her silent all these years about her secret. Maybe her secrecy was inherited. She remembered how Miss Magg, pregnant and nearly forty, hadn't shared the fact that she was expecting a baby with anyone. Somehow she had hidden the pregnancy under big clothes. She didn't go out to church, because she said she had a mysterious ailment. Since she wasn't a big woman, no one knew. Afterward, when Miss Magg delivered her younger sister, Cleo, some fifteen years following Nefertiti's birth, everyone always said her mother really was like an icebox. She really knew how to keep a secret.

32

A woman in a black head scarf and dark shades went inside an unmarked business. Few people would have noticed the woman in this neighborhood, anyhow. It was the neighborhood where the Haitians lived. They often frequented the obeah lady.

"The stuff never worked that you gave me," Roshanne said to the older woman. "He still loves his first wife."

For a price, the woman would start burning the red candles. The woman in the shades handed the obeah lady a picture. It was a picture of Nefertiti. She really wished she could have gotten a piece of her hair.

A mysterious woman watched Nefertiti as she went into the church. She mumbled out loud, "Soon."

33

Nefertiti drove over to the church on Friday to pray about what she should do about finding her daughter, about letting Pharaoh know it was too late, even about talking to her father. She wanted to find her daughter. She wanted to talk to Rev. Luckily, the church's door was opened. She figured someone was in the church when she smelled a pine-scented cleaner coming from the basement. What should her next step be to find her daughter? As she sat in the front pew, she seriously considered some of Rev's old sermons. She remembered how the gold in Rev's chasuble would fade into the purple when he sweated as he got really wound up and preached a good sermon. She had once heard a woman say after service, "Rev know he can dress up some Scriptures."

When she was a child, Nefertiti had never given Rev's sermons a thought. But this afternoon, coming before the altar, she remembered the summer of her conversion and baptism. She was fourteen. Still a virgin, yet, from what Rev preached from the pulpit, bound for the depths of Hell for the lust that was consuming her. They were at a three-day convention, not unlike the one her father was preparing for now, when she was baptized.

"See, God sent all of you here to perform a mission. And when you're not performing your mission, you are not recognized by the guardian angels sent to help you. It's sort of like this car accident I saw today," Rev had said, *"Yes, Lord!*

"I knew someone had been hurt and it looked bad. When I asked if I could donate blood, the ambulance attendant said, 'This man is type O. What type are you?' When I told him that I was type A, the attendant said that my blood would kill this man.

"So you see, many of us are running around with type O people and business in our life, when we are type A. That's why we are killing ourselves."

Lord, was she like the person running around with type O people and business in her life when she was type A? Was she on the wrong path by not keeping her child? Had she been wrong to go along with her parents? Now she couldn't find her child, and had no clue as to what else to try.

"Oh, Father, what am I to do?" Nefertiti had closed her eyes as she prayed. When she opened them, Isaac, who was sitting in the pew behind her, startled her.

"I want to talk to you, Titi."

"What do you mean?"

"Wait a minute. We always get off on the wrong foot. Can we talk?"

"Go ahead. You have ten minutes."

"You know, I've had a lot of time to think."

"And?"

"Do you remember the time we were up all night with Little Isaac?"

Nefertiti was silent. Certain things, such as the good times in her first marriage, she'd found healthier to block out of her memory. She had found if she never looked back on that marriage, she could move forward.

"There were some good times, too," Isaac added.

"I'm not denying that. But that was yesterday."

"Please let me talk, Titi."

"What do you call this that we're doing now? And, anyway, are you following me, Isaac?"

"No, Nefertiti, I'm not following you. I just want to talk. Can we talk?"

"Go ahead. I've got to get to my mother's. She's having dinner for everyone tonight."

"All right. This is it." Isaac splayed his fingers in both hands, like he did whenever he was trying to explain his writing to his audience.

"And?"

"Do you believe in good and evil?"

"Yes, but what has that got to do with the cost of bread and butter?"

"No, I mean it. That there are some evil people in the world . . . who do evil things."

"Look, Isaac, get to the point."

He reached behind his pew and handed Nefertiti a dozen red roses. When she handed them back, he handed her a copy of a manuscript, which she glanced at cursorily.

"Please?"

Nefertiti had always been his best critic. She had an unerring instinct for what was good and what was fodder.

"*House of Mourning,* not a good working title, I'd say."

"I know, Titi. I took it from Ecclesiastes. But it's about us. I felt it in my gut when I wrote it. It's an aspect of the black experience seldom looked at. Childhood sweethearts."

"Isaac, we were never childhood sweethearts."

"But I've loved you since I was a boy."

"Well, you could have fooled me when we were married."

"I know. I believe Roshanne—that crazy woman—put something in my food, Titi. I swear, I was out of my head. I wasn't even myself."

"You looked like yourself to me. You seemed quite happy at the time when you were having your fun. What's the matter? The excitement's gone now?"

Isaac was quiet for a long time. Finally he cleared his throat, and said, "But back to the play. I think the title works on two levels. The story is set in a funeral home, and it's referring to that day of reckoning. Now I know what the Scripture meant by the heart of the wise one is in the house of mourning."

"Isaac, get to the point."

"Nefertiti, I want to come back home. It's like I'm dying."

"And you think it is as simple as that?"

"It means that we should always consider our day of death whenever we make choices. Titi, I made a bad choice. Would you give a brother another chance?"

"Oh? Are you crazy? You know I'm married to Ford. In fact," Nefertiti paused, then said something she didn't know was in her heart, "he's been real good to me, and I love him."

"No, but, Titi, I'm dying inside without you."

"Stop talking about dying. It's too depressing. But no. We can't get back together, if that's what you're thinking. There's just too much water under the bridge."

"Titi, I know what I did to you was wrong and all. But you've got to know I didn't mean to hurt you."

"Wait, let's get one thing straight. I don't fault you for what I allowed you to do. I gave you carte blanche. I should have left your behind the first time you stayed out all night. But you always held my baby over my head, like you had done me a favor to marry me. So I fault myself for believing that your love was worth allowing you to abuse me. No, Isaac, it would never work. I'm a different person now. And I've got a new husband."

After she left the church, Isaac sat considering Titi's rejection. Why did he just have to have *her*? What was it about her? Neither a whore nor a virgin—he could not place what it was about her. She was his Helen of Troy, and like Menelaus, he was on a quest to take her back from her new husband. But unlike Menelaus, he couldn't say that his Helen had left him for another man,

Paris. He'd been the fool. He was the one who had thrown her love away. Perhaps he couldn't wage a war like the Trojan War, but he could use other weapons he had at his disposal. His play *House of Mourning* might help win her back.

Nefertiti didn't know. He was going to use his writing like a Trojan horse. He had eased it into her hands. He was hopeful. Although she'd refused the roses, she hadn't given the manuscript back. She had taken it with her. Once she started reading his work again, she'd see how he had changed. And before she knew it, she would realize that she still loved him—his love of words, his creativity, his spirit.

If Isaac was to look back over the terrains of his life, the loss of Nefertiti had become his cross to bear. Maybe their breakup had been inevitable— he didn't know—but to think it had been over Roshanne. . . .

No, there's a cross for everyone. . . .

He thought about last night when he'd gone home late, and had used the back door. When he noticed the red light flashing on the answering machine, he had picked up the downstairs extension phone. Simultaneously he heard Roshanne upstairs pick up the phone. Isaac didn't say anything. Roshanne must not have heard him come in or pick up the phone.

It was an unidentified male voice.

"Hey, what's going on?"

"Hey, what's happening? I told you about calling my house."

"Well, when am I going to see you again?"

"I told you my husband's ex was in town. I gotta see what's going on around my own house."

"You cold, Roshanne. You know I'd never try to mess up your home."

"Well, be cool. I'll see you next week when this bitch is gone back to California."

Isaac had not been surprised. In fact, he was relieved. Now he knew he would leave Roshanne. There was no way he was going to stay with her after this. And there would be nothing she could do or say about it. He started planning his move. For some reason, Isaac had remained cool. He almost had to laugh at the joke his life had become. History repeating itself.

His life was like one big Greek tragedy. Roshanne was his Cressida. His mother, Calissa, all over. At least Titi had never cheated on him, he was sure of that.

Since their divorce, Isaac had even written a poem, the only one he'd ever penned—a poem about his love for Titi. He remembered how in the poem he had compared their love to the sedative quality of a passionflower. (Once, when he was drunk, he told a strange bartender, "She freed my mind, man. She was like a sedative.") The poem had described their coupling as the blood-heat center of the passionflower's calyx, their communion to the ecstasy of His crown of thorns, and their eventual breakup, he had likened to the agony of Jesus' wounds.

After Isaac eased the phone receiver back into the cradle, he saw his photo album from the years he'd spent with Titi. Opening it up, he first noticed that Titi's head had been cut off in most of the pictures. The second thing he saw was that there was a clean space where a picture of Titi had once been. Suddenly he smelled something fetid. Looking in the drawer under the console near the phone stand, he found a black plastic bag. It smelled worse than raw, spoiled sardines. Isaac picked up the bag and put it in his briefcase. Why did she lop Titi's head off the picture? Did she mean his ex-wife any harm? He wanted to get to the bottom of this.

34

Isaac heard her before he saw her. He didn't think anyone else was in the church with him. He had just retrieved the rejected roses, when she came up from the church's basement, mop bucket still in her hand and apron around her waist. Everything he had missed in his life, every disappointment, exploded within him. All he knew was that he was hurting.

About a year after his mother had left, Isaac had found out where Calissa lived. His mother lived down by the railroads, near the stockyards— on the other side of the world, as far as he was concerned—but he was determined that he would see her. His father had forbidden him to ever speak to, let alone visit, his mother again. So one afternoon, he skipped school and sneaked over to her house.

When Isaac arrived at the frame house, he found the front door unlocked. At first, he thought that the house was empty. But suddenly he became aware of moans and groans coming from the bedroom. It sounded as if someone was sick or crying. With a growing curiosity and concern, he had crawled along the hallway to where the noise was.

On his knees, Isaac peeked through the keyhole and saw the man, who he'd learned later was called Pay Dirt, straddling his mother. She lay spread-eagled in bed. His first thought was that Pay Dirt was hurting his mother, the way she was crying out in whimpering sounds.

"Let her go, you dirty old bastard." Isaac hurtled himself into the room like a small brown torpedo.

"What the . . . ?" Pay Dirt raised up, the sheet draped about his large shoulders like a child playing Superman. Isaac's eyes were frozen on the sword, the turgid mushroom attached to the man's nude body. Then he understood what it was. It was like his. Only bigger.

The next thing he remembered, the smell of Lily of the Valley cologne assaulted his nostrils. But Isaac wanted to see his mother's face. He needed to see her eyes so that he would know.

With the first glimpse of his mother, Isaac could see that Calissa, who was grasping at the covers to cover her nudity, was not in any pain. In fact, he could tell by the shame flushing her face that she had been enjoying herself. Looking at his mother's face, he knew right away that she was not being attacked, that she was a willing participant in this nasty act. Before they realized Isaac was in the room, it was as if they had been two children innocently frolicking in the bed. Afterward, he would often think of the couple as looking

ashamed—as if they had done something dirty—
in the same way Adam and Eve must have looked
when God returned to the Garden of Eden after
they'd eaten from the Tree of Knowledge.

"Isaac!" his mother shrieked. "What are you
doing here?"

For a moment, his eyes had locked on the
lusty, dreamy look in his mother's eyes. Is this
what she had left him for? He knew from watching animals that they had coupled like his dog,
Queenie, and the stray dogs who would come
sniffing around after her. Before his mother had
left home, Isaac had always slept with her. He
had been her little man. He'd never seen his parents kiss, let alone "do the nasty." He didn't even
think his mother knew about this type of back-
alley, kid's-dirty-joke thing. He thought this act
was something children made up.

He felt as sickened as a cuckolded husband
who stumbled upon his wife defiling their marriage bed. If he had been old enough to carry a
gun, he would have pinned them both to the
bed in a shower of bullets.

Isaac felt a burning lava in his throat before he
realized that he was vomiting as he stumbled out
of the room, out of that house of sin and pleasure,
never to return. From that point on, he would
always hate the smell of his mother's cologne, Lily
of the Valley. In the same way that the damp musk
of spring collides with the sweet aroma of lilac, he
would always associate a lady's perfume with the
civilized veneer of a woman, coupled by a wildness
underneath that threatened to take over. And he

would always want to make love at night—when the lights were out—like decent people.

Finally, snatched back to the present, he blurted out, "Calissa, tell me one thing. Why did you do it? Did you ever think about me?"

His mother was quiet for a long time as she studied Isaac. Her son was a grown man, yet his tears still had the power to pull at her womb and her breasts like a nursing baby. Helpless to ease his pain, she died inside.

"Son, I thought about you all the time."

"Thought about me? No, you didn't. If you had, you would have never left."

"I couldn't stay, Isaac."

"Well, would you do the same thing, if you were faced with that choice again?"

"Probably. Some things don't change. Yesterday is one of those things."

"So you're trying to say it was your destiny? Is that all you can say? Don't you see what your choices have done to my life?"

"What do you mean?"

"What you did made me wind up throwing away the only woman I ever loved."

"Boy, what are you talking about?"

"You know what you did, Calissa."

"No. I know what people say I did. But I want to hear what I did to you, out of your mouth."

"I didn't know how to love, after what you did. Now, after all these years, all you can tell me is if you had it to do again, you'd do the same thing. Woman, are you heartless?"

Calissa paused for a long time.

"I was dying, Isaac. Can't you understand?"

"I wish I had never been born to you. I hate you!" He threw the roses on the floor and stomped on them, as if for emphasis.

"Isaac, how dare you talk to your mother like that!"

Isaac turned and saw Nefertiti standing behind him and Calissa. Once again, she'd seen him in a bad light. Speechless with rage, Isaac stomped out of the church and sped off in his Mercedes.

Nefertiti was so shocked at his outburst, she had to gather her wits before she went over to the pew to get her purse, which she had left behind accidentally. She was embarrassed and hurt for Calissa. Calissa had always been nice to her, even if distant, when she had been her mother-in-law. Nefertiti was going to leave quietly after witnessing such a painful scene between Isaac and his mother, but Calissa held out her hand and gently touched her arm.

"Nefertiti, can we talk?"

"He doesn't hate you, Calissa."

"I know it, but poor child, he thinks he does. Anyhow, if I had known Isaac was going to be here, I would have come to the church to clean it earlier. I never want to hurt my child again in life. But I had promised your mother I'd do something for your father's dinner. You know, I'm not invited, but, still, I like being here by myself. It gives me time to think about my memories."

"What memories?" Nefertiti asked.

"My memories of my life with Isaac's father. I was being buried alive by his father. He was only concerned with public front. Behind doors, he hadn't hardly touched me since Isaac was born. Even then it was 'wham bam, thank you, ma'am.' He wanted to be assured that he had God's anointed son. He said sex was only for making babies. He'd done his part. I guess maybe that's why I overdid motherhood with Isaac, his being sick and having a form of cerebral palsy. He didn't walk until he was two. He don't remember, but I made over him so because I was a lonely, love-starved woman.

"His father slept in one room. Isaac and I slept in another. One day, when he was eight, I kicked him out of my bed. He had almost become like my little man, to replace his father."

"What?"

"No, I never molested him. But as he grew older I knew it was becoming unnatural for him to sleep with me. Even if he was at the foot of the bed, I needed human closeness, and I felt like he was the only one who cared. What went on between us was nothing dirty, just a sick needy kind of love. Even though I knew it wasn't healthy, it took all my strength to get him out of my bed. That's when I knew I needed a man of my own.

"I remember, when I was a teenager, I used to babysit for my mother's sister Kaytree, the wild one. Even back then, she was tipping around on her husband. She used to pay me to babysit while she went out with the man. Sometimes she'd pay me not to tell her husband. Well, she had been seeing this older man for years, and even though all of her sisters knew about it, they never told her husband.

"One day, after a romantic rendezvous with the outside man, he had a heart attack and dropped dead right in my aunt's bed. She had to think fast. She called all of her sisters, who came over and dressed the dead man. They got him out of the house before my aunt's husband came home."

"Why are you telling me this?"

"Why? I just want to say I couldn't cheat like that. It was either all or none. Either I was going to be with Deacon Thorne or I wasn't. He threatened to kill me if I even tried to take Isaac with me. Back in those days, most women did not work. I was a housewife and had no way of supporting Isaac. I got tired of living around death all the time at the funeral home. Seems Deacon Thorne only knew how to dress up the dead. He didn't seem to have any more use for the living.

"One night, I let a neighbor talk me into going to a club where they played the blues. And that's when I saw Pay Dirt. He looked like a black Adonis, feet planted squarely on the floor, holding that bronze metal, hitting those keys just right. When he played the saxophone, it was as if he would fill his body and soul with the music, and it would come out in your pores. Pay Dirt could caress each note like he was making love to a woman. That's what made me want him. His ability to take the air and make something out of it. 'I'mgonnaloveyou,' he screamed into that sax all night. I heard him.

"And that's when I knew that he was the man who I wanted, and that he would give me what I needed. To be alive. To be a fulfilled woman. The river can cut two courses through the earth— one, the easy smooth path, and one, the crooked one. I took the crooked one.

"Yes, I got a bad reputation behind the whole thing. But I swear, the Deacon and Pay Dirt were the only two men I ever had in my entire life. I married one to get free and found myself in shackles, and I lived with one, against all the world, and found myself free.

"An old lady—one who had been a lady of the night, so to speak—once told me something. It's not much, but I want you to hear it, anyway. It's a shame how we as women shortchange ourselves.

Settle into loveless marriages for the money. It's worse than being a whore, I think. To marry without loving someone . . . like I did with Deacon Thorne.

"Anyhow, this is what Queen Esther, the prostitute, told me. There are a lot of men in the world whose wives have never known satisfaction with their husbands. Every man can't please any woman. Some women are just made to be pleased by that one man.

"Yes, I was the Gravedigger's wife, and I had been buried before my time. Later, everyone said Pay Dirt had done obeah to me, or put something on me, but I'll tell you this. He put something on me, all right. I was one satisfied woman until the day Pay Dirt closed his eyes in death. Although we lived in a one-bedroom house by the stockyard, I was happy. All the money in the world can't buy happiness.

"But that gal Isaac's married to. You watch her. She's an evil something. I know she deals in all that voodoo, but remember one thing. It can't hurt you as long as you don't eat their food, or as long as they can't get hold of nothing that belonged to you. A lot of time, when you don't believe in it, you're strong enough to ward it off. And another thing. Remember, any love worth having is worth fighting for.

"I know it's a horrible thing when a woman is old and by herself. But one thing—before I die, I can say that I lived. Yes, I snatched the nails off my coffin and came back to life, just when I thought I was being buried alive. I can say I lived before I leave this cold place."

When she finished her story, Calissa began to laugh. "You're the first person from Shallow's Corner that I ever told my side of the story to." Halfway through her laugh, Calissa covered her mouth.

"What's wrong, Miss Calissa?"

"What day is it today?"

"Friday."

"I just remembered the old saying 'He that laughs on a Friday will cry by Sunday.'"

36

The moment Tiger boarded the 7:00 A.M. flight to Michigan, he knew he was lucky. Here he was flying standby and hadn't had to wait all night. But instead of feeling happy, he had a grimness in his spirit.

Over and over, he kept thumbing a yellowed paper he had in his hand.

"I never would have thought . . ."

When the news went off, Reverend was silent. Although Miss Magg had heard the same thing that he'd heard, she didn't realize the impact of what the broadcast had just announced. She sat at her dresser table and began putting up her hair. She'd already washed her face and lathered it in Pond's cream.

"See what I said about our young people is true. I don't know why Huttleson would try to embezzle money out of a charitable fund. They say he was getting kickbacks on securities, bonds, and other notes. Now, if he needed campaign money, he should have done it fair and square. Pretty soon, we're not goin' to have any more colored officials."

Holding a pink sponge roller midair, Miss Magg looked back at Reverend's image in the mirror.

"Are you all right, Joshua? You look kind of gray. Did you take your pill? Joshua?"

37

Reverend Joshua Godbolt

The first time I got the calling, I didn't answer. I was like Jonah. I tried to head in the other direction. That was why I went North. I thought I could stop the call.

I went through my conversion after my daddy died, when I was fourteen. I was searching for you and didn't believe it when you answered me, Father. I had to make sense of our family's life. I was sitting on the mourning bench that Sunday. Although I went down on the threshing floor, I didn't surrender. Yes, I fought you, Father, because I doubted.

The second time, I was only eighteen, working as a short-order cook in a restaurant in Detroit. I worked the late shift, so I thought I was just sleepy. I was lying in bed when the Lord picked me up and hurled me onto the floor. I lay there, scared to death as noises surrounded me like a train engine. *Oh, Lord, I must be dying,* I thought.

I tried to get up, and something knocked me back down. I said to myself, "Father, help me. What do you want me to do?"

I heard a voice in my head say, *"Preach. Go make disciples, Joshua."*

I didn't even have any money saved. The next Sunday, when I preached at the church as a visitor, they collected enough money for me to get on the traveling circuit and go through the South preaching for the next ten years.

I used to travel in the deep South, where a colored man couldn't even be served in a restaurant or get a bed in a motel. We had to be put up with colored families. That's how I was able to get in good with Big Mama Lily. She the reason Miss Magg married me. I know it in my heart.

Lord, you know I've tried to be a good man. I got the calling when I was only eighteen. In over forty years of marriage, I ain't never once stepped out on my wife. Not that I didn't have chances, right there in the church. And I was a young man. If I must say so myself, I had the tools to garden with, so it wasn't that I wasn't like any other red-blooded young buck, as they used to call them. But I always believed what you said about adultery. To even look at a woman with lust in your heart was same as committing it. Miss Magg is the only woman I ever laid with. I loved Miss Magg. I thought I was an uxorious husband. She didn't want for nothing. Closet full of clothes. An allowance each month. Now I have to admit, maybe I was wrong.

Something weighs heavy on my heart. When I laid up in the hospital, so close to death I could feel it creeping up my legs, I said, "Lord, I don't want to feel like Job's wife did. I don't want to curse you and die. But maybe my whole life has been a lie." Maybe I was wrong to take Miss Magg from Tiger. Maybe they would have at least been happy together. I don't ever think I made her happy. Maybe what happened would never have happened. . . .

Lies. The whole thing has been a bunch of lies. Going to church when I didn't feel like it. Preaching sermons that I didn't believe in my heart anymore. Like Zephaniah says, "All a man's gold and silver can't get him into Heaven." But now, here I'm knocking at those pearly gates. Job said, "I was born naked." I'm truly going back that way. And now that Huttleson has been indicted for embezzling funds from a charity—if that don't beat all—the little position I thought I'd have, the little money I thought I would have to leave my family, is all gone. Ashes to ashes. Dust to dust.

How many times have I said those words? But now, I'm saying them for the lies I done told. Father, I done lied about a will. I done lied about the land I told Josh I was leaving him. I sold all that land back in the 1970s, and Tiger was right. I didn't share it with him, and that was heir property.

Lord knows, I haven't got any money but a little insurance money to leave my family. I'm too old to start over. Lord, Almighty God, I'm tired.

38

The sun was shrouded by a ring of cumulus clouds when Nefertiti drove home from the church. Her head felt so heavy, she felt it would snap her neck in half like a windblown hollyhock. A black mountain of clouds resembling soapsuds huddled and plodded. The damp air only added to her dark mood. She felt bad for Calissa's and Isaac's relationship. Would her daughter feel the same hate for her that Isaac seemed to hold for his mother? Should she keep searching? At least Calissa had been true to her feelings and followed her passion. She had not hidden her sin, as Nefertiti had.

In her rearview mirror, Nefertiti suddenly noticed someone following her. When she turned the corner suddenly, she no longer saw the car. It was a red Toyota.

By the time she reached Black Stone Drive, rain had begun to pour in a torrential storm. Thunder clapped like one of the saints on the mourning bench. Hail, as large as white mothballs, began to pelt her windshield. Each splash made her more depressed. Something was wrong.

Nefertiti felt an overwhelming sense of foreboding, but she couldn't put her finger on what it was.

Would she be able to find her daughter? *Desiree, where are you?*

"If it ain't one thing, it's another," Miss Magg exclaimed, looking out of her front window.

There was an angry sky with turbulent clouds threatening to explode the night Miss Magg cooked her family dinner. Nothing was going right. Little Josh and them had called and said they couldn't make it back until morning, because of the weather warnings. Thunder and lightning crackled through the haze a good hour before it rained, making the air feel cloying and sticky.

Although she was disappointed that none of her children were there (Nefertiti had gone God-knows where, "that girl sure been acting strange"), Miss Magg had set out her best china, and she was glad that Tiger was there to see the spread she had fixed. She had her starched lemon-yellow linen tablecloth on the table. She had matching cloth napkins. She used her cornflower ceramic tureens with their matching ladles for her turtle soup, and a gumbo loaded with crab, shrimp, chicken, okra, and sausage. She had a bowl of turnip greens dotted with diced turnips and hot corn bread. She served dirty rice as a side dish. Freshly squeezed lemonade was served in one of Big Mama Lily's old pitchers with the blue cornflowers painted on the side. That pitcher had to be at least sixty years old. Miss Magg remembered it from when she was a little girl. She admired her centerpiece, which was made of white orchids, lilies, and baby's breath. She had started to serve Mogen David table wine, but she remembered that Tiger had been sober for about five years now. No sense in tempting him with the ignorant oil.

Reverend had seemed real happy that Tiger was able to fly standby and get there by Friday evening. Just before he left to pick him up from the airport, Miss Magg noticed Reverend had read the newspaper, folded it up, and tucked it under his armpits.

"Where's the kids?" Miss Magg overheard Tiger ask Reverend as he took off his trench coat in the foyer when they made it from the airport. Tiger was dressed in an impeccably cut navy blue dinner jacket and slate-gray pants. That was one thing about Tiger—a black Casanova. He'd always met women who liked to dress him up. Here he was, a middle-aged man, still dressing like a sporting man.

She heard Reverend tell Tiger, "Cleo went with Little Josh and his family up to Niagara Falls. I don't know where Nefertiti is. She has been gone the whole visit."

After Reverend said grace, the dinner commenced. For a while, the three gray heads were bowed quietly. The only sounds in the room were the clicking of the spoons and knives and forks on the bowls or china.

Tiger had made such smacking and slurping sounds while he ate, Reverend thought it was almost indecent. Being a sensuous man, Tiger had always been a connoisseur of fine wines (before he stopped drinking), gourmet food, and exotic women.

After Tiger had knocked some of the chill off his hunger, he turned his attention to Miss Magg.

"Your cooking is still delightful as ever, Miss Magg. I have lived in Japan. I have dined on shark, on caviar, and on sushi. I've eaten the finest French cuisine. But your food is better than any great chef's food."

Miss Magg ducked her head to hide her blushing. "Oh, you embarrass me, Tiger. Have a second helping."

The rest of the meal was eaten before they turned to each other to talk. Only Tiger and Miss Magg seemed to have something to say. They talked about the foods from different regions and parts of the world and their similarities and differences. While the two talked, it was as if Reverend were no longer in the room. He cleared his throat to make his presence known.

Reverend cleared his throat again. "Tiger, so what have you been doing with yourself?"

"I just started a new job. Life couldn't be better."

"Well, I hope you stick with this one. Have you ever paid enough into Social Security to draw anything?"

"Well, if what the news tells me is correct, I'll be in good company. There won't be any money for those who have paid into it, either."

"But still, Tiger, maybe it's time you settled down."

"I missed my chance. I think we only get one

chance in this life. When you miss an opportunity, it means it either makes you or breaks you. It's like you've missed your boat. Like a ship that never sets sail."

"That's yesterday, Tiger. Leave it be now."

Miss Magg started twisting in her chair. She reached over to dish Reverend some more soup.

Looking uncomfortable, Reverend coughed against his fist.

Tiger's lips were pursed in a determined line. "Well, I wish I could. I need to talk to you about something," he continued.

"What?" Reverend lifted an eyebrow.

"Man, why did you do it?"

"What are you talking about?"

"Man, you know damn well what I'm talking about." Tiger took his fist and slammed it on the table, causing his lemonade to spill.

Miss Magg was so flustered, she didn't know what to do. She began to nervously dab at the tablecloth with her napkin.

"Don't disrespect my house, Tiger."

"Stop hiding behind that collar, man. I found out that you took all the proceeds from the land that Grandpa's Grandpa Samson left and sold it. Is that how you built your church? On stolen money? Yeah, I might have been the black sheep in the family, but I ain't so sure about that now."

"Is that why you did what you did?"

"What?" Tiger retorted.

"You know what you did." Reverend's tone of voice was choleric.

"No, I don't, big brother. Please enlighten me."

"Well, I might as well say it. I'm an old man, now,

ready to meet my Maker. I don't want to carry this to the grave with me . . . but I'll never forgive you for what you did while I was in the war. I should've killed you and her both. Why, every time I look at that child—but no, we've already had enough bloodshed in this family. It's already like a curse upon this family."

"What? Are you crazy? What are you trying to tell me?"

"I've said it once. I don't intend to repeat myself."

"Wait a minute, Rev. Are you trying to tell me you think that something went on between me and your wife when you were in Korea? Boy, are you crazy? That's my sister-in law! My brother's wife. I have never felt nothing but the highest respect for Miss Magg. How she put up with your crazy butt is the only thing I wonder about her. Oh, I see now. So that's why you have always acted funny when I come around. My Lord, I've heard everything now."

"Don't go callin' on the Lord now. How could me and Miss Magg have a child this dark?"

"Now, if you going on the basis of color, how about us?" Tiger pounded his chest with his open, splayed hand for emphasis. "I took color after Grandpa Bryce. You took color after Mama and Pretty. Don't you know, the way we is all mixed up with Indian and white blood, kids can be a throwback on they ancestors? Are you referring to Lil' Bit? She look just like Grandpa Bryce. What's wrong with you? You color struck?"

Reverend turned to Miss Magg and lashed out. "I watched you, Miss Magg. Y'all thought I was gon' die last spring. I guess you and Tiger could've picked up where you left off with me out of the way. But I fooled you. No, I'll be here to put dirt in y'all face."

Tiger raised up from his chair.

"Pardon me, but I don't believe in messin' all up in the family."

"Man, don't be yelling at my dinner table. In fact, you can get out of my house."

"Well, 'scuse us niggers. Before I leave, I want to say one thing. Is that why you always treated my niece different from the other two? Because you thought she was for me? That she belonged to me?"

"What is all this talk about belonging to somebody? I belong to myself. I don't belong to no man."

No one had heard Nefertiti come in. It was as if she had blown in on a monsoon. Miss Magg, hand over her heart, looked as if she might fall over any minute with palpitations. She spoke up as she stared at Nefertiti, afraid of her reaction.

"Joshua, you know that's not true. Why you listen to idle gossip? I've had it with you."

"Wait a minute. Do you mean to tell me all this time, I've been thinking something was wrong with me, when all this happened before I was born?" Nefertiti's voice was going soprano again. She stood on the floor with her arms akimbo.

"Forget it, Lil' Bit," Uncle Tiger said. "I know one thing. This clock is my inheritance, since your daddy cheated me out of all my land. I'm taking Big Ben and get whatever I can get from an antique dealer I know. He's already told me he's willing to give a few thousand for it."

When Tiger went to lift Big Ben, her father raised up in his maple dining-room chair, knocking it over on the floor. As old as he was, he landed a right punch on Tiger's shoulder. Tiger was so stunned, he turned around and let the clock fall to the floor. Big Ben's breakfront shattered into shards as loud as the thunder booming outside the house.

Reverend began to clutch his heart.

"I can't breathe."

Between Rev's gasps, Uncle Tiger loosened Reverend's tie. Miss Magg ran to the phone and called 911.

While the flurry of motion was going on around her, Nefertiti noticed the bas-relief on the back wall of the clock. It was in the shape of an ankh. It seared a hole into her brain.

In spite of the pandemonium, she had the presence of mind to slip an envelope she found among the wreckage into her pocket.

39

That night, after Reverend had been rushed by ambulance to the hospital for chest pains, Nefertiti sat with her hands in her lap, dazed. Without thinking about it, she knew she was waiting for Miss Magg to return from the hospital. She was so glad that Joshua and his snooty wife, Gloria, and Cleo had gone to Niagara Falls. She was happy they hadn't witnessed this fiasco.

If it wasn't so sad, it might have been funny. A seventy-five-year-old man and a sixty-six-year-old man trying to duke it out. Brothers at that!

How had what started off as a simple dinner turned into a sudden squall on the seas of family tranquility? How many battles had been set off at the dinner table? How many other lives destroyed? In fact, how many bombs had gone off over dinner tables, that one place touted for family love and unity? Nefertiti had been so stunned, she had stood outside the dining-room door and listened in from the point of the "bloodshed in the family." She couldn't take any more when she'd burst into the dining room.

She'd just gotten in from the church, and she hadn't expected them to wait for her for dinner. She was going to go freshen up before going in to dinner, and had headed up the stairs. When she'd heard her uncle Tiger's voice, she'd almost rushed into the dining room, but the angry tones had stopped her. She had never heard her uncle Tiger argue with Rev, who was his big brother, and almost like a father to him. The only thought that crossed her mind was that more misery and hatred were shared at the dining-room table than in any place in history. So this was the truth that had been beneath all the difference in her during the years. When she had lunch with Sweet, she had begun suspecting that maybe she had been fathered by another man, but her uncle Tiger? What was the world coming to?

When push came to shove, as long as she lived, Nefertiti would never understand how anyone could make her more irrational than family. She tried to keep crazy people out of her life. Why put up with this? What a conundrum!

Why had she returned home? Why hadn't she continued to deal with them on a long-distance basis?

But she knew the answer. Somehow, the ties of blood ran an emotional river through her so that she did not feel whole until she returned to the delta's source and dealt with her family. Besides that, they were her spirit's only resting place of unconditional love.

For all their tussling and wrestling, Uncle Tiger rode in the ambulance with Reverend, holding his hand and crying like an inconsolable baby. The vagaries of the heart.

When she heard her mother come in and go to her bedroom, Nefertiti waited for a decent amount of time before going to her bedroom door, tentatively knocking. But once she got in, she went straight to the point.

"Wait a minute, Miss Magg. Let me see if I have this straight. Tiger is supposed to be my father? Now I've just about heard everything. Miss Magg, all these years, I thought something was wrong with me. And now I find out our whole family has been built upon a lie? You're telling me my whole life has been a lie? So I'm your dirty little secret? Is that right?"

"No, Nefertiti. That's a lie your father made up. He built it up in his mind."

"But why would he think that?"

"Why does anyone do the things they do? Nefertiti, I don't know why, but it is not true."

"When we were growing up, my childhood was filled with 'You-can't-do-this, you-can't-do-that. What will people say?' We always had to act a certain way. We couldn't be normal. 'You're the minister's daughter,' people used to say. I just wanted to be me. I wanted him to accept me for me."

"I think your spirit is too free for him."

"Free? How can I be free, when I'm still looking for his approval? Miss Magg, why doesn't Rev love me?"

"I know you think I was never young, but once upon a time, I entertained foolish ideas, too. Never having a mother to tell me things, it stunted me. I know Big Mama was like a mother, but I was never sure of myself. I know you think I'm stupid for how your father talks to me, but over the years I learned to overlook him. He might have been overzealous, but what if he had been like your uncle Tiger? Have you ever known me to have to work?"

"But, Miss Magg, how could you have lived your life? It seems like your whole life was lived washing, cleaning, and taking care of everybody else. How about what you wanted?"

"Somebody had to do it. We can't all be like you, Nefertiti. Some of us have to be in the background, keeping the home fires burning. You were always courageous. Strong-spirited, even when you were a child. That's why I know you're more like Rev than his other spineless children. They're more like me. Have to be safe. Take the known way out.

"You know, I had given you the name Nefertiti because I had big dreams for you. And you have lived them. Nefertiti, look at you. Educated. Traveled. Have been to Europe. Can hold your own with the best of them. I'm proud of you."

Nefertiti was quiet for a moment, trying to absorb what her mother was saying. However, she didn't want to get sidetracked; so she blurted out what had been on her mind since she'd come home.

"Why didn't you stand up to Rev and help me keep my baby?"

"Those were different times then."

"You had three children. Now tell me, which one of us would you have wanted to give away?"

Miss Magg didn't answer the question. "Your life would have been ruint," she said simply.

"How do you know that?"

"I don't know. I'm just not as strong as you, Nefertiti. Don't want to talk about it anymore. Your father is a good man. He is just a small man . . . sometimes."

She just had to ask, anyway. "Miss Magg, was there another man? Is there someone else who was my father?"

Miss Magg answered without equivocation. "No."

Nefertiti left the room, still unsatisfied with the answers she'd received. And Miss Magg, too, had so many things she wished she could tell to Nefertiti, but all these years later, she knew that these were secrets she would take with her to the grave. . . .

As she sat alone with her thoughts, Miss Magg had never dreamed the day would come that Nefertiti would confront her about the past, when her daughter would ask her why she had encouraged her to give her child away.

Well, for one, she knew the Children's Home Society had a nice home picked out for the baby. The child wouldn't grow up being unwanted, like she'd felt—except for Big Mama Lily and Paw Paw. She wouldn't wish her childhood on anyone. Not that they weren't good to Miss Magg. It was just she wanted young parents.

Funny thing, she used to cry all the time for Betty Lee and whoever her real father was. That's probably why she hadn't been as strong as Nefertiti. Say what you want, but a man in the house puts a little more starch in a kid's backbone. Miss Magg really believed that. For that reason, she'd wanted Nefertiti's baby to have two parents.

She didn't know, though. You wouldn't know it by Little Josh. Looking back, she thought Rev ruint that boy. Was too hard on him. Didn't build his confidence up enough. But most of all, Nefertiti had been her child. Big Mama Lily said that Rev would make the better husband. And he had been. He was a good man, with all of his faults. Yes, she guessed Joshua did turn out to be the better man of the two brothers.

If she had married Tiger, her life might have ended up like poor Calissa's. *I'd be out there scratching my ass someplace.* But probably she would have had that . . . that passion.

Miss Magg and Joshua hadn't slept together in over fifteen years. *Not that I miss it. It was always only his pleasure. Now I'm old and all dried up, anyway. . . .*

She almost left Joshua once. And to this day, Joshua knew why. She guessed she did the right thing . . . staying with Joshua and all.

It all started when Joshua had Tiger come live with them. Tiger had been down on his luck, and Reverend hadn't seen him in such a long time. Shortly after, Reverend was drafted in the Korean War as a chaplain for the black soldiers. *He told Tiger to look out for me. . . .*

The only time Joshua ever accused Miss Magg of anything was when he came home on leave from the Korean War ten months later and Miss Magg was about to deliver Nefertiti.

When Miss Magg went into labor, Reverend

got so ornery, he wouldn't even take her to the hospital. A midwife had to deliver her baby right there in the kitchen of their home.

Here, they all looked kind of Creole, and Nefertiti came into the world looking kind of fudge-colored. But, secretly, she was always Miss Magg's favorite child. Anyhow, Nefertiti was more like Rev than his namesake, but he couldn't see for looking.

They already had Little Josh, who was about three by then. Miss Magg had two miscarriages, and had just about given up on ever having another baby.

Joshua never wanted much to do with Nefertiti after she was born. That was the only time Joshua ever slapped Miss Magg. When she cried, "Why?" Joshua looked over at the baby and he turned away. From that day to the present, he never mentioned it again. Although he had threatened her recently, he never laid a hand on Miss Magg since, but she always saw the difference he made in Nefertiti.

That was when Miss Magg wrote Big Mama Lily and Paw Paw Bullocks and asked them to come stay with her. When they first came, they intended to stay for a visit. Back then, it was not unusual for kinfolk to come visit for six months. But it didn't take long for Big Mama Lily to look around and see what was going on. Maybe she thought that Reverend was going to kill Miss Magg. Or worse, kill Nefertiti. Whatever, after Big Mama Lily came, Nefertiti never wanted for any love.

Big Mama Lily was the cornerstone of this family. Seemed like hating her white daddy, who was some big-time mayor down South, made her back strong. Her daddy had raped her mother, Summer Rose, when she weren't but a girl. Big Mama Lily hated her father to the day he closed his blue eyes, but it seemed like she got satisfaction from it. She even hated all white folks, because of her father. You would have thought, as light as she was, she would not have been this way.

She made a fuss over her little fudge great-grand like Nefertiti was the actual queen she was named after. Perhaps she hoped that it would make up for all the ignoring Joshua did of the child. The time he whipped Nefertiti over Big Ben, Miss Magg and Joshua had a big fight later that night.

"Why you whipping her over an old clock?"

"That's a family heirloom. It's all I got of my people."

"So she ain't your people, too?"

Joshua never answered.

"I'll tell you what. Don't you ever lay a hand on my child again."

Yeah, Joshua took care of Nefertiti, but he only did it by the letter of the law, not by the spirit.

There were just some things Miss Magg hadn't told a living soul, and she guessed she was just going to have to take them to the grave with her. Just like they never talked about Nefertiti's baby, her first grandchild, there were some things Reverend and she never talked about. But it had always been there. Like a cancer. Eating away at their marriage.

But she guessed some things were better left unsaid. Maybe Big Mama Lily was right. All chickens do come home to roost.

40

When Nefertiti went to her room, she went straight to her laptop. A puzzle had been turning in her mind. She logged on to the Internet. Next she pulled up adoptions. She found a lady who was purported to have handled more than fourteen thousand requests to help adoptees and natural parents find each other. The lady had access to a CD-Rom phone, which kept a database of adoptees and birth parents.

"Could you put in a Desiree Godbolt, adoptee, born in Wilcox Hospital, in Shallow's Corner, Michigan, in 1967?"

That night, Nefertiti dreamed she was in a flood. She was drowning in the churling, swirling water. Yet, her eyes were open and she saw a whale come and swallow her whole. I don't want to go through with this, *she told herself.* I can't go through with this. I must turn back. *Before she knows it, she is swimming in the whale's belly. She thinks she is going to die, but the next thing she knows, she is spit out whole. Like Jonah, the*

*whale spits her out on solid ground. She knows she
must not turn back on her mission. Just as Jonah had
been returned to Nineveh, she must return to her obligation. She was going to put it to rest.*

*Somehow, she fell back in the water, and was drown-
ing again. Everyone on the shore called her a different
name, and she didn't know who to answer to. Her
mother called her "gul." Big Mama and Tiger called her
"Little Bit." Her father called her "Nefertiti." Pharaoh
called her "Nefertiti," but in his lilting accent. Isaac
called her "Titi." Ford called her "Mother of the Earth."
But who was she?*

*She saw the adoptive parents, their fear. Their an-
guish. They felt like birth parents. After all, hadn't they
gotten up three, four times a night when the baby had
colic? They hadn't been able to have their own babies,
and when they got this baby, she was all "theirs." "We
own her." "She belongs to us." Who is this woman
threatening what we have built in our sinew, sweat,
and blood? Who is she who only had but a moment of
pleasure? We've had years of struggle. The scraped
knees. The hurts and pains.*

*Desiree does not belong to anyone. I don't belong to
anyone. You can't own what was never yours to own.*

41

Nefertiti barely had closed her eyes, when she saw the first whispers of daylight slanting into the room and sliding in across the doorsill. Perhaps she had dozed, but the rest was so fitful, she felt like she was sleep-deprived when she woke up. She couldn't remember having dreamed anything until just before she woke up, but she felt like she'd had more than one dream. In her last dream, Nefertiti had dreamed of Big Mama Lily and Big Ben. They were heading on a trip, but forgot to pack Big Ben. When Nefertiti went back to get the clock, she found it had been stolen.

When she woke up, Nefertiti tried to decipher her dream. Was her time being stolen? Was she running out of time to find her daughter? Oh, what was it? She knew she needed to get back to her business. And hadn't she dreamed something else? Earlier in the night. Someone was calling for a light, or was it a spirit? A woman's voice was calling someone beautiful. Or was it pretty? She couldn't remember.

Without questioning it, Nefertiti followed her instincts to the entrance hallway and looked closer at Big Ben. With its guts still lying busted up on the floor, the old clock looked like a wrecked car. She opened the cabinet door and looked on the back wall. The outline of an ankh had been carved into it. The ankh was like the one she'd found in the letter to her great-grandfather. She also found another important paper. She read the paper, which was the deed to the Douglass land, and then several bills of sale for various acreages of this land at various auctions held in different parts of Alabama.

The first thing she did was go to the attic and get the picture of the couple she'd seen earlier. The second thing she did was go check the carving she found inside Big Ben and the piece of paper.

The next thing she did was go to the bathroom, look under the medicine cabinet, and find a bottle of hyssop. She poured it into her bathwater. As a child, she'd learned the Bible backward and forward, even if against her will. Now she remembered that hyssop was for cleansing and purification. She remembered the account in Leviticus of hyssop being used to cure leprosy. Maybe she did need to be purified. Wasn't that what Big Mama Lily was trying to tell her in her dream? Clean out your house. Well, your house was your own spirit. She couldn't help but feel like someone had been following her. Like someone was stalking her. Was it Pharaoh? Was someone trying to harm her? She didn't know. This house needed to be purified of its ghosts of sins—committed and not committed. Was there something blocking her? Was she cursed? Maybe she was the one who needed to be cleansed and purified of all these ghosts, all these secrets, all this past.

Without asking her mother if she wanted to go, she drove straight to the hospital. Her mother had already called Josh and Cleo up in Canada. They were driving back. All Nefertiti knew was that she was at a crossroad in her life.

She would have to go and confront Reverend and find out what was going on.

"Daddy, did Grandpa Bryce ever tell you the story about his Grandpa Samson?"

"No. How did you find out about Grandpa and them?"

"Never mind. So what you're saying is no one ever told you that Samson changed his name after he ran away, and that he may be related to some Douglasses?"

"I don't recollect all that."

"Well, then, how did you get the deed to the Douglass land? And from what I can see, there is a bill of sale, as though you sold off quite a bit of it. Is that how you got your church?"

"No, that's not true. I found the Douglasses when I was traveling on the circuit. They had the clock with the ankh carved in it, and I just put two and two together that this was my grandfather's grandfather. Of course, he had been long dead."

"But isn't this your handwriting on this bill of sale for four hundred acres of timberland?"

"Look, Nefertiti, I don't have to discuss this with you. That's between me and my Maker."

"Well, tell me, where are the Douglasses? I might want to get in touch with them."

"I lost touch with the rest of them that I met when we moved north."

"And who is this in this picture?"

"That's my grandfather, Bryce, and his wife, Light Spirit. She was Indian. Cherokee, I think."

"Don't I have the same color as your grandfather? Doesn't that look like me? Why didn't you tell me about the Douglasses? Daddy, if you want, I can take a blood test. To find out if I'm your child."

Nefertiti felt a lump in her throat, and the next thing she knew, she was drowning in her own tears, her head buried in her father's sheet near the foot of the bed. She cried for all the days Rev had rejected her. She cried for Desiree. Not knowing whether she was dead or alive. She cried for Pharaoh, whose mind was destroyed. She even cried for the black baby who had died inside Violet. She cried for all the black mothers whose children had been sold from them in slavery.

At first, it had felt like a flutter, like the first kicking of a fetus—the quickening process. Then, softly, gently, almost tentatively, she felt a hand touch her on the head. Suddenly she realized something. Her father had never willingly touched her in her life. She started a fresh wave of wailing.

"It's been so much pain in the family, it's better left unsaid. Don't do that, Nefertiti."

The room was quiet, save for Nefertiti's weeping. The two sat frozen in position, a freeze frame, with Rev's hand still touching her head. Finally, when Nefertiti lifted her head, she took a tissue from the box next to his bed. She blew her nose, trying to compose herself. When she came to herself, she noticed Rev's golden hand had taken her sable one into his.

Nefertiti looked her father in the eye. "Well, is there at least one of the Douglasses I might get in touch with?"

"I don't know. I might have one of Great-Aunt Millie's niece's phone number. She would be in her nineties now. She's probably senile."

"Well, when you get well, you might tell me. Please, Daddy. But what I really want to know is, what did you mean when you told Uncle Tiger that there had been enough bloodshed in the family already?"

Her father was silent. He turned away, looking out the hospital window. Tears streamed down his face the way the rain had run down the tin roof of their shotgun shack that night back in Alabama. "Nefertiti, I'm going to tell you a story. I can still see that night like it happened yesterday."

One Saturday night, when Joshua was not yet thirteen, his father, along with Uncle Ulysses, Uncle Theo, Uncle Silo, and Grandpa Bryce, had gone carousing into town. Tiger was only three, so he never remembered what had happened, unless Joshua told him.

This was the three brothers', and their father's, typical Saturday-night routine—go down to the juke joint, get inebriated, and come home arguing. Joshua, who slept in the back bedroom with his baby brother, Tiger, woke up first to the loud sounds of thunder and flicker of lightning. Then he recognized the usual Saturday-night sounds of loud arguing in the kitchen. He ran to get the stick they kept against the door at night, thinking it was his father fighting his mother again.

When he reached the kitchen at the center of their shack, he saw his uncles, his grandfather, and his father, all sloppy drunk.

"She's my woman," Ulysses muttered. His voice was slurred, and he seemed to get tripped up on his own tongue.

"Now, she ain't, she mine." Pretty argued.

"You a-lie. I had her first." Grandpa Bryce's voice was slurred, too.

"Her"—the subject of the heated debate—turned out to be Sally, the slatternly woman Joshua always heard his mother call "the neighborhood barfly."

Bertha, who had gotten more nervy than when she was young, came out of her bedroom, threatening the men with a broom.

"Look, you bunch of hard legs. Y'all got wives, 'ceptin' Grandpa Bryce, here, and y'all got the nerve to be up in my house, talkin' about some barfly. Get out in the barn, if y'all want to be talking all up under women's clothes. I mean it now, Pretty."

The men never made it to the barn. Out of nowhere, Uncle Ulysses had pulled out an old .45-caliber Springfield and pointed the gun at his father, Grandpa Bryce.

"No," Pretty had hollered, tackling Uncle Ulysses. Somehow in the tussle, the muzzle of the gun, pointed in the opposite direction, went off, and ripped away Uncle Ulysses' face. Time became gelid. Glacierlike. Like a Jell-O mold slightly trembling on a barefaced plate. No one moved a muscle. Everyone's face seemed suspended on the ceiling after the gun blast.

The first movement that Joshua remembered seeing was his father, Pretty, as he sat, his tears running like slimy okra mixed with blood, cuddling his faceless brother's corpse. He cried over and over.

"Don't die on me, man. Ulysses! No! No! No!" Afterward, Pretty stared at his hands, as though he could only see in them the destruction they had wrought. The instruments of his brother's death. Cain and Abel.

Grandpa Bryce became so crazed from seeing what had happened to his son, he ran to the bridge and almost didn't stop running until Uncle Theo tackled him. In a daze, Joshua had helped his mother mop up the puddles of blood. Blood, lightning, and barfly women would forever be connected in Joshua's mind.

This medley of homicide and chance, this debacle, was to haunt Pretty for the rest of his life. No one was ever prosecuted, but Pretty condemned himself. It seemed as if a pall fell over the fields, over the house, over their very lives. After Uncle Ulysses' death, nothing was ever the same with Pretty. He no longer went to the fields to work. He even stopped frequenting the juke joints. Overnight, he aged, hair turning white, his once-burnished skin crinkling up like a raisin. After the day he accidentally killed his brother, Joshua's father simply had never been the same man. He hadn't meant to harm Ulysses. He and his brother had often gotten drunk, fought, then made up when they were sober. It was like a ritual with them.

From that day forth, the family never had

enough food to eat. The fields became so barren
that they had to move to another farm, then to another, "just like itinerant workers," then to another,
and eventually to the harsh, rawboned poverty of
the city.

Just as the rain and blood of his brother soaked
into the ground, leaving no hint of the devasta-
tion, Pretty became a quarter-moon shadow of the
man he used to be, spending most of his time lying
in bed, drinking corn liquor. Joshua never remembered hearing his father speak again, until about
a year later, when he died, crying out "Ulysses.
Mama." Although the death certificate listed the
cause of death as natural, Pretty died from grief.

Bertha, a victim of the same whooping-cough-
type privation, died within the next three years,
leaving Joshua an orphan at seventeen, alone to
figure out his fate in a hostile sea of white faces in
the South. That's when, figuring he had nothing
to lose, Joshua hopped a freight and went up
North, seeking his fortune. When he returned to
the South, he was already an ordained minister,
but by then, it was too late to help his baby brother,
Tiger, who was already lost to the ways of the flesh.
So he left the South without Tiger, but he did have
someone else with him. His new teenage bride,
Vijay Bullocks. He also had in his care and keeping
a beautiful grandfather clock, his only family heirloom, which he named Big Ben. He decided to
settle in Shallow's Corner, where his congregation
later built his home, two doors away from the First
Solid Rock Baptist Church.

Only Grandpa Bryce, who finished half-raising
Tiger, lived on in the South, in the wake of this

tragedy, taking it on the cuff, as he'd always lived life. He knew no other way but "to keep on, keeping on." From what Joshua learned years later, Grandpa Bryce had stared in the face of death and watched his own father, Shilo, who had owned fifty acres of timberland, die at the end of a lynch rope. Bryce had been hiding in the woods. Because of that, Bryce always chose life. From then on, there was nothing in life that could break him. He lived—chasing women, drinking, juke jointing, and all—to the ripe old age of ninety.

After Nefertiti left, Reverend stared into space. Maybe his grandmother, Light Spirit, had known what it was to be true to her Cherokee heritage. Maybe it had been the lack of love and connection to knowing his dual heritage that had destroyed his father, Pretty.

He didn't know. Try as he would, all these years, he had been unable to forgive Pretty. All of a sudden, Reverend heard a loud *swoosh* in his soul. The space where he'd hated his father all of these years formed a vacuum, which was so wide, it almost swallowed him into a vortex of his own tears.

Before Nefertiti could leave the hospital, she ran into Cleo and Little Josh in the lobby.

"What did you do to him?" Cleo shouted at her.

"What the hell do you mean, what did I do to him? Rev already had a pacemaker."

"Little Josh was telling me how you had a baby when I was born. I never knew about this. All of you don't tell me shit in this family."

"Look, the whole group of us are dysfunctional."

"What are you talking about? We are not dysfunctional." Josh had jumped into the argument.

"Good-bye, y'all." Throwing her hands in the air, Nefertiti left her brother and sister standing, mouths wide open, in the lobby. She felt too good to spoil this moment. Even if Reverend didn't apologize, his reaching to touch her head meant he accepted her.

In her room, Nefertiti read once more the letter she'd found inside Big Ben.

March 17, 1968

Dear Nefertiti,
I am so far on the other side of the world, sometimes this feels like a dream. I think about you all the time and that one summer we had together. I am watching the moon and wondering if this is the same moon I knew in the world. I wonder if I will ever see you again. What will become of us? Please wait for me, Nefertiti.
Love,
Pharaoh

Nefertiti sat and tried to absorb the letter. So Pharaoh had tried to get in touch with her while he was in Vietnam. Although she didn't love him anymore, it made her feel better to know that he had tried to find her.

Nefertiti closed her eyes to rest before the dinner. Before she knew it, she saw Desiree, or a young woman she thought might be Desiree, going through a merry-go-round of doors. She had a key in her hand. She kept saying, *"I have the wrong key."*

42

Isaac absentmindedly backed his Mercedes out of his driveway. His mind was made up; he was determined. He had to go see Nefertiti and let her know that he was packed and ready to leave Roshanne. Where he'd take it from there—who knew? He just had to do this. From rote, he turned his neck to check the street for oncoming traffic, backed out swiftly, and headed west for the Godbolt house. At first, he thought it was his imagination. Something cold and metallic was pushed into his neck. The word "carjacking" flashed in his consciousness, but it was the voice that made his heart leapfrog.

"Don't turn around. Keep driving."

He relaxed a little, since he recognized the voice. It was Pharaoh's.

"What the—"

"Man, shut up. You got that phone in here? Good, 'cause you gon' need it. Drive to the cemetery. We're going to finish what we started twenty-six years ago."

* * *

Roshanne had a funny feeling that Isaac was acting strange. At first, she wasn't upset when she'd found his packed suitcase hidden at the back of the hall closet. Only for a minute, she worried if he knew about her "spare tire," as she called her boyfriend, Benny. No, Isaac was too stupid to know any difference, she decided. But what was that suitcase for? He generally let her know if he was going out of town. Then it hit her. It was that Nefertiti! The kids weren't with her. *That bitch! He's going over to see her again.* And worse—her heart almost seesawed—no, he didn't think he was trying to leave her? Even if she had been a shrew during their years together, she'd never believed he would change on her. Well, she was going to follow him to see what he was up to. She'd make sure the potion worked on Nefertiti this time.

If that don't just about beat all. Here, all this time, Nefertiti had thought Rev just didn't like her for herself, and it had been because he thought she was Uncle Tiger's child. Here, she was just beginning to suspect Miss Magg had had an affair with some unknown lover who'd fathered her, when all the time, it was Uncle Tiger whom her father had suspected. And then to find out that none of it was true at all—that she just looked like Grandpa Bryce.

Now, if she wasn't a strong person, this would be the time in the movies that she'd just gracefully go off and have her genteel nervous breakdown. But

she didn't know how to act like "normal" people
and go crazy when the world got to be too much.
She would just keep plugging away, broken-down,
worn-out, half-crazy, but holding on by her toe-
nails, if necessary.

She really wanted to be alone. To sort out her
feelings. But when she saw how her mother, Miss
Magg, took charge and carried everything out,
Nefertiti felt compelled to go on to the big church
dinner. Miss Magg had said that since all the tickets had been printed and sold, they would just
have to rise to the occasion as a family.

For the moment, Little Josh, Cleo, and Nefertiti had silently called a truce. Nefertiti thought it
was a little strange when Uncle Tiger turned down
her invitation to ride to the dinner with her, and
instead rode with Little Josh and his family, but
she didn't worry about it. It gave her more time
to apply her makeup and fix her tunic, which
wrapped around her.

Miss Magg had made arrangements for the
presiding pastor, Reverend McCullough, to do
the benediction. Miss Magg had decided that she
would accept the Community Service Award on
the Reverend's behalf. And with Councilman
Huttleson being indicted for misusing funds—
well, he would just be dropped from the program. He had already dropped out of the race for
mayor. He was out of jail on bail, and had bigger
legal concerns to deal with than an award dinner.

Nefertiti had already bathed and put her makeup on when a chill went through her. Full moons,

for some reason, always bothered her. The news said that there was going to be a lunar eclipse later that night. The wind seemed a little higher again. Spume, as heavy as a thundercloud, encircled the street in a heavy fog.

The phone rang just as Nefertiti was going out the door.

As soon as she put the receiver to her ear, she heard shouts before a voice came on the phone. The call had the static sound of a mobile phone.

"Nefertiti, this is Pharaoh. I need to see you. We've got to talk." Pharaoh's words came tumbling out.

A voice in the background shouted, "Don't come, Titi. He has a gun! He's crazy. He's tripping. He's thinking he's back in Vietnam." It was Isaac.

"Shut up, man. You're the one who did the fragging to my road dog. I'ma kill you, Charlie."

"Where are you?" Nefertiti screamed into the phone.

"At the back of the cemetery."

"I'll be right there. Don't do anything crazy, Pharaoh."

Just as Nefertiti rushed to go out of the door, she ran into a girl about Cleo's age coming in the door.

"Hey, are you one of Cleo's friends? I'm in a hurry. She's gone to the church for the ceremony."

"No, I'm not looking for Cleo."

"Well, come on out with it. What do you want? I'm in a hurry."

"This won't take but a moment. Nefertiti, I have to ask you something."

Nefertiti noticed a camera hung around the girl's neck. "Aren't you supposed to be the one taking the pictures? What's your name again?"

"Zora."

"Oh, yes, the photographer. Well, Zora, you caught me at a bad time. Like I said, I was just leaving and I'm kind of in a hurry. I have an emergency."

"Did you put a request on the Internet? Online?"

"Yes, I don't know, I'm so busy. Please, this is just not a good time."

"Nefertiti, do you know what date this is?" Zora asked as she handed Nefertiti a small piece of paper.

Nefertiti stopped, cold blood running down to her toes when she saw the date written down.

Who was this who knew so much about her business? There it was again. The secret.

"Why do you want to know?" Nefertiti held her breath. Was somebody trying to blackmail her? Well, if that was the case, when had her store started turning that big of a profit to pay out blackmailers?

But then, Nefertiti stopped and really looked at the landscape of the mahogany face in front of her. Really scrutinized it. The face that had Big Mama Lily's heart shape. The widow's peak, like hers. The slender, tall build, like Pharaoh's. Like a bid whist player laying down a Boston, the young woman handed Nefertiti a copy of an amended birth certificate for Zora Desiree Fairchild, a copy of Desiree Godbolt's original birth certificate, Nefertiti's marriage license to Isaac, and even a copy of her Social Security number.

"Well, if you do, you may be my mother." The girl spoke in a rush. "I just got these papers in the past couple of weeks. I am twenty-six years old and I don't know my history. I don't know if I have heart disease in my family. I don't know if I have cancer in the family. This is all I want to know. I don't need you as a mother. My mama has been my mother."

Nefertiti didn't have to hear the words. She knew it in her blood gelling around her marrow, pounding against the walls of her veins. It was the girl she had seen at the hairdresser's. It was the person who had been following her for the past two days.

Nefertiti didn't know if she wanted to cry—she felt such a hard cramp cross her stomach—but it passed as fast as it hit her. "I know this is crazy, but you must come with me. It's urgent."

"Where are we going?" *Don't tell me she's as crazy desperate now as she was when I was born,* Zora thought.

Before Nefertiti left, she ran back upstairs for one more mission.

"Wait a minute. Let me get this ankh. It's from one of our ancestors. We're going to need somebody's spirit tonight. Oh, Big Mama Lily, help us! God, Jesus Christ, we need you!"

"What's going on, Nefertiti?"

"Your father is trying to kill your sister and brother's father. I know the shortcut. Let's go! Hurry! This could be a matter of life or death."

Had Nefertiti thought about it, she would have thought of the irony that she and her daughter ran through the same field she took as a young girl to meet Pharaoh. The night air was filled with the sweet breath of wisteria and honeysuckle.

Milkweed, bramble, and nightshade slapped and snarled at their legs. Only the full moon provided light as the two women ran under the night's ebony canopy. A moonbeam lit their path. A miasma of evil clung to the air.

The meadow had grown up until it felt like a forest. The two women were no longer mother and daughter, but humans caught up in a crisis. They ran with an urgency. Nefertiti hadn't come to the cemetery at night since the riot—the night she and Sweet both had seen a diaphanous shadow of a pregnant woman, who stood between them and the National Guardsman when he pointed his flashlight on them. To this day, Nefertiti had never understood why the Guardsman couldn't see them when he was standing right in front of them, but now she knew that it was Violet's ghost.

They heard them before they saw them. When the two women arrived at the cemetery, they found the two men arguing in raised voices. Pharaoh no longer seemed to be hallucinating about Vietnam.

"You're gonna pay for what you did to me, man," he was telling Isaac.

"What? I don't have Nefertiti, either. What's wrong with you?"

"No, we are going to finish what we started twenty-six years ago. I should have kicked your ass that night, anyway, jumping in between man-woman business. Well, we can get it on now."

"Man, you are crazy." Isaac threw his hands up in exasperation. "Hey, bring your old, tired, burned-out ass over here, and see what ya get. I'm not in no playing mood today. I've been through too much. You best put that gun down."

"Oh, I will. I don't need no gun to deal with your lame ass. I'll wax the floor with your behind."

"Well, drop it. We'll see who's the baddest."

"Look, if it hadn't been for you, maybe she and I would have had a chance. Oh, so now you bad, huh? I'll put it down when I get good and ready, see? But Rev kept pushing you up in her face."

"Well, here Titi is. You can ask her yourself. If she wanted to be with you, nothing in the world could have stopped her. Not me, not Rev, not the war, not nobody."

Both men turned and stared at Nefertiti. They were so involved in their argument, they failed to notice the tall young woman standing by her. Pharaoh was no longer pointing the gun at Isaac.

"Not Rev, not me, not nobody!" Isaac emphasized.

"Stop, Pharaoh. Stop, Isaac. Stop! Pharaoh, here's your daughter. Please don't do this in front of her!" Nefertiti shouted.

"What do you mean, this girl is my daughter? You're not fooling me, Nefertiti. I know Cleo is the baby you had and *pretended* to give away."

"Pharaoh, that's not true. This girl here, I named her Desiree—her name is Zora Desiree. She is your daughter—*our* daughter. Pharaoh, we were too young. What kind of parents do you think we would have made? Look, the people who raised her gave her a good home. I couldn't be prouder of her. She's gone to college. She is a photographer. She even likes art, like you do."

Nefertiti felt like Scheherazade, only she was trying to save Isaac's life, not her own. She silently prayed to God and called upon Violet—and Pharaoh suddenly threw the gun to the side.

"Who did you say this girl—I mean, young woman—is?" Pharaoh asked.

Before Nefertiti could respond, she looked into Roshanne's ghoulish face. Where had she come from? Hate had disfigured her features worse than any hoodoo.

"Bitch, I'll get you out of his head. You've been gone for seven years, and he's still chasing behind you."

Roshanne dashed for the gun lying on the ground. Within a heartbeat, she pointed the gun at Nefertiti and pulled the trigger. At the same time, both Isaac and Pharaoh jumped on Roshanne, tackling her, trying to wrestle the gun out of her hand. The shot pierced the night's air. Nefertiti had been knocked down in the struggle. At first, Nefertiti thought she'd been shot when she felt the wetness on her tunic.

Until she heard Isaac say, "Call my mother," she didn't know it was Isaac who'd been hit. Nefertiti never remembered how she had the presence of mind to call Calissa on the phone in Isaac's car. Pharaoh was the one who had told her that Isaac's Mercedes came equipped with a phone. When she returned from the car, she found Pharaoh hugging Isaac to him, crying softly. Zora stood near Pharaoh, patting his shoulder as if he were a baby. She vaguely remembered Calissa getting to the cemetery before the ambulance arrived. She never remembered seeing Roshanne after the gun went off.

* * *

Lying there, feeling his blood gush out of him like a geyser, Isaac remembered reading once in a Chinese book, the *Tao Te Ching*, that the word for "freedom," in the first written language, meant "return to mother."

"Mama, I hurt." Isaac sounded like a little boy.

"Son!" Calissa cradled Isaac's head. The blood continued to gush out of the wound in his chest. "Oh, baby. Oh, my baby boy. I love you. Please forgive me."

"Mama, I didn't mean it."

"I know."

Calissa began to sing one of Isaac's nursery favorites.

Jesus loves me! This I know,
For the Bible tells me so.
Little ones to Him belong . . .

Air raced in and out of his nostrils. Isaac stared over the branch behind Calissa's shoulder. The moon shimmered on the branch, resembling a lightning rod. Lilac still played its jazz notes on the spring breeze. Then suddenly the moon was eclipsed.

He heard Big Mama Lily's rooster, Mannish, crowing. He tried to remember that line in a blues song. Now, how did it go? *"That old rooster don't want to crow no more"?*

He tried to smile, but the pain caused his heart to burst. He felt peace as he flew away, free as a nightingale.

43

In his own way, Rev had tried to show that he loved her before he died. However, he never did come to visit her in California, saying he was too old to fly. But at least he did ask Nefertiti about Ford and sent his greetings whenever they talked on the phone the last year of his life.

And as he died, Nefertiti had flown back to Shallow's Corner and made it to his bedside before he closed his eyes. With tears in his eyes, Rev tried to tell her something. Nefertiti shushed him. "I know, Daddy. You don't have to say anything." She could still remember how he'd given her away at her first wedding. The fact that he had asked for her before he died had been enough.

It was Uncle Tiger who'd changed toward Nefertiti, after that family dinner. He never called her anymore. When she thought about it, he hadn't called her since Rev's funeral, and he'd been dead for two years.

Isaac had been dead for three years now, and she still hadn't gotten over it. That was something else she'd have to deal with—the fact that Isaac had taken a bullet meant for her.

Maybe that was why she held on to his play *House of Mourning* like a shrine.

His agent, Robert Winthrop, had recently contacted her. "Before he passed, Isaac told me he gave you the only copy he had of *House of Mourning*."

When Nefertiti admitted she had the manuscript, Mr. Winthrop asked her if she'd be willing to act as executor on behalf of his estate, as the mother of Isaac's children.

"Why?"

"I've gotten a little interest from publishers who would like to publish this play posthumously."

"I'll think about it."

At that point, Nefertiti didn't feel strong enough to part with this personal offering to the world . . . yet. Her children really grieved for their father, and sometimes she felt they resented her for what had happened. Why did everyone blame the mother for everything? How did that old saying go? What herb was more bruised than woman?

Well, at least Roshanne had been given fifteen years for manslaughter of Isaac, with intent to commit murder on Nefertiti.

Since she'd hung the painting that Pharaoh had given her in her store, a white female who was not a regular customer had offered her two thousand dollars for it. The painting was of a pair of black lovers holding hands in a field of jasmine and freesia. Monarch butterflies floated on the edge of the freesia. In a flame of yellow, red, and purple, the young couple stood so close to a crimson sunset on the horizon, it looked as if they were both kissing the sun. Perhaps the woman had felt the longing, the wistfulness, of the picture. Nefertiti had named the painting *Remembrance.*

Which reminded Nefertiti of letting go of old pains. Her parents had done the best they could. Just as she had done the best she could, under the circumstances, when Desiree was born. In the same way she had chosen to give Desiree away, as the lesser of two evils. After all these years, Desiree seemed to have forgiven her, though.

Through Desiree's example, Nefertiti had forgiven Rev and Miss Magg. They'd done the best they could. Rev had just been mistrustful of Miss Magg. Uncle Tiger wasn't her father. People could believe things in the head, until they almost came true. Just as Nefertiti had found her own truth, Desiree would have to find her truths for herself.

Maybe some loves, like hers and Pharaoh's, or like her great-great-great-grandparents, Samson and Violet's, just weren't meant to be. Maybe, from the start, they were doomed like chaff in a wasteland. . . . Perhaps the phantoms of those doomed loves wandered in a purgatory, never being put to rest. Always haunting, down to the end of time. And not for any lack of love, either.

All Nefertiti knew was that she felt whole again, now that she had Desiree back in her life. Thinking of her, she picked up the phone to call her. The two had planned a trip to the South to do some genealogy research on the family.

"How's Ford and the kids?" Desiree always asked about Ford, Savasia, and Ike.

Desiree had made two trips to visit Nefertiti
and her family over the last couple of years. It
was uncomfortable at times, but they were growing used to one another. The times that bothered Nefertiti the most were when she would
catch Desiree staring off in the distance, looking
so alone, so fragile. She remembered the lines
from an old poem she'd read in a book while she
was searching for Desiree:

*"Oh, why does the wind blow upon me so wild? Is it
because I am nobody's child?"*

And those were the days that Nefertiti had to
wrestle with the guilt her decision had wrought. . . .

However, Ford's acceptance of Desiree had
definitely tilted the scales in his favor with Nefertiti. Now she didn't care what anyone said about
him. Or about his color.

"How's your father doing?"

"Which one? My daddy is doing fine," Desiree
answered.

"Pharaoh?"

"He has his good days. He has his bad."

"I just wanted to thank you, Desiree. I know he
and I haven't been much of parents to you. It's
beyond nice of you, how you got your father into
the VA Hospital. Miss Magg tells me how you go
and see about him regularly."

"He gave me life. He is my father."

Which made her think of Rev, again. Since his
death, she was remembering many of the good
things he'd done for her. Tried to keep her on the
straight and narrow. Always had been hard on her,

making her do her best. Even if he hadn't pampered her, he'd made her strong. And she was finally free to love him for who he had been.

Just finding the truth about her daughter had freed her to love her husband, Ford, and she was no longer held hostage by lies.

Yes, she was finally free to be herself. It made her think. Maybe Calissa had been a free spirit long before her time. It's a dangerous thing, when a woman is too free. But a man? Even a free spirit like Uncle Tiger was risky. Was that what had destroyed Pharaoh? That he couldn't be free? Or had it been because of her?

Epilogue

Five years later

Heavy footsteps clicked on the flagstone to the verandah on Black Stone Drive.

"What you know good?"

The lilac cluster of wisteria on the porch's columns laughed in the wind. It almost mocked the man's expensive aftershave lotion, which his entrance left wafting in the air.

Sitting under the fragrant white canopy of stephanotis covering the trellis on one side of the porch, the woman nodded in greeting. She sat on the swing, which moved gently to and fro.

"I came to talk to you about our daughter."

"You know that girl is a grown woman now. Where were you when she was growing up?"

"It's not my fault."

"What do you mean? No one's blaming anyone now. That is just how things were."

"Until five years ago, I never even knew."

"Do tell."

"But it was only that one time. I never thought—"

"Hush. What was I to do? Did I say you should have done anything?"

"But you're the one who passed her off as someone else's daughter."

"Wasn't I the almighty Reverend Godbolt's wife? Too many lives would have been destroyed. Look, we make choices. We live with them."

"How you making it since he been gone?"

"Not bad. Reverend had gotten a life insurance policy in the later years, not a lot, but I'm comfortable. I also get a little Social Security check for my disability."

Tiger sat down on the swing next to Miss Magg, putting his dark parched hand over her albino-looking hand. He took his fingers and began to trace the lifeline in her palm. The long rivers forked about midway in her hand, turned into two branches, then took a jagged turn, until it ended in its source at the delta found near her frail wrist. Turning her hand over, he took his fingers and kneaded the network of lines on the back of Miss Magg's hand; the veins mapped out the mountains, furrows, and valleys she'd faced.

"It's a beautiful *daylean*."

"What did you say?"

"That's Gullah for when the sun is leaning to the west. I hadn't thought about that word in years."

"I always liked to hear your Creole accent."

The two were quiet.

"He was a good man," she said. "I miss him."

"I miss him, too."

They both continued to swing, just two old people, shadows melding together in the falling vermilion sun. Twilight settled on their shoulders like a golden powder and encircled them both in the wind's lavender.

Reading Group Guide

1. In 1967, having a child and not being married was frowned upon in society in general, and among working-class blacks in particular. Do you think Nefertiti, who at fifteen gave her child away, made the right decision?

2. Do you think slavery has had an impact on how the separation between mother and child is viewed among African-Americans?

3. Do you think family secrets can become like a generational curse on a family?

4. How far back can you go in your family tree?

5. Why do you think Pharaoh and Isaac wanted to fight over ownership of Nefertiti?

6. What are your views on closed adoptions?

7. Are there historical stories in your family similar to the one Nefertiti discovered in the attic regarding her ancestor who had escaped from slavery?

8. Do you think Nefertiti and her father, Reverend, made peace before he died?

9. Do you think Miss Magg was cowed to allow Reverend to order her around, or was she simply a woman of her time?

10. Have you ever known a black sheep in a family? Do you think Nefertiti was the black sheep in her family?